The Puddle Variations

WMP

The Puddle Variations

Jeff Alworth

WALKING MAN PRESS
Portland, Oregon

This book is a work of fiction, though given the evolving nature of the category, take that for what it's worth. Names, characters, places, and incidents are products of the author's imagination; however, certain philosophical schools maintain that nothing else is possible, lending further confusion to meaning of "fiction." Any resemblance to actual events, locales, or persons, living or dead, is entirely likely. The author denies any specific connection between his imagination and actual events, locales, or persons, particularly where such associations involve legal counsel. In other cases, and under the application of stout ale, he may admit to more. You didn't hear it here.

Copyright © 2007 by Jeff Alworth

FIRST EDITION

First Walking Man edition November 2007

ISBN 978-0-6151-7184-5

Printed in the United States of America

To my mother,
for keeping the faith.

Reel One

1.

A rasping, thrashing noise. Then, to his left, an enormous box, closing in. A brief struggle and he thrust himself up to face the box, which he recognized once his eyes focused as his apartment's east wall. A plop and the thrashing ended with mail spread on the floor. Hand-delivered, unnecessarily, by the landlord, Mr. Booth.

His head spun and ached, and he hobbled to the bathroom to lap water from the tap and pee. Shuffling, burping, and massaging his sore neck. He put the coffee water on and returned for the mail. Political advertisements, a magazine, and two letters: the first, bearing a Washington D.C. postmark, was addressed to J. Jarmusch; the second to Charles Depaulo. He discarded Depaulo and walked toward the kitchen with Jarmusch. While pouring lukewarm water through a bed of day-old grounds, he read:

> "It is characteristic of wisdom not to do desperate things."
>
> Which leaves you out, my unwise, desperate friend. Two women is bad enough, but mixing sex and money is a doomed venture. Janie is bound to discover. You, of course, will regret it even—pay attention to this—if your sugar mama comes through with the dough. Forget it.

There was a great deal more, written in his friend Carlos's blocky script, which he left unread on the kitchen counter. Perhaps when he had a bit more energy.

With his cold cup of weak coffee, he returned to bed. The alarm clock read 3:13, and dangling from it were two silver hooped earrings. Cascading, it seemed, down toward the bed. The smell of her on the pillow. Charlie, nose deep in the cotton folds, wondering if he could detect the cigarettes she smoked. Absent. Absent from the pillow, never staling her clothes or fouling her dark hair. He fondled her earrings and entered a daze.

When he found himself more alert, he was standing, laundered, in front of the door of his apartment and two hours had passed. He stooped, picked up the letter addressed to Depaulo, and exited.

"Have you had a chance to admire the moon?" Charlie, taunting the walled-in dispatcher.

The voice came back preceded by a loud static buzz, drawing out the first, soft consonant. "Fuck you."

"Startling intensity."

"What do you want, di Paulo?"

"I'm going to do some shooting. I'll let you know when I'm back in the cab."

"All right, you're off the board."

Charlie nosed in next to the factory warehouse. From its sheet-metal face, a beam protruded ten feet, on the end of which was tied, by its own cord, a hooded light bulb. He climbed out and walked to the center of the parking lot, checking for perspective. The bright hood contrasted the shadowy rear end nicely, with the darkness of metal faintly visible in the background, climbing up and out of sight. A scene too dim to pick up on camera, he imagined, but the yellow was of a particular luminescence he found very pleasing to the eye. Perhaps with a bit of backlighting the lens would be able to see the scene as his own eye did.

From the roomy Detroit trunk he removed a gas generator, poles rigged with hardware-store floodlights, a tripod, and his $11 garage-sale Super 8 movie camera. He placed the poles, ran an extension cord back to the generator, and then paused briefly to see who might be disturbed by the drone of an electric generator. In each direction, concrete and metal and silence. A sharp pull on the pull-cord produced a rumble and then a sputter. He adjusted the choke and gave it another yank. The machine literally jumped to life, hopping back and forth on curved, chrome bars, the metallic growl amplified by corrugated walls.

He erected his lamps immediately next to the car, extending the poles to their highest reach, to approximate the direction of the warehouse's light. He placed the tripod 20 feet from the driver's door and looked through the camera. Too bright—the pond-water quality of the light was broken by the harsh spill of his floodlights. He adjusted them, moving one pole back five feet, and directing the other toward the metal wall. Through the camera viewfinder he saw that now the light was too diffuse, bathing the cab in sunny brightness.

After a search, he located four steel wheel rims rusting behind the warehouse. Two under the base of each light, the second light post back, facing the cab, and the effect was much improved. Yet slightly too bright—harsh contrast rather than rich saturation. The lamp furthest back was just about right. He tried it with that one alone. Not enough light. He finally found the right quality of illumination by draping his white T-shirt over the metal flaps along the sides of the second lamp. Yet within seconds, he could smell the shirt as it warmed under the blaze of the 250-watt bulb.

Working very quickly, he ran back to the camera and took a light reading. Above the car, his T-shirt began to smoke. He removed it from its perch, fanned it, and turned off the second light. Starting with a completely cool lamp, he calculated two minutes to combustion.

He spent fifteen minutes prepping the scene, and returned to find the metal flaps cool to the touch. A last look through the viewfinder, and then he settled the rubber band on the broken "play" button. A whine: rolling. He sprinted to the light, threw the T-shirt up and over, and then dove into the cab. Action.

This was the scene: A cabbie resting his head in the crook between the door and seat, as if sleeping. After a three count, he raised his head, leaning forward, as if waking. Without sitting fully up, Charlie adopted a position he hoped suggested dawning wakefulness. Acting now with economy, counting off the seconds in his mind.

The camera watched on as the cab driver's head pivoted away, then back, a cigar between his lips. As the camera waited for him to light it, the image shattered into an explosive, dancing glimmer, as if the sun had suddenly greeted its dilated cornea. In the center of the frame, the barest moment after this happened, the camera could also see, in an almost completely overexposed shot, the man's hand rising to his mouth, tipped with the faint ember of the cab's glowing cigarette lighter coil.

Charlie saw the ignition indirectly, as the hood of the car reflected the fire blossoming above. He stopped lighting the cigar and craned his head out the window to study the situation. Flames were spreading like lapping water down the shirt, away from the lamp. Exiting the frame this time at a jog, he went to the generator and pulled the plug on the light. Thought a moment, and shut off the generator itself.

The fluttering aperture droned as he approached, impassively recording his foibles. Twenty-four frames per second, slices of life so close together as to give the illusion of continuity. Yet separate moments, each one a discrete image. He envisioned looking through his film editor at this footage, frame by frame. In the darkness, his body would enter from the left, a gray blotch, ill-defined, like a ghost. The darkness would shroud all but the front half of his cab, reducing the world to this single point of action. A manageable likeness of reality, edited down to what the director wanted the audience to see.

He looked through the camera at the scene as it appeared now, then opened the lens up all the way and zoomed in toward the T-shirt, wafting ashily on waves of upward convection. Now the point of action was too small to advance the narrative: a few licks of flame floating in the center of blackness. He pushed the slow-motion button, and with a sharper whine, the camera recorded 36 frames per second. The space between each picture now shorter still, the illusion closer to perfect continuity.

The flame died, and he shut off the camera.

"Hey listen Mike, I'm going to go home. I'm done."

"Done driving? It's still early, Charlie boy. You didn't get caught looking through somebody's bedroom window with that camera of yours?"

"Never know."

"All right, you're *still* off the board."

"Thanks. See you tomorrow night."

From the cluttered glove box he retrieved a steno pad on which he recorded, "Roll #14, 40 feet. Scene: non-protagonist cab driver (me) asleep under the light of a warehouse. Shot: LS, night (T-shirt fire)." He returned the notebook and began disassembling his equipment.

When the lamps had cooled, he examined his shirt. The fabric had burned away, but a bit of plasticy decal had fused to the bulb's surface. With the short nail of his index finger, he made an exploratory scratch. It was dense, rubbery. He tried scraping it with his pocket knife. The blade gummed up immediately, and now he had two plastic-coated surfaces. A lost cause. With some effort, he managed to clean the blade fairly well on the edge of a piece corrugated steel. He unscrewed the soiled bulb gingerly, abandoning it to the parking lot.

Sunrise was still two hours away. The night had reached the time between worlds; no night owls remained awake and the early morning workers yet slept. In a few buildings throughout the city, just a few graveyarders: workers slicing silica for computer chips, nurses checking pulses, policemen dozing, a taxicab dispatcher sipping old, burned coffee.

In front of his apartment building, Charlie sat in the cab and listened to the hum of power cables. A car pulled up to the streetlight on 12th Avenue and idled, the driver soon gassing it through the intersection while the light was still red. He got out, went in through the back door and down a narrow, featureless hallway. On his left was the boiler room, rumbling away. At the end of the hall, a 92-year-old elevator with a brass name plate: Otï. Someone had scratched off the s. On the third floor, his footsteps fell, quietly but creaking, on the gray wooden floor of the hallway; he wondered, was anyone listening?

As he undressed, he emptied his pockets: the wadded Depaulo. Above the return address was the picture of an old-fashioned movie camera, and inside were two sheets of paper. The first one, on letterhead, said:

Dear Mr. Depaulo,
Thank you for submitting your film, "Taxicab Triptych," to the Portland Film Festival. We are sorry to inform you that we cannot screen Super-8 films. Unfortunately, our submissions guidelines did not include this information. Thank you for submitting your film; we wish you luck with it elsewhere.

Sincerely,
The PFF Selection Committee

The second was hand-written in large, slanting letters on a piece of note paper:

Charles,

Even though we can't show Super-8's, we watched your film. It's fantastic! Every year the Film Institute has a little grant money to give to a couple local filmmakers. I talked to folks around here and if you wanted some money to re-shoot your film on 16mm, there's a very good chance we could help you out. Usually we give $1,000 and discounts on the use of all our equipment. Call me and I'll tell you more about it.

October Moore

He put the letter on his chest and laid his head back on the pillow. After a moment he said, "Hmm."

First came the sharp pulse of his digital alarm, then razor light shafts sliced into his false night from the fissures between blanket and window. Confused, his consciousness suspended above his head, partly still in his dreamless afternoon sleep, partly in the unreality of his artificially-dark bedroom. He sat upright, sweating, blood pounding in his neck; soon waking reality would crash down over sleeping reality and become a dull ache inside his head.

After a few minutes he removed the navy cotton blanket from his window. A day of more yellow and orange and less gray and blue than he'd expected, judging from the seepage he had seen in the dark. Across the river, the buildings of downtown sparkled with washed light, reflecting sun shining off drops left by autumn rain. The blood rose to his temples, and he perched for a moment on the edge of his bed, breathing deep, REM-sleep breaths, the blanket an abandoned pool on the floor at his feet. Despite six months on the same schedule, his body could not adjust to sleeping during the day.

He stood on rubbery legs and went to the kitchen to make coffee. Only recently had he relented and begun using it to fool the natural cycles of his body. Dependency was unseemly. For years he'd avoided it: avoided the coffee shops on every corner of the city, avoided the trappings of spill-proof mugs and buy-ten-get-one-free cards, grinders, coffee makers, and $10 pounds of scorched Indonesian beans. In a secret pact with himself, he bought 3-pound cans of generic grounds and a pour-through filter, promising that the moment he quit driving cab, everything would go into the garbage. He put on the water to boil.

Toward the end of the first cup, typically about the time he was exiting the bathroom clean and showered, his mind began to clear. Perhaps the shower was an additional aid. Charlie, not given to swings of mood, had become accustomed to them during his morning routine. The panic of waking at midafternoon, most of the day gone, began to evaporate under the clear light of caffeine.

Searching for a clean pair of socks, he heard his neighbor screaming. A rareish event which nevertheless happened more often than he liked, the screaming seemed to indicate displeasure, not distress. Or had, anyway, heretofore. Each time, Charlie stopped to listen for pain or fear.

He cocked his head toward the wall and listened for words; today's version wavered slightly, lacking the sophistication of speech. It was typically atonal and unemotional. Nevertheless, he went to the front door and poked his head out.

He had not been studying his neighbor's door long before it swung wide and Laura swept out elegantly, wearing a stained green robe. "OUT OF CIGARETTES," she said, directing the information back into her empty studio apartment in a clear, flat voice. Flowing regally by, she did not look at Charlie, but offered a stagy "HELLO."

She had nearly reached the corner and was about to glide into the third floor foyer when Charlie saw her feet.

"Laura, no shoes!"

As she vanished, she let a hand trail behind in an affirmative wave. In consideration of these facts, he paused, wondering if she had understood him, acknowledged him with her wave, and was now headed to a neighbor's for a loner unfiltered, or had not understood him, had waved to the greeting she thought she heard, and was now prepared to leave the building, loose change in the pocket of her robe.

But then she reappeared.

"I FORGOT," she said, not to Charlie, but generally. Back into the apartment, announcing her arrival to the couch.

Cement stairs led down to a subterranean entrance behind the cinderblock building. The entire area was a palate of grays, unbroken except briefly and pathetically by a nearly-gray tree, dying on the sidewalk. At the landing below street level, he arrived at a steel door propped open by a three-foot tall brick column, crowned with a toupee of sand and spikes of cigarette butts. Taped to the door was a pink sheet of paper: Portland Film Institute.

Inside, the walls of a small alcove greeted visitors with celluloid advertisements. Cameras for sale, film festival announcements, a section where toothy actors had pinned up soft-toned photographs of themselves. From this alcove, stairs led up and down. Following them up, one arrived at the locked second-floor door. Hopeful first-time visitors invariably turned upward. Charlie, who used the Institute's cheap film developer, headed down.

At the bottom of the stairs, he arrived at an open doorway visible from the landing, beyond which lay a grim vista. First, an open space, more a DMZ than a room, ringed by open doors exposing a network of offices crouched under low ceilings, each containing a 1950s gray metal desk, cracked beige chairs bleeding foam rubber, and one or two groaning computers. Light was mostly artificial, but a few of the offices had small windows near the ceiling, looking out on the ankles of people walking by. Like baggies of white crystals in a drug house, the objects of value—in this case film stock—offset the dreariness of the environment. Their black cases gleamed under the light.

Backed up defensively into a far corner of the open space was a particularly battered desk and on it rested an ironic placard reading, "Information." A man, chatting on the phone behind the desk, did not look up. Charlie placed six rolls of film on the desk in front of the attendant, who, sensing that nothing more would be required of him, nodded.

First task completed, Charlie scanned the rooms for bodies. "Excuse me, I'm looking for October Moore." This, directed to a young woman he hoped might actually be October Moore.

She was holding a length of film under a light, squinting to see its tiny images. Pulling the film through her fingers, she repeated this name very slowly, "Oc. Toe. Ber." She marked a frame by holding it between two fingers, still aloft under the light, and turned her head. She was still squinting.

"I'm sorry, October. You're looking for October?" Her eyes widened.

"Yes, October."

"She should be around somewhere." The woman's head began to move back toward the film.

"What does she look like?"

"Shaved head." And now her eyes were squinting through tiny squares of color and Charlie was forgotten.

He stepped back into the foyer, surveying each office. In one, he saw what was not exactly a bald head but a stubbly head, the skiff of hair dyed brilliant yellow, like the fuzz on a tennis ball. The head rose up an inch above the back a chair, ears sporting a brocade of silver earrings. The head floated there, attached to a bare, corded neck; no other evidence of body could be seen. Amid its surroundings, the yellow head did not seem frivolous, as he expected. It seemed defiant, as if actively engaged in battle against the color-absorbing offices.

Charlie's knuckles, about to descend on the door frame, paused. He stood and the head floated; neither moved. He was fascinated by the visual illusion of the disembodied head. He thought about its power to disburse money to poor filmmakers, to instruct and guide, its strange autonomy. As if it alone, separate from colleagues and selection committees, might have the power to authorize banks to give him large sums of money. Or, for that matter, to float about the room on its own power.

She turned around. As the yellow head gave way to a face, he was surprised to see a woman in her early forties.

"Can I help you?"

"Excuse me—are you October Moore?"

Weather-damaged, lined, tanned, bony around the inset eyes. "Yes." She was dressed in shorts and a yellow tube top, one vestige of the 70s he had not seen recur as fashion.

"Hi, I'm Charlie di Paulo." He stood at the door.

She looked at the end of her nose for a moment, thinking, before saying, "'Taxicab Triptych.'"

"Right."

She stood and offered a muscular hand. "Come on in."

Homes crowded out close to the sidewalk like spectators at a parade. Near the corner, a shaggy beast layered with vines and creepers. The grapes, blackberries, and English ivy rose up like a train from the ground and covered it with a thick green coat. Inside, the cobbler Clay Lapierre dozed heavily.

Charlie banged on the door with increasing vigor, including shouts as the minutes passed. Lapierre's 1972 Cadillac was in the driveway, indicating he was home. Also the time, 6:08 in the morning, Charlie noted without concern, was fairly reliable for catching him in. Ten minutes passed and no Lapierre.

Fifteen minutes later, Charlie was pounding the door again, this time holding a styrofoam cup.

"Lapierre, time to get up. It's a beautiful morning out here. You don't want to miss the sunrise." He sat on the front stairs and waited. Periodically he cupped his hand and called out in the direction of the bedroom window, "Coffee's getting cold. Rise and shine. Let's get a move on." And then after another minute or two, "Cassius!" A name spoken only to provoke him.

Twelve hours before giving birth to her first child, Lapierre's mother was watching television. On the black-and-white screen, Muhammad Ali was speaking after being stripped of his title for his disinclination to kill Vietnamese. Though she did not tell her husband, who mistakenly believed his boy would be named Earl, she decided then to call her son Cassius Clay. And so, his birth certificate made it final.

"Oh, so that's why the old man calls you Earl," Charlie said when he first heard the story. "But why not call you Muhammad Ali?"

"Mom didn't like Muhammad Ali. Felt it was too black."

As Charlie stood to make another assault on the door, it swung open. In the doorway stood Lapierre, completely nude.

"I hope you didn't just go to the Quik Stop for that coffee," he said, nodding in the direction of the convenience-store polystyrene in Charlie's hands. He was nearly a foot taller than Charlie, covered with an even pelt of golden-brown hair, except for his bald head, which glistened oilily. "Well come on, before the neighbors start to get excited." Charlie handed over the cup and followed him inside.

Like many of the old homes of North Portland, the front door opened to a staircase and, to one side, a living room. This one was strewn with scraps of leather, some no bigger than a rat's tail, others the size of throw rugs. He had a new television in a corner of the room and very little else. In the center of the expansive space, which was actually two rooms joined by a broad arch, was a table lamp, on the floor. The greatest concentration of scraps was near the lamp; from the center they spread out in a fairly even pattern, as if they had once formed an enormous piece of brittle leather that had fallen and shattered. Also near the lamp, the cobbler's tools and a few thick leather soles.

Lapierre had become a cobbler out of necessity in the beginning and stayed one out of opportunity. Early in his acting career, Clay had researched clothing for a production of *Emil Duda: A Hero of Poland*, leading him to seek out appropriate footwear for a turn-of-the-century Polish factory worker. He found a reference to *poniedzialek* shoes in a history of factory labor, including a picture. *Poniedzialek*, or "Monday," because in the Polish factories at the turn of the century every day was the start of a new week. They were a cross between rubbers and traditional cap toe oxfords. Of course, he couldn't locate such a pair, so he made them. Soles, nails, needle, thread, advice from Dick Hattaway, of Hattaway Shoe Repair, and a thick slab of black cowhide from Best Leather.

He cobbled four pair for the production, and a fifth for himself. Thereafter he noodled with the craft, studied department-store fashions, and slowly began his own business. He made several styles (men's shoes only), but his signature style were the *poniedzialeks*, which had become a minor fashion in Portland.

"I'm going to put on some drawers."

Charlie went into the kitchen and sat at a round pine table overlooking the back yard. A bright ray of dawn came through the windowpane and warmed the room, making him drowsy. As he was dozing off, he heard the rush of a shower.

When he looked up again, Clay was standing in front of him, wearing a pair of pressed wool pants and black shirt. Without the aid of a mirror, he guided an electric shaver over his head. Like a lawnmower, one strip at a time. Clay paused to look out the window at the unusually clear day. At the end of each swipe, out of contact with skin, the razor whined and rattled. A dull, productive groan, high whine, groan whine, groan whine.

He finished mowing his head and took the razor back to his bathroom. He returned and sat at the table, "So what the hell's this all about?"

Charlie retrieved Depaulo and put it on the table in front of Clay. "Read both of them."

Clay picked up the folded envelope, extracting both notes. He absently took a drink of coffee as he read, spat it back into the cup, then stood up and threw the coffee—styrofoam and all—into the sink. On his way to the refrigerator, he dropped the pages in front of Charlie. "You want some decent coffee?"

"No, I'm going to go to bed in a while."

As he was preparing the coffeemaker, "You give this October woman a call yet?"

"Saw her yesterday when I dropped off my last batch of film."

"Well?"

"She said there are two options. One, re-shoot it on 16mm. That's the obvious way, but there are some problems with it. No equipment, first of all, though she said I would get a discount on whatever they have at the Institute for equipment. The main issue is with the sound and editing. If we shoot it on 16mm, we have to write a script and re-shoot everything with mikes and dialogue. With sound, the editing is a lot more complex. *And* it's very expensive."

"How much?"

"Many thousands. Probably ten or fifteen thousand for a 30-minute film."

"So what's the other option?"

"Yeah, now the second option is interesting. Transferring the film from Super 8to 16. I wasn't even aware you could do it this way. Apparently, it's a relatively easy process. You can also add some visual effects. Of course, sound effects can be added, but no dialogue."

"Okay, so what's that cost?"

"I don't know—a lot cheaper."

Water was entering the coffee machine with a great crackling sound as it hit the heating element. Clay returned to his seat at the table. "Man, ten grand. Same length?" Charlie nodded. "So let me ask you this: now that you know you can make a—what is it, about a half hour?" Charlie nodded. "A half hour film for ten thousand, is this the film you want to spend it on?"

"Absolutely."

"Which one do you want to do, transfer or re-shoot?"

I'm sort of intrigued by transferring it, which would be quick. But I mean, shooting it on 16mm—who can resist that? October suggested the re-shoot as well."

"She liked 'Cabbie Triptych?'"

"Yeah, and she thought it would lend itself to a script really well."

"All right. Sounds like the first thing you need to do is see Ava."

"Nope, that's done. I mean, I may hit her up and see if she wants to help fund this film, but as far as everything else, we're done." A pause. "Janie. Things are seriousing up."

"No kidding?"

"Yeah, in fact, she spent the night a couple of nights back."

Clay, winking, acknowledgement without lasciviousness.

"Slept together, but the clothes stayed on."

"You're an old-fashioned cabbie."

"Still, we passed some kind of no-looking-back point. We laid there all night talking and kissing. We *could have* done something more, but in a way, that might have made it seem less intimate. Kind of crass, you know what I mean?"

"Hmm."

"So I've got to cut Ava off. I mean—"

"Janie doesn't know about Ava"

"Of course not. When was I going to mention it? *How* would I mention it?" Clay, nodded. "Anyway, the whole thing looks pretty seedy, so there'll definitely be no telling her now."

"So. That limits you a bit more on the money front, doesn't it?"

"Yes. Any ideas?"

"About Janie or the money?"

"Money."

"Vic?"

"Only as a last resort."

"Credit?"

"Maxed out."

Clay went to the coffeemaker and poured out a cup. "Sure you don't want any?"

"No, I need to go to bed."

He took a meditative sip. "Well then, we'll have to think about this one."

2.

In the fluorescence of a convenience store parking lot, reading the news.

"Cab 133?"

Charlie smoothed the newspaper, folded it in half, then into quarters, and placed it on the seat next to him.

As he raised the speaker to his mouth, "Cab 133 — hey Charlie, you near the radio?"

"Yeah Mike, I'm right here. Whatcha got?"

"Lady wants you in Irvington, a personal request. Says there's no hurry. You want it?"

"What's the address?"

"2436 NE 17th."

"Okay, I'll take it. You still got her on the line?"

"Yeah."

"Tell her a half hour, give or take. Cab out."

Irvington, wooded thickly by the trees of New England: oaks, maples, walnuts. The settlers to Portland civilized the coniferous Oregon forests, planting their trees among a safe, square grid of homes. Now suitably aged, the trees stretched out their thick arms, small leafy fingers laced together, high above the pavement. Arching up over the streets like a cathedral's ceiling, lit by antique streetlights.

The vast house in front of which he parked had an antebellum quality, with pillars and a porch that wrapped around three sides. In the century since its construction, it had been subdivided to accommodate roomy apartments on each of its three floors. Inside the top one, Janie Prescott waited for his horn.

He had first visited the house a month earlier, by chance. But cab driving is a game of chance; the brief communication of a few digits and a street name, crackling like a fortune-teller's voice across the radio. Older cabbies loaded the dice; to the regular airport crowd, they gave out business cards and offered beck-and-call service any time of the day. During the slow hours, they glided around downtown hotels like carp underneath submerged logs, waiting for a fat, safe target. The more often they could get a good look at a fare before agreeing to take him somewhere, the better.

For Charlie, the risk was part of the fun. He enjoyed the electric shock when Mike radioed — time and space collided, tumbling out in the concrete formulation of an address: his immediate future revealed.

In this case, the address and time of day gave him hope for an airport run. The woman, whose name Mike included with the address, stepped out onto her expansive porch as he pulled up. No luggage. He noticed her appearance vaguely. Attractive, middle-class. It would be a safe fare. He might fear condescension, but not violence.

As always, seeing his fare's harmlessness calmed and reassured him — an emotion that commingled, however, with mild disappointment.

"Front seat or back?" Charlie, ready at the door.

She stopped walking, still ten feet from the car, regarding him as she would an older, devious brother. "Are you allowed to sit in the front?"

"Yeah, sure." He snatched at the door handle, stood back, and let the heavy slab of metal swing open of its own weight. She moved timidly forward, and after pulling abreast of him, darted smiling into the car, as if to avoid losing the opportunity. He noted her height as she passed him. Substantially taller than he.

Inside the cab he asked the usual question. "Where to?"

She turned her whole torso to face him, long fingers resting on her lap, still smiling. He found this odd and slightly unnerving. Before naming a restaurant a short drive away, she sat and watched him for a moment.

And then she continued to watch.

He pulled a U-turn and started back down the street, trying not to return her stare. As he drove, her gaze passed, occasionally, to something on the street that caught her eye. Sitting rigidly, scanning both sides of the street, she looked to him like a little girl traveling to the city for the first time. With each pass of her eyes, she paused at his profile, her stare burrowing into his right temple.

What she saw: his head, a larger-than-average globe out onto the front of which stretched a peninsula of russet hair, ending like a tuft of sod at the top of his forehead. He had green-gray eyes that were set back deep in their sockets, hiding as if by fatigue underneath cantilevered eyebrows. A face just less than good-looking, but compelling.

A cool cabbie, he kept his eyes on the road.

"You don't look like a cab driver."

He eased into a turn without saying anything. Then, "Too skinny."

She smiled.

At the restaurant, he pulled the cab into a parking place, put it into park, turned off the meter. It was a dreary chain restaurant. An advertisement for a "three-dollar breakfast menu" stared at them from a painted window. As she reached for her purse, he returned the favor and gave her a long, careful look. She had dense, chocolate hair, brown eyes so dark they looked black, pale skin freckled at the collarbone, dark semi-circles under each eye. Snowy teeth save one, upper left canine. Yellow.

From a black plastic cube she brought out a rubber coin purse. A five and three singles on a $2.90 fare.

He saw the five and singles and didn't stop to count. It went straight into his breast pocket, joining a fat fold of ones and fives (for change). "Hey, thanks."

She didn't get out. He made a move to open his own door, thinking perhaps she had an expectation that he would open her door. Like old women.

"Can I ask you a question?"

He waited. Noticed that she smelled of gingerbread.

"What was your most interesting fare today?"

Now it was his turn to smile. "That's a good question. I don't believe anyone's ever asked me that before." His eyes seemed to pull further back into their sockets. "Interesting to me or most exotic?"

"To you."

"I just started, actually. How about yesterday?"

"Yesterday's good."

"All right, let me think. Okay, I have one. There's this old guy who lives in one of those apartment buildings for the elderly—I don't know if you're familiar with them. This one was over on Holgate. It was probably 45 degrees by the time I got over there—this was maybe 10 o'clock—and this old man comes out in a seersucker suit. He's also got a cane and a hat. Very dapper, but he must have been freezing."

"He asked to go to this shithole tavern called the Semaphore, which of course is only about three blocks away. That's always the way with the oldsters, they never go very far. On the drive over he didn't say a word, but at one point he took a gold cigarette case out of his breast pocket. He had these massive hands, totally smooth and worn; when he pulled out a cigarette, it looked like a toothpick. He didn't light it, just put it between his lips. And then, when we get to the Semaphore, he pulls out his billfold and inside it is a single twenty-dollar bill, nothing else. No driver's license, credit card, pictures, nothing—just the twenty."

He stopped and looked over at the young woman for a reaction.

She had leaned toward him slightly.

"Though to tell you the truth, I take Henry over to the Semaphore two or three times a week, so maybe that doesn't qualify."

Her eyes were on his lips, watching. "Tell me another one."

The next day she waited until nine before calling for another cab. Charlie, cruising the area, hoping she might, but he had just about given up. They both tried to make it seem coincidental, but both noted that it wasn't. Janie asked for another story, and Charlie, who had prepped one, told her about a favorite stripper of his who was working on a law degree.

The third day she called early—Charlie was downtown and missed her. Instead of him, she found a slick-haired buzzard, Adam's apple bobbing independent of speech, waiting at her curb. His cab smelled like feet, and Janie spent the trip looking out her window gulping fresh air. Charlie cruised the neighborhood until ten thirty before giving up. The fourth day she called again around eight and after that they made it a regular pick-up, no call necessary.

Their relationship developed in increments. Short rides to nearby restaurants. Increasingly long post-arrival chats. Huge, indecent tips, the likes of which he had only previously received from a 6-foot-4, middle-aged transsexual whose hands lingering during payment.

During this period, their conversations were bounded by role and ritual. Janie, the client, asked the questions and prepared the ground for conversation. The ritual was hearing about his fares, coaxing details and observation from him. She liked his sense of people, enjoyed his fascination with the mundane, his suspicion of the gaudy or lurid, his love of odd, his appreciation of common fares.

She learned that when people climbed into his cab, they told him amazing things. All he had to do was wait and listen, make small talk until they told him the questions they really wanted him to ask. Once he showed that his ear was open they seized their chance to unburden themselves. They told him everything: prognoses family members were too afraid to learn; petty crimes and trespasses they had made in silent rebellion against spouses, bosses, parents, children; abuses they had suffered or committed; secrets they didn't want to keep.

Even though she asked him to tell her about his fares, Janie understood that he was in the slow, careful process of pulling details out of her life. He had an observational eye, and even as he was telling stories, he was learning about his favorite fare.

He told her a story about taking a woman to see her children at a foster home in Tualatin, and used it to inquire about her own family. A story about a group of drunken teenagers led to stories about her college days. An old woman with a sick dog became an inquiry about pets Janie had owned. Janie was happy to reveal herself in their parking-lot chats. She wanted him to know her like he knew his other fares, but slowly. She meted out the facts knowing that he was stowing them away, filling her out in his mind.

Charlie did gather the details, putting them into a mental dossier he constructed over the course of a dozen or more chats. By the time their relationship advanced beyond cabbie and fare, he had put together the main features of her biography.

She was a recent immigrant to Portland, arriving just three months before their first meeting. She had splashed onto the banks of the Willamette with the vanguard of young tech professionals, drawn to the suburban campuses where engineers coded software. A woman of specific skills but vague goals, she had migrated west from Minneapolis because the West Coast was where tech was happening. Shivering Midwesterners recommended the Pacific Northwest for its mild winters; savvy hipsters said Portland was cooler than Seattle and way less pretentious. And her ability — translating the binary code of the engineers into short, declarative sentences — was in especial shortage in the burgeoning silicon forest: she would be able to write her own ticket.

So far, though, Portland had been a bust. The gray skies, to begin with. They had come early that year, sporadic in late August and regular by mid-September. To a woman whose body chemistry had been honed by the brutal extremes of Minnesota's climate, the weather's unremitting softness was debilitating. Like the taut muscles of an astronaut suddenly deprived of gravity, her body and mind lost their focus.

She noticed that she wasn't alone; low-grade torpor seemed the natural state for Portlanders. They self-medicated with caffeine, but to no great effect. They were minimally polite but uncommunicative: on buses and trains, in stores and restaurants, they responded with wan smiles and straightforward answers to her queries, but offered never so much as a nod of the head if left to themselves. Their brain waves dully active, they stood on empty street corners waiting for the "walk" sign to prod them into motion. Even though she was sliding into this native sluggishness, she charged past them and out into traffic.

Her irritation at the city was heightened by the residents' inexplicable pride. Despite the lack of evidence to support such a position, they were slavish in their love of Portland. Every time she mentioned she was new in town, someone invariably asked, "Isn't it such a great town?" They didn't want to hear "no." Janie hadn't yet formed a definitive position on the city, but she knew that the constant badgering was making her hate it. They praised their restaurants (average), their local art scene (meager), and their local bookstores (these she admitted were pretty great). In rebellion, she refused the city's so-called virtues — which explained why she ate at faceless chain restaurants.

Her job was providing no refuge. She traveled each day by light-rail to a network of desolate concrete pods in the suburbs on the east side of town, only to be greeted by an insular (and self-satisfied) world of protected, white, male software designers. They spoke of consumer products, new cars, landscaping, and children.

The square concrete pods of her office "campus" were connected by walkways; each was a single story tall and consisting of a field of square cubicles. Each cubicle in turn was composed of square desks, square chairs, and cubical computers. On the square walls of each cubicle were tacked square bits of paper and photographs which expressed the "personality" of the inhabitant, though Janie saw the same pictures of perky, slightly-overweight faces, the same fuzzy-animal calendars, the same "Far Side" clippings repeated in each one. The pods' only roundness: lumpy men in khakis with computers reflected in their fisheye glasses, balding foreheads shiny from overhead lights. She described it all as a fractal of squareness.

Janie's unnoticed revolt was in heterodoxy. She nurtured a layer of dust on the walls and surfaces and allowed the scatter of colored pushpins to remain where they had been replaced, haphazardly, after her predecessor's departure. She looked like a squatter — or would, had anyone bothered to notice. Three months in and thus far no one had asked about it. She described her anonymity to Charlie with relish.

In the dry, crisp Midwestern air, she had been an outdoor person. She had ridden her bike to work, gone cross-country skiing in the winter, swum one of the ten thousand lakes in the summer. She did none of this in her new town. In their place, a sole new activity, another private rebellion: she had taken up smoking. Several times during the day, she interrupted dreary conversations with, "Sorry, I need a cigarette." Outside the pods, alone, she blew jets of her own polluted air at dodging engineers as they went to the parking lot. Bad breath and nicotine stains, but still worth it.

The story went back earlier, to Minnesota, but the information grew sketchier the further back it went. She had a younger sister who was just now entering Macalester College — her own alma matter. Her father worked for the government and her mother was a bookkeeper. After college, she had worked for a software company that maintained a database for dairy farmers — which was dull enough to cause her to consider radical change. Up until her move away from home, she had been waiting for the pleasure of life to begin. And so she had set off to Portland for the fun, except that so far it had been in short supply.

Except for Charlie (and this he had to intuit from observation). His cab became the world into which she waited to slip, his colorful nights a tonic to her gray world. She waited for his unembellished stories that seemed almost vivid enough to see. They gave ballast to help her ground her life as it floated each day into the surreal concrete pods. His tales were flat, like police reports of little old women, eight a.m. drunks, and debutantes who actually lived and breathed in this city she had not yet come to know.

Unlike Charlie, however, she asked pointed questions during their conversations. These he evaded. During their conversations, she also probed the cabbie for information on his life, and these he also dodged. He asked oblique questions and got tons of information; she asked direct ones and learned nothing. To the question of where he was from, he answered, "Here." Yet she had already learned that his father lived in Arizona. Discrepancy? Something had happened to his mother but she couldn't discover what. "Gone," he said.

Friends occasionally appeared in his stories — ghostlike beings who entered only to advance plot. She assumed he wasn't on the career cabbie track, but even this remained unclear. Other interests? He hadn't said. One thing she had clarified: no girlfriend. She asked about it the second or third time she saw him, casually, but it had been too early. He'd said, "Now?" But once, after he'd told a story about a hip artist he knew, she asked him again, pointedly. For once, he answered it quickly, "No."

The arrangement held course for three weeks, a ritual of little variation: arrival, small talk and trip to a restaurant, story, foolish wide smiles, and departure.

Finally, in the parking lot of the Lloyd Center Village Inn, the first variation of routine. "Would you like to do something for me?" It was di Paulo, which surprised them both.

"Depends."

"It's easy. I've been shooting a Super-8 film for a few months, about the cab driving. I want you to do a scene."

"No kidding. Wow, a movie. You're a movie maker?"

"It's just a short. Let's not make too much out of it."

"Finally, I'm getting a little action over here."

"Quit it."

"What else do you want to tell me?"

"Do you want to talk about this or not?"

"Oooooh, big talk. Okay, what's it about?"

"It's a little hard to explain. It takes place in the cab."

"That clarifies everything. Thanks." They squared off, nose to nose. He smiled; she kept a straight face. "What do I have to do?"

"Be yourself, play a regular fare."

"Oh, I've been demoted to a 'regular' fare now, have I?"

"I mean you don't have to dress up or get in character."

"Well, I need to know what it's about first."

"It's about the cab."

"Are you the star?"

"No, my friend Clay plays the cabbie."

"Clay, hmm? Which one is he, again?"

"Friend of mine."

"I see. What's the plot?"

"I told you, it's about cab driving."

"You suck. I'm not doing anything until I hear what it's about."

"All right, all right. Well, it's kind of a concept piece, which is why it's hard to explain. There's no sound in Super 8, so it limits what you can do. You tend to see a lot of Charlie Chaplin or concept pieces as a result. The worst part of it is that I'm pretty bad with plots as it is, so without sound, it's even more dangerous. I once tried to write a screenplay and ended up with ten pages of dialogue and 30 pages of camera angles."

"Would you get *on* with it?"

"Hang on. God. So in this movie, I've been filming Clay. The idea is that I take a 'day in the life' and then break it down into three different stories."

"From different perspectives."

"No. What you see are three separate stories. In the first one, the cabbie picks up a sinister-looking guy. He drives him around for a little while, but when he drops him off, the sinister man asks him to come by later and pick him up again. Then there's a few scenes of him doing his usual cabbie thing before picking the guy up again. It appears like he's scared of the guy all day long."

"Does anything happen to him?"

"No; in the end the sinister man gets out and the cabbie looks relieved."

"Okay, got it."

"The second segment shows the cabbie having a rough day—he gets lost, he gets a flat, everyone shafts him on the tip. But then he picks up this little old lady, and she's such a sweetheart that his whole day turns around."

"That seems a little simplistic."

"Thanks." He leaned in toward her until she smiled. "It's supposed to be. It's supposed to be sentimental and sappy. Bad music, soft focus, that kind of thing. Then in the final part, it's all the footage cut together—you see the cabbie has a very normal day. The sinister-looking man is in there, the old woman, plus a lot of additional footage that you haven't seen before, but it's all shot without any kind of slant, so it amounts to nothing."

"I see what you mean by concept piece."

"It's supposed to be commentary on the way we make movies. You know, the standard plot is like, 'boy meets girl' — they show you all the events related to them meeting, but none of the other stuff going on. Real life is messier."

"I could see it being fascinating, but also not. So is it good?"

"You'll have to judge for yourself."

"It's done? What do you need me for?"

"It's mostly done, but I may tinker with another edit. You can never have too much footage."

"I see. So how do you get all the actors?"

"I fill in with other friends as fares, or occasionally an actual fare if I think they'll be interested. It's a little bit harder then because I have to shoot around the fact that Clay's not there. But I've gotten some great stuff that way. I tempt them with a free ride."

"What's it called?"

"'Taxicab Triptych.'"

"Oooh, clever."

"Yeah, titles aren't my strength, either."

"Well, you might be able to talk me into it. Cause you know, I did a little acting in college. What do you want me to do?"

"Let's just try some stuff. We can start here if you're game."

She considered this for a moment while looking at her shoes: black, stylish, new. "I don't know if I like what I'm wearing."

Charlie, looking up through the windshield at the sky. "Well, it's pretty dark now anyway. Probably too dark. What about tomorrow? I could pick you up a little earlier."

"Maybe, but before we start all this, mister, there's something I want to know."

"Yeah, what's that?"

She leaned in and lowered her voice. "Am I a friend or a free ride?"

He noticed that when she laughed, he could see a small flash of silver at the back of her mouth.

The day they planned to do the shoot, Charlie was late to pick her up and there was some screwing around at dinner and so they overshot the optimum filming conditions. Back at her apartment at seven o'clock and the light was already poor. The sun had dipped underneath the tree line: now blotches of intense orange and yellow streamed though trees, punctuating pools of shadow. He looked through the camera and into the murky evening.

"How's it look?"

"Perfect," he lied.

They began by staging the shot, extemporaneously. "Why don't you turn the light off in your apartment, then back on for a few seconds, then off, like you were on your way before realizing you forgot something. Then zip down as quick as you can and I'll pan down to the front door and catch you coming out."

"What then?"

"Yeah, let's think. Okay, you just glance at the cab once — almost a reflex — then come down the stairs while you root around in your purse."

"What am I looking for?" Nudging his elbow. "Come *on*, what kind of director are you? I haven't even *asked* what my motivation for the scene is."

"Oh, for crying out loud. The talent's already getting pissy." He smiled. "How 'bout you're looking for your sunglasses." Halfway between the cab and house, he found an orange-tipped maple leaf. "Okay, as you're digging around, keep your eye open for this." He placed the leaf in the center of the sidewalk, fifteen feet from the curb. "When you see it, pull out your sunglasses, put them on, and about six feet before you reach the cab, look up at the camera."

"Going for a bit of the glamour thing, are you Mr. di Paulo?"

"Exactly right. In fact, if you want to give your hair a bit of a toss as you're looking up, that might be nice too."

"Over the top."

"You think so? All right, no hair toss."

"Give me a few minutes to check myself in the mirror — I'll holler out the window when I'm ready."

"Yeah, that's good. I have to set the camera up and take a light reading."

He watched her climb the stairs and disappear through the great oak door before he set about prepping the scene. He positioned the camera so that the initial shot would be framed by the car's trunk and back window as Janie walked down the path. He panned from her window, down to the door, followed the path toward the cab—it was pretty nice composition for a rush job.

The light was getting soupier and Janie was still fooling around with her clothes. He gave her a blast of the horn. A moment later, the window flew open.

"Okay, okay. God!" From the window, Janie's glamorous head of hair. "I'm ready."

"Count to five—one one-thousand, two one-thousand, like that—and then turn off the light."

"Yep, here I go!"

On the first take, Janie was slow in getting down to the front door. She came out laughing. "I tripped coming down the stairs." Cut.

Take two, timing fairly good, Janie came out the door, gave Charlie a glance and . . . laughter. Cut.

Take three was the big winner. Light off, back on, count of four, off. A slow pan down the front of the building from window to door from which, by rare film serendipity, Janie instantly emerged. Distracted look at the cab, descending the stairs and rummaging, leaf, glasses out and on the face. A glance (without laughter), then the subtlest of hair tosses, and out of the frame.

Perfect. It was a rare (in his experience) aligning of director and actor. The light would ruin it, probably. One chance in ten that the visual quality of the shot would look intentional, but he could hope.

Skipping toward the talent. "Janie, that was amazing!" He gave her a spontaneous hug as she came around the corner of the cab. Arms around her waist, eyes at her chin, a new sense of proportion. He let go.

"I told you I did a little acting in college." This time a full, Hollywood hair toss.

Full dusk. They tried one half-hearted attempt at close-ups and then he threw in the towel. While he packed up his equipment, Janie went upstairs to make coffee and herbal tea.

In her sparse living room, Charlie sat on a reproduction 1940s red velvet couch. When Janie came bearing beverages, she reclined on the matching armchair. "That was a total blast."

"Yeah, I love shooting. I love it all, actually. Editing is fun, too."

The conversation began on the topic of film. Which were his favorites, hers. As he watched her talk about *Reds*, Charlie noticed how keenly he was taking things in. His deepening infatuation with Janie was manifesting as sharp awareness. He could feel the moment imprinting itself onto his brain. The walls were painted a bold adobe, which made the maple floor look almost white. On the wall next to the door was a sole picture: a framed, blurry photograph of a small girl spinning in a raincoat. He looked at the blond coffee table, the cream throw rug. If there had been a list of Latin declensions on the table, it would have gone into the memory forever, too.

She was leaning in toward him, a rim of brown on her lower lip from the coffee. More animated than when they were in his car, she was the one talking, mostly. He noticed the temperature of the room, the heat that came off her sunlit wall, the quality of the light coming from the floor lamp sitting between them.

"Hey, what are you looking at?"

"Your apartment."

"You've seen it before."

"Once, briefly. I've never had a chance to study it."

"Trying to figure me out?"

"Sort of, yeah. I don't know. Normally I wouldn't think an apartment would say much."

"But?"

"Well, I mean, for example you've got orange walls and red furniture. You've gone out on a decorating limb there."

"You think so? What do you think it says about me?"

"I'm still drawing my conclusions."

"Well, you've got me at a disadvantage. I've never seen *your* apartment."

"I guess that's true."

"We should go see it."

"Now?"

"Sure, why not?"

"No, it's a bit messy."

"Oh, messy. There's a hell of an excuse. What are you hiding?"

"Bodies? A wife? I tell you what. Why don't you come over tomorrow and I'll make you dinner?"

"Well, it's all right—as a back-up plan. Can you cook?"

"Canned soup or cereal, take your pick."

"I guess it will be worth it to see inside your life, analyze you."

"Excellent."

"I'll bring my pen and take notes."

By this time, he had learned a fair amount about Janie's culinary tastes. She liked lusty meals of meat and starch and red wine. Preferred bold flavors to subtle, admired tradition in dining. An intermediate chef, Charlie selected from his pool of mastered entrees broiled salmon. Steaks, steeped in a sake marinade, broiled in tinfoil. He decided on a second pocket for roasting vegetables but pondered—use diced potatoes in the vegetable medley or wrap up whole russets for Janie? They would be less elegant, but she might appreciate the familiarity. In the end, the potatoes went in alone, also in coats of tin.

An hour before he picked her up, he prepared the tinfoil packets and put them in the refrigerator. Made a last tidying pass, put out a bowl of fruit on the dinette. All that remained was to pick her up at 6:30. He had chosen the early hour because his building appeared less institutional in the daylight, the apartment larger and more cheery.

At her place, he didn't honk from the curb as usual, but buzzed from outside the front door.

A hissing came through the speaker and he hollered, "It's me." The machine went dead and he waited. After five minutes he wondered if she had heard him at all. He went out to the front yard and looked up at her apartment—and at that moment she came out the front door.

"Are you looking at something there?"

"The hang of your eaves. By the way, you didn't happen to call for a cab, did you?"

The day was overcast, a fact Charlie regretted as they pulled up to the VMC, which now had a municipal look, like a high school in red brick. It even had thief-proofing wrought iron on the lower windows. In the sunlight it looked somehow English. But now just grim.

Nevertheless, Janie bounded out of the car, admiring it. "Wow, cool place." She especially liked Oti, its inside accordion door, mechanical pushbuttons, and the lurch as it started grinding up to the third floor.

"Wow, this place is great. Why were you holding out on me?"

A bit of sunlight poked through a cloud when they came into his apartment. It seemed light, airy, clean and even Charlie saw its antique chic.

"It was an issue of tidiness, not coolness."

Janie surveyed the apartment. From the front door she saw the two stairs that led up to the bathroom, causing a smile to flash. She charged at them. "Hey, what's up there?" He allowed her to linger in a moment of admiration for his clawfoot tub before showing her how each apartment had a pull-out bed that extended into the neighboring apartment, accounting for the two steps up. Like a bar-room magic trick, he pulled his own bed through the wall and out from underneath neighbor Laura's bathroom.

"Ingenious," she said, rolling the bed in and out.

"Can I get you something to drink?"

"Whatcha got?"

"Alcoholic or non?"

"Alcoholic."

"Beer. Two varieties: stout or India pale ale."

"You don't have any wine?"

"You're in Portland now; you've got to kick that wine habit. This is a beer town."

"Beer's icky."

He went to the table where he had left a paper sack next to the fruit bowl. He selected two bottles of beer, went to the kitchen and poured them into glasses. Thick and black as oil. "You just haven't been drinking the right beer."

"Ewww. This is going to be *so* icky. *Look* at it." But she took the glass. "So when do we eat, mister?"

"Food will take a half hour to cook, roundabout. When do you want to eat?"

"Now."

"Hmm, well. I'll see what I can do." From the kitchen, "Put some music on."

He set the oven to preheat, pulled out the food, and put the rest of the beer in the fridge. While he puttered, he heard her testing music in the living room. A few notes of the Clash, silence. He put in the veggies, pulled out the salad, and tossed it. He came out of the kitchen to the sound of jazz, but then saw her stop the music. Eject. She picked up a handful of CDs and thumbed through them, stopping from time to time to read the back cover of one. Charlie, watching, noticing that she took sizeable swallows of her beer.

She finally settled on a 70s funk compilation. Decisively dropping the CD in the player, she pressed play and spun away from the stereo.

"Hey. How long have you been standing there?"

"Just came out."

She turned back for her beer, sitting next to the stereo. "I don't believe you. You were spying on me." He didn't say anything; didn't move. She walked up to him, too close, looked down her nose at him. "You little spier." Her assessment punctuated with another swallow of beer.

"See, stout. Tasty."

She looked at the remaining inch of liquid in her glass, then back at him. Leaned back. "Do you like my music selection?" They listened to a fat bass line roll out of the speakers and let smiles bloom.

"I do."

The evening sped by and lasted forever. Janie complimented Charlie's "delicate Oregon cooking." Charlie noted that Janie had become, in one evening, quite a "beerhound." They talked about her work, his film. They went out on his two-by-five balcony while Janie smoked. They drank all their beer, walked to the grocery store for more. Their bodies moved closer together, their hands found ways to touch each other. Janie manned the stereo, selecting Charlie's oddest music, challenging him to protest.

On the balcony around 11, Arvo Pärt's drums banging minimally from inside the apartment. "Here, I want you to smoke one." Janie, proffering a Marlboro.

"No thanks. Talk about icky. You should just be happy I don't care if you smoke."

She put the cigarette in her mouth, lit it and handed it to him. "Here, smoke it."

He took it, examined it for a moment, inhaled. His lungs were used to smoke of a different kind, and he didn't cough, but his chest burned. As they looked forward, east toward 13th Avenue, an icy choir serenaded them in Estonian. Charlie blew jets of smoke through his nose like a dragon until his head began to spin. To control the balcony's bucking, he stepped forward and took hold of the railing. His cigarette, half smoked, sailed to the street.

Janie looked at him, took a last drag of her own, wholly-smoked cigarette, and sent it after his. Then she stepped to swaying Charlie and put her hand on his arm and turned him around. She leaned in and gave him a gentle lippy kiss. Her hair fell down around their faces and they stayed still, lips touching but not moving. Finally, hands on his face, holding him there, not taking her lips off his, she said, "See. Now we both smell like smoke."

He spent a few seconds feeling the electricity of their close bodies, their faces joined by skin and hair. Then he took her hands and led her back into the apartment, over to the stereo. He didn't let go of her hands but moved them to his waist, fixing them like clamps. Arvo out, a cassette, laying handily (but not accidentally) near, in. Hands back down to hers, still clamped to his hips. Then music rolled out of the speakers—dancing music, something Janie didn't recognize. Ska maybe.

Charlie started to swing his hips and backed up, a reverse conga line of two back into the open space in front of his couch. Alcohol limbs began swaying, pivoting on alcohol joints. He spun around, put his arms around Janie's neck, moved lewdly under her hands.

Half time to the music, bodies apart, hands now on hands, eyes on eyes. Grooving. A mix tape of fast and slow rhythm, but the two bodies moved at their own speed. Catlike, circling. During a slow number, Janie tried to pull Charlie in, but he skittered away. He turned his back and shook his ass at her, smiled over his shoulder.

The next song was fast and he danced around her in a circle until she sped up. Bobbing, weaving, nothing touching now. A trickle of sweat ran down Charlie's temple and he saw that the hair at Janie's scalp was also damp. Black tendrils of damp hair curled around her forehead down to her jaw. They came together at high speed, let hands grab bodies, let bodies pull sweatily close. Spinning slower until they were at a shuffle, a wall of energetic music no longer accompaniment. Soundtrack.

Their faces came together again, lips on lips. Then tongues on tongues. Not hungry, as he expected, but soft and gentle. Also their embrace, light and caressing as if they didn't want to damage something fragile. The music ended on a long, sharp note and the apartment seemed to reverberate in the silence. Still shuffling and swaying, they moved eventually toward the couch and sat down. They kissed and hugged and held hands so gently they could feel the ridges of their fingerprints hop against each other.

From the curb, he studied the yellow light of her living room window, draped out the sill and across the porch like a length of cloth. A scene from Edward Hopper. He imagined his gaze rising on a dolly, level with the window. Slow zoom. The window filled the frame, a couch and coffee table beyond the fluttering curtain. In the foreground, the arm of a human rested, with an ashtray, on the arm of an overstuffed chair. It was a naked limb, lightly tanned, with feminine curves. The camera entered the window and swung around toward her face. After a tight zoom, it revealed a single eye and a lock of black hair, a line of smoke curling through the frame.

He gave three short honks on his horn. Inside the apartment, the light went off, came back on for scant seconds, went back off. He got out of the cab, ambled up the sidewalk, and inhaled, detecting notes of autumn decay on the breeze.

Out the front door, rolling down the steps like a Labrador retriever.

"Hey Shorty," She stopped mostly before contact, and gave him a chesty squeeze. "You hungry?"

"I might be."

Heading south. "What does the lady fancy tonight?"

"You pick, I don't care."

"You know I'll go for Thai every time."

"But I told you I don't care."

"All right then. Thai it is."

Janie was antsy, smiling at nothing. Her words were punctuated by squeezes of Charlie's right elbow. For the first time since he'd known her, she pulled out a cigarette in the cab. Her energy, ready to consume him; he leaned in, waiting to be consumed.

Their relationship, driving along Northeast 15th Avenue, was at the moment of exquisite potential. From the slow comfort of their chats they had raced forward. The film shoot at Janie's apartment, the dinner at Charlie's. Everything was stretching out in front of them. His brain soaked it in.

At the Thai restaurant, Janie was a bit calmer. Their hands were stretched out across the table, laced. Heads low, ducked toward each other.

"Oh, I have something for you." He leaned back and dug around in his pocket for her silver hoops.

"You left these at my apartment."

| 3.

New to Portland, standing in a line of three for a screening of *Touch of Evil* at the Zale Theater. At the ticket booth a lithe blonde argued for a senior discount. Next in line, Charlie's compact girlfriend Molly. Last, Charlie wondering what the big deal was.

"You'll see," she said.

The Zale was a dingy 1928 structure at the corner of 34th and Belmont. He examined the dull brown-brick façade, the pebble-sized tile murky under a patina of grime at his feet. Strips of metal dangled from the marquee, handprints smeared the glass door. Two chrome poster boxes hung at either side of the entrance, glass long gone; one was empty, the other contained a piece of notebook paper. Handwritten in pink marker: LOCAL FILMS SCREENED EVERY THIRD MONDAY AT 7PM.

Charlie, a recent college drop-out, on his first visit to the Zale, lured by Welles and Molly.

At the front of the line the dispute continued. An indistinct, cement-colored man, his face fractured by three snaking cracks in the window, croaked through the speaker. Eventually the dispute ended, the blonde losing on appeal to the manager.

The threadbare lobby held no greater promise: yellowed wallpaper; a single, ancient light fixture giving off a dim glow; a desiccated green couch outside the bathroom doors. And then the concessionaire, a lumpy teen with thick glasses, started scooping their popcorn from a clear plastic garbage bag underneath the counter.

"Hey, why don't you give us the fresh stuff?" Charlie asked, pointing to a machine cascading with drifts of popcorn behind the boy.

"The machine breaks all the time, so we store up a bunch," he said, handing a tub of pre-bagged to Molly.

"It's working now."

The teen gave a suspicious glance at the machine. "Well, okay. I guess it doesn't matter."

Molly, returning the tub, fidgeted. Then to Charlie, softly. "It all tastes the same."

"Ah, he doesn't care." He grinned at the kid as he took the fresh tub.

From the lobby, warm popcorn in one hand, irritated Molly in the other, he aimed at two heavy wooden doors, carved with art-deco sun rays. He admitted privately that they, at least, were pretty cool.

"Are you ready?" Molly asked, hand on the theater door.

Inside, a cathedral shimmered in white. The curtain, centerpiece of the theater, was a lustrous white velvet, folds heavy like the curves of fresh snow. Gracefully tall, crowned by scalloped ruffles, fleshy feet brushing a four-foot stage. The seats were crystalline cubes of frosted chiffon, divided in three sections by two spits of icy carpet. Sconces embossed with opaque *fleurs-de-lis* glowed amid walls dancing and shimmering in a ghostly taffeta blouse.

"See," she said. "What did I tell you—fucking cool, huh?"

Lit nightly in monochrome, as images from Hollywood's golden era turned the Zale into a glinting winter cave. Charlie had thus discovered a second home.

In front of a stylish 1951 ranch home, idling. The lower half of the house was white brick, the upper wood panels, black. From a three-paned, walnut front door curved a cement path, dotted at three-foot intervals by carefully-snipped beach ball shrubs. A picture window that overlooked this suburban idyll was flanked by two antique-looking but quite new white curtains. A house from which it appeared Fred MacMurray might soon emerge.

Inside, in the shadows beyond the reach of the mid-afternoon sun, resided the actress/director and Portland grand dame of independent film, Ava Zale. An elegant woman in an inelegant age, she infused her fashion with the same care employed on the theater, spoke in a languid Parisian accent, and glided underneath flowing garments as if on castors. Owing to her unique sense of personal style—European wardrobe, sculpted, formal coiffure—and appearance, she might have been five years on either side of 45, though Charlie had extrapolated from her personal history a more accurate dating: 48.

She was not exactly a recluse, but a woman for whom visiting hours were strictly prescribed (between 10 p.m. and 1 a.m.), and visits strictly scheduled. Among the few on her short list of allowed guests were those who could be relied upon to follow the rules. Ava Zale did not tolerate the pop in.

Charlie, however, was afforded unique rights of contact due to a special relationship with Ms. Zale. He was exercising those rights now, in his cab outside the house. On the days Ava was awake, properly adorned, and in the mood, she would pass by the front window. Charlie, after parking a minimum of a block away, was then allowed to visit.

Today no appearance. After fifteen minutes, he drove off. He went back out onto Barbur Boulevard and to a gas station, where he placed a call from the parking lot.

"Charles, dear, how are you? It's early for you to be calling."

"I'm sorry to bother you, Ava. I need to talk. Is there any chance you could meet me at the theater around five?" He selected the earliest time she might possibly consent to leave her home.

"You sound so serious. It must concern your film."

"No, it's not about the film."

"Oh well, relax then, Charles. How serious can it be?"

"Can you make it?"

"Yes, fine. Let's make it five-thirty, though, hmm?"

That the Zale Theater was named for Arturo Zale, not Ava, was a rare bit of trivia. In Portland, the theater and the woman were synonymous. Arturo was a forgotten, insubstantial footnote in the history of cinema. To the patrons of the Zale, he was—if anything at all—Ava's dead husband. An old guy who had something to do with the movies, maybe.

In fact, he was something more than that.

In the 1940s, Zale had been a promising Spanish director, an early practitioner of neo-realism. This was the first phase of his career. Then, in the fifties and sixties, he directed a unique style of a blue melodrama, retrospectively known as sexual noir. This was the second phase. Of those who were familiar with his work, few were familiar with *both* phases.

The first phase reached its zenith in 1948 with his masterwork, *The Last Cow*. After seven years in production, it was a victim of bad timing; delays in distribution led to a late-December premiere in Madrid, weeks after De Sica's *The Bicycle Thief* had begun to take fire in Italy. *Cow* was subsequently labeled derivative. Nevertheless, he continued with his small morality plays, his mostly-amateur casts, his themes of struggle and loss. But audiences of the early 1950s were seeking shiny new cars and happy consumers, not broken plows and dying Spanish peasants. Even the critics abandoned him by the final film of his first phase, *Cold Sunrise*, in 1954.

After a year of dangling his treatment of *Bread and Water* in front of his old investors (who declined due to the failure of his previous three projects), then new investors (who declined because of the grim, unmarketable plot), then friends (who just declined), and finally family (who had no money to give), he admitted it was over. He sold his Bell and Howell and took a job from his cousin Franco managing a Barcelona grocery store.

The second phase of his career began a continent away, of someone else's volition, in the dingy Escondido office of Cosmopolitan Films. Ed Setzke, using a print of *The Last Cow* as a visual prop, pitched the concept to his partner.

"Look at this luscious piece of tail, Marty." Ed stood in front of the screen and poked a thick finger at Antonia de la Paz, Zale's heroine. He had been struck by Zale's eye in capturing the radiance of de la Paz, the fullness of her lips and the throatiness of her voice, in which he thought he heard the purr of suggestion.

A stylist more than a storyteller, Zale had let the spectacle of his films carry his message. Central to his theme was always a woman of generous curves like de la Paz who evoked fertility and creation— a metaphor for motherhood. To Zale, she was like the wholesome land to which the peasants fled from the bombed-out (or to Zale, corrupt) city. Her own fecundity, like the land's, providing a metaphysical kind of sustenance.

Setzke had a different vision. "See, look here, in this shot—this broad is ready to go!" More purr, less nurture.

The first Cosmopolitan production went without Zale, to save money. A proto sexual noir featuring de la Paz as a dark seductress, a foreign divorcee waiting at the end of the bar to capture a man. Not for marriage—she's done with that. For companionship, for . . . . But Zaleless de la Paz came off as slutty, unsophisticated and fat. The light was too revealing, the pace too quick. Lurid.

And so for the next film, *Indigo Vixen*, Setzke decided to pop for the old master, whom he found in cousin Franco's grocery, handing out packets of cigarettes.

This next phase lasted 10 years and produced four times as many films as the first. Not quite stag films, but neither regular-theater fare. They were pushed back to midnight "special screenings" and were called "foreign" even though they were filmed in English, shot in California, and peopled almost exclusively by Americans. But they starred a series of foreign-born actresses—Marina del Mar, Beverly Hackett, Nina Carmichael—with throaty voices and exotic accents (which 42-year-old Wisconsin car dealers instantly recognized, like Setzke, as the sound of sexual experience). Waitresses, cigarette girls, and cashiers with heavy, smoky features who seduced older married men and exposed them to wild affairs, shook them out of the doldrums of their middle-class lives. No on-screen sex, but bare breasts, panties, silk stockings.

The second phase ended as it began, overtaking Zale, as had the failure of phase one and the beginning of phase two, without his participation. It came in the form of 22-year-old Ava Roos, a platinum blonde in Capri pants, five four in three-inch heels, recently arrived from France. Cast to play Gina (renamed Claire), the innocent in the film, a little-sister type who was fiercely guarded by Nina Carmichael, the cynical waitress with a heart of gold at the restaurant where they both worked.

For Zale, it was a bit of adventuresome casting. Roos, whom he billed as Ava Rose, possessed the essence of a Zale Lady (hips, breasts, lips, accent). But in contrast to the typically raven-haired Spanish and Italian women who were his trademark heroines, Roos was Baltic by parentage, and underneath her (natural) whitish tresses was a face of strawberry and cream cheeks, rose petal lips.

Little Ava, sweet Ava, young Ava, for whom Zale felt especially pleased to be doing this great kindness.

Little Ava, smart Ava, not-so-young Ava, not plucked out of the blue by beneficent Zale, but actually, drawn to Escondido because of him. In order to save *him*.

🎬

She hadn't arrived, like so many, a naive Kentucky (or in the case of Zale's ladies, Tuscan) farm girl. No. The only daughter of Lithuanian refugees, Ava was born in Paris in 1944. About the same time *The Bald Soprano* premiered at Théâtre des Noctambules, Ava was becoming a conscious being. France, blessedly and finally done with the physicality of human conflict, was emerging into the comfort of the intellect. Parisian artists of all disciplines, at last out from underneath the oppressive yoke of moral absolutism, dove into the fresh, healing pool of ambiguity. While the rest of the world rebuilt, repressed, and tried to reassert control, in Paris they mocked. In plays and essays and novels and music they said: "Now that we have seen, we cannot pretend otherwise."

Ava Roos was a quiet, literate girl; she soaked in the waves of thought wafting through open windows and doors and her mind became attuned to them. She preferred books to toys, conversation to games. An austere girl, she sifted through objects, ideas, activities, and people, selecting only the gems. Anything that did not thrill her she forgot effortlessly, without prejudice. Was on to the next thing.

Ava Roos as a pre-adolescent sifted through interests, discarding, discarding. Flute, ballet, piano, cuisine, couture. Her parents thought they had found something when Ava began taking snapshots on the family Leica. They watched with interest. But after a month, when her father offered to buy her her own camera, she was disinterested.

"I don't care about the camera; I'm collecting places." When he looked through her hatbox full of photos he saw streets, buildings, doorways, windows, and sidewalks. For another year, Ava continued to wander and collect places until she had reconstructed her neighborhood in three-by-five blocks of black and white on her bedroom wall. Then the camera joined the culled. She rejected more activities: violin, sculpture, tennis. To pass the time, she gobbled mystery novels or wandered the neighborhood.

It wasn't until she was fourteen, inside the *Théâtre de Chimère*, three blocks from where her father worked as a *pharmacien*, that she finally discovered the kernel of wheat amid childhood's chaffy offerings.

On Saturdays, Ava spent the afternoon with her father at the *pharmacie*, usually happy to read and help with inventory. On that particular day, it was hot and slow and her novel was tedious, and so she launched a campaign to go to the movies where it was at least cool. At around one, her father hung a sign in the window, locked the door, and walked her over to the theater.

The *Chimère* was run-down: musty, loose seats, sticky floors. During the week it showed second-run films, but on the weekend, matinees were usually American slapstick—Three Stooges, Abbot and Costello, The Little Rascals.

A Mickey Mouse cartoon was ending when she arrived; she waited until her eyes had adjusted and then sat in the back row, where the wall braced the rickety seats. There was a pause in the cool darkness, and then the feature began.

It was unlike anything Ava had seen—a strange, barren landscape, a skinny, angular man sitting on a rock; then a horseman riding across some desolate rocky ground that looked to her like the moon. During all this, a queer song rolled along, spare as the landscape. After three minutes the screen went blank. It started again for a few seconds, went blank. Cursing drifted down from the projection booth; heads craned to see what the trouble was.

Another five minutes and a hunched, scarecrow-looking man came out to explain that the wrong movie had been sent in the Laurel and Hardy can—an American film called *High Noon*. Everyone who wished would receive a refund. He started to leave, hesitated, and then admitted that it wasn't a comedy, to which the audience responded with grumbles and hisses. But it was dubbed and although not at all like Laurel and Hardy, was supposed to be pretty good. Ava, transfixed by the footage she had already seen, didn't dream of leaving.

After a sizeable number of people filed out, the film lurched back into motion. The barren landscape, the joining together of the skinny man, the horseman, and another cowboy, the three of them galloping off to the rhythm of the song.

Like a cat finally striking a fish that has come to the surface of a pond, Ava's life went from potential to kinetic. She spent all her energy, all her time, and all her money on film. Hitchcock, Kurosawa, Bergman—whatever was playing. The best, though, were the raw American films. Brutal, nonconversational, active. *On the Waterfront*, *Shane*, *Red River*, *Double Indemnity*. She read movie magazines and biographies, ingesting film whenever she could, in whatever form was available.

At fifteen she began reallocating her finances into her own project, an ongoing series of shorts shot on her father's home movie camera; a Super 8. They followed the adventures of Jean (played by her best friend, also called Jean), a boy who roamed the streets of Paris looking for empty spaces and solitude. The buildings from her snapshots reappeared, with only subtly more motion as Jean walked into the frame and stood, taking in his environment. For Ava, there was something about the freedom and danger of wide open spaces. She loved the stoicism of the leading men, as if they had very grave things on their minds and was gripped by their desire to be outside the influence of society and law. She did her best to make Paris look like the American West through wide angle long shots.

Her life was wholly focused on film. She took courses, studied *Les Cahiers du Cinema*, continued to watch two or three films a week, shot Jean walking, standing, smoking. She even started an English language class so she could understand the actors and not miss the action while reading the subtitles.

In 1962, as she neared the end of school, Ava began to wonder about traveling to America. Paris was providing poor inspiration. The settings were wrong—too domesticated. The people were wrong—too talky, too soft around the jaw line. Even the movies were wrong—too . . . French. The New Wave had arrived, and France was leading in yet another medium, the rest of the world trailing along behind. Especially *Breathless* and *The 400 Blows* she admired, yet they didn't resonate with her. So cramped, oppressed by the weight of society, the constant crush of bodies. She wanted the severity of the American desert, the flat stares of American men. She liked the cerebral, but not the overly emotional.

The air of Paris, whatever its effect on the rest of the citizens, suffocated Ava. By the time she completed her baccalaureate, her long-range plan had become the United States. She lived at home and worked a job at her father's *pharmacie*, tucking her money into a bank account she called John (for John Ford), planning to go to California in order to launch her career as an American auteur.

In the summer of 1965, after three years of saving, Ava liquidated John and moved to Los Angeles, one of the hundred kids who arrived each day to unleash themselves on the movie biz. She had done her research, though; she had a plan. Stardom wasn't her goal, but connections and the money to shoot her first film. She waitressed, took night classes at Los Angeles Community College, roomed with an aspiring actress, and kept her ears open. In her first year, she learned the business of the business, the motivation of the business—not art as in the case of the Parisian idealists, but in bottom-line, American fashion—money.

In the spring of 1966, Zale was putting together *The Seduction of George McArdle*, a fact brought to Ava's attention by June, her roommate, who was hoping to fake a good Spanish accent.

"Yeah, he makes these kinda blue pictures. I know, I know, but Ava honey, I haven't had a decent role in *months*, and I—"

"*Arturo* Zale, the Spanish director?"

"I don't know, probably."

"Arturo Zale who made *The Last Cow*? He's making stag films?"

"They're *not* stag films!"

For fun, Ava tagged along with June. She wanted to see if the great director would be there—to see if it even *was* the great director, to see, if it was him, how he had gotten from *Cow* to *McArdle*.

It was worse than she imagined. The reading was at a tiny office in Escondido—an embarrassing, tawdry shack. Outside the building, a line of gum-popping girls practicing their lines. And inside a fake-wood paneled room was the great master, Zale, looking very tired even at the start and catatonic before they were half-way through the line of girls giving abysmal readings in bad accents.

Setzke was with Zale, whispering to him and interacting with the girls. Asking them to read a line again or stop, telling them he'd be in touch. After each reading, Zale shook his head once to the left, slightly, a cancer patient rejecting food. And then Setzke would make him go through it again.

June read near the end of the day, bad as the rest, and then Setzke said everyone else would have to come back in the morning.

As she watched the spectacle, Ava wanted to intercede on Zale's behalf. As each new aspiring actress was called forward, she wanted to leap up and intercept her, give her some direction. The best came off as simple and coquettish, the worst as unintentional vaudeville, parodies of European women. What Zale needed was a decent reading, an understated reading. By the end of the day, when it was clear none of these girls was capable of such a thing, Ava began toying with the idea of giving it herself. At first, she was still thinking of Zale, but later, she started thinking of herself, *working* with Zale. By the time she and June were back home, Ava had resolved to land the part.

She arrived the next day in Escondido before seven and still wasn't the first one there. Two other girls paced on the sidewalk, puckered lips mouthing their lines.

Ava approached the role like a director would. She looked through Zale's camera and saw the performance she needed to give: innocent but not naive, virginal but in possession of adolescent nurturing, the potential of all Zale's Ladies, waiting to blossom. Presence, confidence. She sat in June's car and watched other girls trickle in and join the murmuring actresses in their pacings. At 7:20, she got out of her car and leaned against the building. Lucky number seven.

The casting debacle resumed at 8:30. The first two read for a distracted, decaffeinated Setzke, who sipped coffee and coughed out a sharp "Next!" in between their readings. The third girl had started when Zale shuffled into the room. She hadn't been doing too badly, but the director unnerved her. She started, stopped, started. Shaky, accent evaporating, the performance ended in tears.

By the time it was Ava's turn, Setzke's "Next" had been softened by a cup and a half of coffee. She started her reading while Zale slouched, fist under his chin, listening to Setzke whisper into his ear. Midway through the reading, Zale's chin came off his fist, attracted not by Ava, but by Millie, reading the Nina Carmichael role. Her voice was no longer a place-keeping drone, but human. The short blonde was working *with* her, interacting with nuance, subsuming her performance to the dominant lead role. For once the scene was natural, believable.

Zale leaned over to Setzke and whispered loudly. He stopped, looked up at the scene for a few seconds, then leaned over to Setzke again. Before they were done with the reading, he got up and left the room. Setzke interrupted Ava.

"Okay girls, that's it. The director has found his Gina."

On the set, Ava continued to give Zale what he needed. Like an on-court player/coach, Ava the actress/Assistant Director placed the camera, shuttled bodies, checked the lighting. The start of the shoot, for her, was an exercise in keeping the frown of despair off his seasoned face. This was her real audition.

Zale's mood improved each day under the influence of Ava's scurrying. He relaxed and, to the wonder of the crew, smiled from time to time. The right corner of his lip rose unconsciously at the industry of the young woman, at her intuitive sense of the production, at the relief of having the obscene movie lifted gently out of his hands. The whole shoot took 19 days and the last two went off without him even on the set, Ava doing a little clean-up work with the extras.

And that was it for Zale's career. Ava's respect for *Last-Cow*-Zale burned off the last bit of inclination he had toward being Cosmopolitan-Films-Zale. Over the course of the production, working with Ava had begun to refocus his attention. Seeing her reminded him of himself at a young age, of all directors with vision. For the first time in years, he had hope of a new legacy.

Ava, taking the reins, had passed the audition.

After *McArdle*, Ava shot her first 16mm short. This was to be the beginning of her career as a filmmaker, the beginning of Zale's career as a mentor. And things started out well. Before it was completed, a few weeks before the two-year anniversary of the Cosmopolitan casting call, she and Zale married. Zale did his part, prying money and equipment from Setzke on the false promise that, after Ava's short was complete, he would make another picture for Cosmopolitan.

The 23-minute film was essentially a reprise of the adventures of Jean, this one set in the California desert with a steely-eyed American standing in for her young friend. It wasn't a bad effort; Zale admired her landscape shots, the stillness, the emptiness. But perhaps too little happened, he suggested; film is after all a medium of motion.

Ava's next picture was a feature, a more ambitious project that she wrote as well as directed. It was an unfortunate failure. An adaptation of a Matt Shenk potboiler, she plucked the hero out of New Orleans and dropped him into late 19th-century Cheyenne. She had chosen the idea as a way of adding action, but the story couldn't stand the translation from city to frontier.

The husband and wife did not despair. The first film had shown promise; this one was merely too far out of her comfort zone. The next would prove her skill.

But the next one, her final film, never made it to post-production. She had gone back to her obsession with emptiness, tried to mine her vision and produce a lyrical film that adequately illustrated it. The action followed a drifter who abandoned the city to wander. She tried to enliven the picture, sending him to the mountains instead of the desert. She shot hour after hour of her drifter drifting, hoping to find a narrative in the editing room.

While Zale had managed to get Setzke to pony up for the second picture as a favor with still more promises, the final one was self-financed. In the end, Ava was unable to bring her dream from mind to reality. Looking into the block of stone for something to echo her vision, for a statue to draw out. But she was unable to see it, unable to reveal it. What she had given birth to was a disfigured golem unable to breathe on its own. She took a serious look at her footage and saw it for what it was: pretentious, confused, unwatchable. No editor could save it.

In 1975, Zale told Setzke that Los Angeles was no good for his health. Which wasn't far from the truth, though it was Ava, more than he, who suffered to live in a city built of celluloid and façades. Relatively well-off from his stint at Cosmopolitan, they decided to move north so Zale could enjoy his golden years. They tarried in Marin County, then in Ashland, Oregon, and finally stopped when they came to Portland.

Arturo and Ava told themselves that perhaps after a few years Ava would return to filmmaking. In the meantime, they put away some money and waited for her to craft her masterpiece.

In retirement, Zale took to gardening. Ava puttered around the house for a few years before searching for something to occupy her time. Again she began discarding. Jobs because she had no skills, hobbies because of their transparent uselessness.

She continued to ponder film, to consider the story she wanted to tell. She tried to coax it out and when that failed, spent part of the saved money traveling, trying to open her mind up so a story could enter. One never did. She didn't give up the idea of directing again, but quit fostering the idea as an active enterprise.

Finally she arrived at proprietorship as a useful alternative and began sifting again, a process that concluded in 1981 when, unable to abandon film, she decided to buy the Belmont Theater.

In 1983, she approached the Film Institute with the idea of hosting a festival of local filmmakers. The Institute declined—they already had a film festival—and so she organized it on her own. Fourteen films ranging in length from two to forty-eight minutes, just two evenings' worth of footage. Of the group, perhaps two were not painful to watch.

Yet from that inauspicious start, Ava became the patron of a ragtag group of filmmakers, opening up the theater to regular screenings, a kind of open mike for filmmakers. They showed their films—their rough cuts, single scenes, sometimes even their unedited footage—and then discussed them, went home and reworked them, and brought them back the next month to show again. She continued to host her annual film festival, the quality of which improved year by year until in 1990, she actually had to institute a screening process. Suddenly, Portland had a lively local film community—all orbiting around the elegant, aloof, accented Ice Queen.

The owner of the Zale had once laid greater plans. A small girl in Paris, sitting in a theater watching *High Noon*, she knew film would be her life. But she had imagined it differently. Not to be, as she had become in a strange little American city, a patron of film, but a creator of it. She imagined that her contribution to the world would be film, *her* films. Instead, her contribution was other people's films. She supported and nurtured and gave birth to them by proxy, her contribution generosity, not art. She got thanks, admiration, and a minor, local celebrity.

She took it.

Charlie parked in one of the three spaces in the alley behind the theater. The back door was inside a square compound of chain-link fencing, slatted with strips of thin red metal. He unlocked the padlock on the fence, side-shuffled around the dumpster and let himself in through the iron door.

Autumn sunshine carved a triangle of orange light in the space immediately behind the open door, beyond which was cool, still blackness. Door closed, Charlie felt around for the light switch. To his left, a hallway lit by dim globes ran alongside the theater. To his right, the back of the movie screen rose up, catching just enough light to glow phosphorescent silver.

He waited until his eyes adjusted to the theater lighting, then passed through the curtain doorway into the auditorium.

"Ha!" he yelled, listening to it reverberate. Then he raised his arms like airplane wings, spun, ran to the back of the theater, lips thpp thpp thpping the sound of a propeller.

Ava leased most of the films that showed at the Zale, but in the projection booth, she hid a small cache of her own. Charlie put on the first reel of *North by Northwest* and went back into the theater.

Halfway through the second reel, the queen glided into her palace. Black blouse and slacks and a white scarf that picked up the light in her silver hair. She found Charlie sprawled and dozing, so she sat in the row behind him, one seat to his left. She rested her chin on the back of the chair and watched him sleep.

When the heavy smell of her floral perfume reached his nostrils he came out of his doze with a snuffle. Blinking, squinting, turning to the source of the smell.

"Hello, Charles." She purred, drawing his face to hers with a soft, manicured hand, jangling with jade. He felt wet warmth on his left earlobe and he imagined the waxy red on his ear.

He looked at the screen, yawned. "Sorry about that."

"So tell me, Charles, what is your important news?"

"Well, there are really two things. The first is good news. The Film Institute is going to help me re-shoot the film on 16mm." He draping his legs over the seat next to him and turned to face her. "They liked the Super 8."

"Excellent! This *is* wonderful news."

"There's a woman there—do you know October Moore?"

"Of course. She showed her first film in here."

"She's also cutting me a deal on equipment."

"I'm very excited for you, Charles. Have you begun writing the script?"

"No, no. Not yet. Actually, I want to talk about it, but, there's something else."

"Yes?"

"I'm just going to go ahead and say it."

"Yes, please do."

"I met this woman. I've been dating her. I didn't mention it to you before because it didn't seem important. But it's gotten a little serious." He looked at her to gauge her reaction, but she was looking at his knee. "I don't think we should see each other any more."

She smiled. "See each other? Charles, have we been 'seeing' each other?"

"Of course we have. Or— What would you call it?"

She put a hand on his shoulder and watched her index finger as it traced lines in plaid. "Don't let her be a distraction. Men have such little focus, such little determination. Keep your mind on the film. That's the most important thing for you to work on now. The relationships will always be there—always another woman. But this is a good opportunity for your film—you don't want to lose it."

"Me seeing this woman doesn't bother you then?"

"You have heard that Arturo spent seven years on *The Last Cow*, yes? It's true that it took him seven years to finish it, but he wasn't 'laboring with difficulty' all those years. He was screwing his star, getting drunk on wine and doing no work. Years later he woke up and found her fat and unappealing to him. Only then could he continue with the film."

And then without theatricality and with only a trace of her accent, she said, "Make sure you finish the film Charlie, you'll be much happier." It was the voice she allowed him to hear only when they lay in bed, when her hair was tangled, make-up smeared, skin exposed and drooping. When she was Ava Roos, the 48-year-old theater owner and he was Charlie the cab driver, her 26-year-old lover.

"But of course, have relations with whomever you choose." She looked him in the eyes. "You have something else to tell me?"

"Really, it's okay?"

A pause and then a slight nod. "What else?"

"Hmm, yes. Well, you know how it is with film. I'm either going to transfer this thing or re-shoot it, and either way I'm going to have to come up with some money. The Institute's giving me a thousand. I was just wondering if you had a fund or something for local projects?"

"Of course I'm happy to give you as much money as I can. You're a talented filmmaker, Charles. But give—please, no loans, eh? Loans are no good for friendships." She moved further forward, shifted her body to face his. "Now come here."

She put both hands around the back of his head and gave him a deep, probing kiss. Toothpaste, coffee, something sweet (liquor?), and in the end his mouth was messy with her lipstick. "A goodbye kiss for an old friend. A real kiss." She stood up, and walked toward the rear exit.

"Goodbye, Charles."

| 4.

"Okay, let's put together a strategy." Lapierre, sitting next to Charlie at his kitchen table, pen poised over white tablet. "Let's forget about the total for a minute." Charlie nodded assent to the small businessman. "A thousand from Ava, a thousand from the Film Institute. That's clear money. Now, what other sources do you have? Friends, family. Any other groups?"

"Credit cards and that kind of thing—"

"Okay, we'll call that 'other.'" But I mean, like for example the guy who owns Yellow Cab. Anyone like that?"

"Blakemore—that chiseler, are you kidding? No, I don't really know any of the big boys."

"Just think. What about your regulars, there's a lot of money there. Business friends of your family—Vic's, say?"

"No, nothing like that." Thinking. "Wait a minute, do *you* know anyone?"

Lapierre looked at him. "Good, that's how you gotta think. But no." He printed FRIENDS, FAMILY, and OTHER on the tablet.

"Let's start with the family."

"Okay, that's easy—Vic."

"Who else?"

"That's it."

"Oh, come on. You have to have some cousins or uncles or something."

"No, seriously. Vic's got some relatives in Italy, but they probably don't have a pot to piss in. He also has two daughters from a previous marriage that I've never met. I'm the last of the di Paulos. Well, Vic's side, anyway."

"That's ironic. The di Paulo line's going to change a little."

Charlie rubbed his hair. "Funny, huh?"

"Okay, nothing in family." He wrote Vic di Paulo under FAMILY. Pointing the pen at the next column. "All right, friends."

Charlie rattled off a list. Then: "But you know, they're not gonna give much."

"Keep thinking. It helps to brainstorm like this; sometimes you come across someone you haven't thought of."

"I think that's really it. In fact, there are a few people on your list who aren't going to give me a dime."

"What about Janie?"

"No way."

"She'd give you some serious cash. She's got it and I bet she'd love to."

"No." He paused. "I'll put it this way—if you were in my position, would you ask her?"

"Okay, I see what you mean. What about her co-workers?"

"No, forget it. I don't want her knowing about this money thing, at least not immediately."

They continued on, fleshing out the OTHER with arts foundations, credit, odd jobs. Lapierre totaled the amounts.

"Well, looks like you've got a maximum potential of around ten thousand here. Not bad. Now, if we drop out Vic and the arts foundations and lower the take from friends, it's—" adding—"about three grand. That's including Ava and the Film Center."

"That's about what I figured."

"Three grand's a lot of money."

"I need to do better than that."

"You need Vic, then."

"Yep. That's the way it looks."

Charlie had been here before, on a more limited scale. Super-8 "Taxicab Triptych," initially envisioned as a three-minute short, had set him back $600. As his vision expanded, so did his needs: his own camera, a tripod, a set of lights. Then film and developing, and then editing equipment and finally a projector. Not very far into it, his own cabbie money ran out.

So he went off to friends, rattling his cup for spare change, sheepishly. Lapierre threw in $100. Soft touch. From D.C., letter-writing Carlos wrote him, explaining in nine pages why he was unable to offer even a small sum, referencing Marx, Camus, and Tolstoy. Then two days later a check for fifty bucks arrived with no explanation. Also a soft touch.

A call to Vic and another $100, ill-gotten, after a lie about paying off a speeding ticket. And from other friends another $137, once he'd promised them bit roles as fares. A bit of the old Tom Sawyer, that had been. Of course, $600 wasn't ten thousand.

He was gauging the play of light to see if it was bright enough to pick up the cobblestones running underneath the east side of the Morrison Bridge. Next to him were Clay and Janie, standing in front of Patty's Royal Café while preparing for the shoot. On Lapierre's advice, Charlie had decided to produce a promotional short so that investors in "Taxicab Triptych" could feel they'd received something more tangible than the satisfaction of helping a friend. Also, according to Clay, this would enhance his credibility to prospective donors.

It was Charlie's favorite place in the city. Warehouses, storage, fenced lots of steel and concrete, the rumble of freight trucks and trains framed overhead by bridges and freeways. Although it was just across the Willamette River from downtown, it was an invisible section of the city. Six blocks wide and twenty long. The kind of place that defined a city, that only locals know about but consider unremarkable.

It remained a preserved piece of history, still lively with fruit distributors, furniture warehouses and machine shops, all lodged in 100-year-old buildings. Across the river, people sat in cubicles and studied columns of numbers. When they made decisions about inventory, it was as unreal as a few keystrokes, but here those line items represented boxed goods that needed to be loaded on trucks.

The bridge was supported by massive ribs of concrete, framing the cobbled, single-lane street like the columns of a cathedral. The bridge was only as wide as the narrow space between buildings would allow, and it descended slowly from its arch above the river through the Fruit District, bound on either side by a one-foot buffer of space that gave way to a vertical plane of brick and glass. Underneath, the street was lit by the light that fell through clefts at the edges, sharp when you looked up, but diffuse at street level, the light of a forest floor.

"Okay, looks like we're going to have to drive the wrong way here, but I don't think it'll matter now."

"How come?" Janie asked.

"The light." Clay showed her its slant with his hand. "See how it comes down at an angle? If we go—what is it, east?—it will be on my face. But if we go with the flow of traffic, I'll be in a shadow."

"It's all right. Nobody drives fast on these streets, even if we do see someone. The real problem is that the road slopes down like a bastard on the sides here. You see that; it's not flat."

He looked skeptically at the trough of parking places. "I think I've got a good light reading here: why don't we take a practice run."

Starting at River Avenue, headed east. Lapierre had the cab in the center of the street, arm out the window, eyes forward. "Let's keep it right around 5 miles an hour." Next to the cab was Clay's Caddy, where Charlie gave instruction from the passenger seat. "You got it?" Nods from his drivers. He raised the camera and looked through the viewfinder. "Okay, ready? Action."

Both cars paused. One beat. Then Lapierre pulled forward, Janie lurching to catch up, see-sawing for twenty feet before they found the same speed. He would definitely be shooting from a funny low angle, but it looked pretty good through the viewfinder. The shot highlighted the street, the cabbie's connection to it. The light was pretty good, too.

At the end of their first run, Janie suggested a mark-set-go start to see if they could stay flush from the outset. A second practice run and a third, with subtle refinements to the method. They all agreed it would be an excellent visual to capture Clay turning the corner at Patty's and continuing on down Third. A fourth practice run and a left at Patty's, then continuing down to Stark. The turn seemed inelegant to Charlie's eye. The Caddy had to come to a stop while the cab swung wide to make the turn. But it couldn't be helped. Already the pavement was bouncing his camera enough that there would be no illusion of a perfectly invisible observer.

"We've got it down. Come on, let's *film* it." Janie, with more enthusiasm than frustration.

"Yep, I think so. You ready, cab man?" Charlie said to his star.

Lapierre, left hand on the wheel, leaned out of the window and winked. "You heard the lady."

Ava's discovery of film had been like a thunderbolt; for Charlie it had been like a dawning day. Ava, the visualist, understood the allure of film the first time she saw *High Noon*. But Charlie felt art more than he saw it. A child of television, he had been consuming moving pictures since infancy. Movies were more deliberate, focused versions of the same thing he watched on Vic's giant Zenith at home. Entertainment, disposable.

Charlie's early passion was music. The Ramones, Sex Pistols—they stimulated some ancient receptor at the base of his skull. When he was thirteen, he started strumming along with Joey Ramone on a ten-dollar, garage-sale guitar. He found a book—*Teach Yourself Guitar*—and learned some basic chords, though his style of play was never very melodic. He tended to slip into rhythm with the beat and play a percussive accompaniment.

His opinion about movies changed during the Christmas vacation of his sophomore year in high school. A two-punch, *The Elephant Man* and *Raging Bull*, neither of which had he intended to see. Vic tried to drag him to a Christmas matinee of *The Elephant Man*—a startling event for its rarity. Vic was more a TV guy, but he'd just finished a book about John Merrick. Charlie, still regarding movies as entertainment, thought he could find a better way to spend two hours than with a deformed Victorian Englishman.

"It's going to be fascinating. Trust me."

"Sounds boring."

"Come on—the Elephant Man! A fifteen-year-old should love that kind of thing. Wooo, weird!"

"I don't know."

Vic prevailed, and against his better judgment, Charlie was immediately engaged by John Hurt's performance. Yet it wasn't until very near the end of the film that he realized how dramatically his mood had changed. As they walked from Lynch's dark, English world into the bright Arizona light of his youth, he observed how his brain still swam in the dreamlike movie world. The sensation wasn't explosive like when he played music, but somehow more comprehensive. It swamped his entire mood and carried him away. It was an enlightening experience, but fleeting. It didn't take.

But then, just a week later, he and two friends returned to Camelview 3. As they exited a showing of *Smokey and the Bandit II*, Greg Gordon expressed their collective review: "That sucked ass."

They went to the bathroom and began cataloguing the ways in which Burt Reynolds and Jackie Gleason sucked.

About Gleason: "My dad says he was huge once."

Tony Reid and Charlie, together, "He's still huge!"

"He's fat and stupid."

"I heard Reynolds wears a toupee."

"Who cares?"

"Yeah, who cares—he's an asshole."

They emerged from the bathroom and Greg, wised-up by two older brothers, pointed at the door to theater 2. "That's supposed to be awesome." They looked at the door.

"It's an R," Charlie said, to his instant regret.

"This theater owes us something for that piece of shit we just saw," said Tony, affecting a fairly authentic swagger.

Greg and Tony started for the door. *"It's an R!"* Greg said in little-boy voice as he walked past Charlie into the theater. "Douchebag."

The film, which didn't seem like awesome material, was about boxing. *And* it was in black and white. Charlie bided his time and honed his comeback to the douchebag comment, readying it for after the movie.

Of course, he never got to use it. The movie—*Raging Bull*—was in fact awesome. By the time the three boys staggered out of the theater, Charlie was hooked. The light of film had fully dawned.

It didn't occur to Charlie right away that he could make movies, however. Whereas they were immediately tangible to Ava, to Charlie they seemed otherworldly, not the product of human hands. No one in Phoenix made them—or wanted to.

For Charlie, being a film buff was enough to make him exotic, if not especially hot, property. He put stills of obscure movies on his notebooks—black and white pictures that seemed, to him, to come from a hip parallel universe. He memorized dialogue. He owned a Betamax. When his friends talked about movies, he peppered the conversation with arcane references.

"Stripes wasn't really worth a shit." Sitting on the bleachers, speaking blasphemy over joints of barely psychotropic shake ganja. "Bill Murray's cool, but the third reel was a sellout."

He paused long enough to let them consider the phrase "third reel," and then added pretentiously, "*Dr. Strangelove* was a lot funnier. Kubrick's a genius."

"Listen to Charlie Douchebag. *Kubrick.*" Greg Gordon was turning into a jerk, but he expressed the general mood. Charlie's film appreciation remained a solo pursuit.

It remained that way until he discovered the Zale. After the first visit with Molly, he returned the following Monday for Ava's monthly screening of local films. The lights were up, and there was a group of filmmakers clustered near the front of the theater (regular viewers to the local screenings were few). Charlie sat in the back row and watched the crude offerings. Their lack of polish encouraged him.

"You can get Super 8s at garage sales all the time," one of the filmmakers told him. "Like twenty bucks."

He was right: Charlie found his camera at an old woman's sale just down from the VMC. Soon he had several reels—mostly of Molly walking or Molly sitting or Molly watching television. He augmented his experiments with research material—used paperbacks from Powell's with titles like *The Art of Film*, *Lighting the Set*, and *Screenwriting*.

From experimentation and these resources, he learned the basics—how to make a dolly from a used wheelchair and how to rig a car battery as a source of power for lights. As the film came back and he started putting the narratives together, he learned more nuanced lessons: how camera angles told different stories, how drama is heightened by what you don't show, not what you do; how not acting is the best acting.

Two years into his filmmaking career, Charlie was starting to work on more involved pieces, but he was finding that his friends were running out of patience as actors. Four hours and they lost interest. Girlfriends were more readily available, but didn't take direction well. While he was digging around for actors, he caught a lucky break.

He had just taken a job as a pizza maker at a place on 23rd—back when New York-style pizza-by-the-slice was still a novelty on the West Coast. The guy who owned the restaurant actually came from Brooklyn, and he had an accent Charlie was dying to film.

Charlie's first job was pie-throwing, a task he learned from a huge, meaty-armed guy whose personality appeared to consist of grunts and shrugs. For several hours a day, they would stand at the front of the store, tossing dough above their heads in a silent competition over who could come closest to the ceiling without touching. It was a fairly dull job, and Charlie spent his time trying to get the New Yorker to agree to at least do an interview he could use as voice-over.

"Come on, man, I've got a short written up specifically for your voice."

"Nah. . . ."

Over time, with his cabdriver's latent ability to pull stories out of even the most reticent, Charlie slowly made friends with his co-tosser. He would work on the owner, then work on the big guy. It took him a month, but eventually he discovered a valuable piece of information—Mr. Meaty was an aspiring actor. At about that time, Charlie had convinced the owner to do a voice-over. ("Just five minutes, all right?") And then he got Mr. Meaty to agree to do some acting. It was Clay Lapierre.

Each phase of filmmaking required a different set of skills. On the set, flexibility. You tried to be as organized as possible—location scouted, storyboards prepared, equipment, props, and costumes organized and handy. And then you improvised because the factors beyond your control—weather, noise, equipment malfunction, illness, crew unrest—dominated every shoot. Charlie had the right temperament for shooting: unflappable, decisive, democratic.

For the editing phase, though, one required attributes of order and control. Stories had to be drawn from images, connected only by juxtaposition. Editing required a structured mind, one able to attend to details and larger narrative simultaneously. The process entailed reducing raw footage to strips, some a foot or two long, some a dozen. Each piece was numbered, with a label affixed to the clip's head in masking tape. All the numbers were recorded in a notebook with a description of the scene. It took a particular kind of mind to keep all the pieces separate, to know how they fit into the larger context, but to not lose track of the details.

For this Charlie was less appropriately gifted. It was like cramming for a final; he sequestered himself away and focused all his effort on keeping the pieces together in his mind. Dark room, Bob Marley, no sleep. The end result usually requiring another edit.

Toward the end of editing the promo, a buzz from the intercom jolted his concentration.

His apartment had taken on the aspect of a lair. The shades were drawn, music on low, strips of film hanging from a wall, the kitchen table in the center of the apartment topped by a film editor and lamp, writhing with curls of cut film. On the floor beneath the table were two pizza boxes and a scattering of bottles. He answered the door in shorts and tank top.

"Uggh, how *long* have you been doing this?" Janie, refusing to enter.

"Oh, I don't know, couple days." He stepped away from the door so she could come in. They looked at each other, waited.

"It smells like feet in there. Gross. How about opening a window?"

"Just get in here, will you?"

Sniffing him as she went by. "Well, at least the smell is generalized. Look, I brought you fruit." He opened a window, pulled up the blinds, and allowed fresh air and light to pour into the apartment. He blinked in the light. "So how's it going?"

"Not bad." He took an orange she was pushing on him. "This is a really easy edit, as edits go. I've got the rough cut. Just a little monkeying with the timing is all that's left."

"Is it ready?"

"Now?"

"Yes."

"I don't know. The audio might not exactly match the visual right now. But it's together—I just watched it. You want to see it?"

"Are you sure?"

"Sure."

"Well let's go, man."

He found a plastic spool the size of a chewing tobacco tin amid the snakes on the table. It looked to her like FBI spy film. He threaded it by hand through a projector that was facing a bare wall. He stopped the CD that was playing and put in a cassette that said, "Lapierre – rhythm tracks."

"Okay, I need your help. Go over to the projector and push the white button when I tell you."

"This is so cool. You know, I've never seen any of your film before — even the stuff with *me*."

He cued the tape. "Ready? On three push the button."

The screen played blackness for a moment while a guitar faded in, rolling and jangly. A shot of the cab next to Patty's Royal Cafe faded in and then out to blackness. It faded back in with Lapierre at the wheel of the cab, the camera following alongside him while the bridge supports flitted by to the beat of the music.

Janie yipped. "Oh my God, there he is!"

The scene lasted a minute. The day they'd filmed the promo, they'd shot Clay driving the cab in five different locations. Each time, Charlie had filmed from the car right next to him, each shot framed the same way. Thus, the focus of the shot — Clay, in the cab — remained constant; only the backgrounds differed: under the bridge by Patty's, on busy Grand Avenue, downtown, coming over the Broadway Bridge, and in a desolate residential neighborhood off Foster. When he'd cut the film together, he'd used the shoot at Patty's as the baseline, but during the parts where the guitar started a driving, percussive chorus, Charlie had spliced in the scenes from the other locations, which made the image appear to flutter as the background changed. All the while, though, Lapierre stayed in the center of the frame, a placid, neutral focus. As she watched, Janie noticed that the fluttering background was roughly timed with the changes of the music.

After the last series of flutters, the image stopped with a frozen background — the cab was now still as the last note of the guitar resonated. Lapierre was parked in front of Patty's, still in the same position, face forward, arm out. Then it was the camera that was in motion, passing along the cab's side and swinging around to the front of the car, hood stretching out toward Lapierre through the windshield. Lapierre fixed the camera with an inscrutable gaze. A beat and then the image went black.

"That's it."

Janie sat.

"It's pretty close, I just have to tighten the cuts where the backgrounds change — they're not in perfect time with the music."

She looked at him and then got up, grabbed his head in her hands and kissed him. Hard.

He dubbed a voiceover for each of the friends he hoped would give $50 or more, and then a general one to show to the poor and cheap. He went back to Patty's and took a photo of Clay in the cab, which he used for a label on the promo boxes. He added a handwritten "Thanks from Charlie" to the corner of each one for that personalized feel.

Then the road show.

Ava first, as a matter of course. Again he went through the usual process—a phone call and an agreement to meet at the Zale. But this time he wheeled a video player out of the office and down into the theater. He was in the concessions making a fresh batch of popcorn when she arrived.

"Hello, Charles."

"A little something for the show. To jazz it up."

No real pitch accompanied the first screening. Because she'd already made a donation, it was a thanks to her. They went into the theater and sat on the aisle near the video projector. Charlie handed Ava the popcorn and said, "All right, then."

When it ended, Ava asked him to rewind it and play it a second time. Afterward, she sat and looked at the blank screen. "Once more, Charles."

Afterward, they went back to her little office next to the projection booth. Ava went to the desk, rooted around the lap drawer.

"Oh, I remember now." She found a file on top of the desk and removed a check. "Here you are. You have a great deal of talent, but you know the test is in the final cut. Don't get a large head."

Then on to other friends, starting with the small fry to perfect his appeal. He learned that silence was the best. After a screening, he sat and waited—the first time because he didn't know what to say. He was surprised to get a check for $50. A few more pitches and he realized he didn't mind hitting up his friends. He didn't care if they gave him money and he told them so. And then they did. He understood why; he would have given them money, too. A Ben Franklin to help a friend along. Pretty cheap when you thought about it.

Based on Clay's figures, he had thought $1,000 was reasonable from friends. But when the fundraising was done, he had $1,400 and change.

At seven on a Tuesday morning he arrived at Lapierre's door, cup of espresso-shop coffee balanced atop a video cassette. A modest hour, he thought.

"Oh *no*." Nude.

"Look at this," Charlie grinning and nodding to the stylish black paper coffee cup. "The good stuff."

"For fuck's sake, di Paulo, you're going to hit *me* up for dough, too?"

Charlie elbowed into the house. "Don't be crass, I'm here to *thank* you." Inside, he coerced Clay to take the coffee and then produced a small memo pad. "Besides, I want to show you how the fundraising's going. I'm pretty pleased about it, but you'll see we're still a little short."

"Well, let me shower first."

The morning routine: Charlie dozed in the kitchen while Clay bathed and groomed. The doze was finally interrupted by the snap of shoes and the grind of a chair dragged across linoleum.

"All right, let's see the numbers."

"No, let's look at the video first. It *is* actually a thank you."

They watched it standing in Clay's leather-strewn, furnitureless living room. Charlie in turn looked at his friend while his friend watched himself on the screen. The video stopped and Lapierre held his chin and continued to look at the television.

"You're trying to appeal to my vanity."

"Yeah. And I've got you twice. First, you see how pretty you are and then you congratulate yourself on thinking up the video."

"How much do you need?" They walked back to the kitchen and sat down in front of the memo pad.

"Well, let's see—sixty-six hundred and I won't have to go to Phoenix."

"Sixty-six? Wait, you've already got $3,400?"

"Hey, good job with the math."

"You did better than we expected."

"The tape was genius—the idea, I mean."

"What'd you end up spending on it?"

"Not that much—probably $150 for the whole thing."

He studied the figures, looking through the list of names and amounts written next to them.

"This is excellent. Really. But it's still gonna come down to Vic, isn't it?"

"Well, he definitely has the dough. We'll see." They sat and Clay sipped his coffee and Charlie looked at the memo pad. He closed it, put it in his back pocket, and stood up. "So, what do you think—can I put you down for a hundred, round out the total at a clean thirty-five?"

| 5.

Through the smoke and darkness poked red faces to leer. Or speak, after they had stroked a beaded bottle of beer or four.

"Hey sugar, when you off?"

"Two, hon. Why? — you wanna show me a good time?" The smart ones caught the mustard she put on "good" and stopped right there.

The stupid and drunk: "You bet, sugar, I'll show you a *real* good time."

She would then let her voice rise to bimbo register, at a near shout, "Okay, but we'll have to swing by my house first, cause I got four little ones at home and they *all* got the flu. Oh, I *know!* — maybe you can even help me. Make sure they're all tucked in safe and sound? You do like kids, don't you, mister?" Thereafter she would continue to praise the man's generosity — his intent on finally giving her kids someone to call "Daddy" — until he vanished, generally leaving behind a pile of money. A ransom more than a tip.

Lima, Montana, population 234 — one bar, a combination gas station/grocery/hardware store, a gun shop, and a Methodist church. Everyone passed through the gas station: ranchers, miners, hunters, tourists, the Tuesday Greyhound bus. The gun shop nearly everyone, at least for licenses or ammunition. The bar mainly locals and hunters. And the church very few.

Inside the Bar X Bar, Charlie's mother reinvented her life to ward off drunk men, writing in new burly husbands, running them off, then finding burlier, meaner ones; she conjured small cherubs, let them drown or die from meningitis, Mack grilles, or house fires, then had more. She cried for their little souls in new performances weekly.

The rest of the work was a less creative endeavor: she poured beer and shots until it was time to cut off drunks and load them into their trucks; she talked to the regulars, Pete and Ernie, about the weather; she filled the jukebox with change from the cash register, trying to drown out the conversations she'd heard a thousand times.

Beyond this, Charlie's history—narrative and genetic—was mostly unknown to him. Mary Shaver, only daughter of George and Sadie Shaver of Lima, Montana. They lived in a farmhouse just down Highway 6. George was a mechanic at the filling station, Sadie a schoolteacher and then housewife. After high school, Mary started working at the bar, and soon after that her parents started dying. George went first, of a heart attack. A couple years later, Sadie died from complications related to breast cancer.

For Charlie, the descriptions of her previous activities were limited to those that occurred in the Bar X Bar; everything else consisted of orphaned facts, references that added little to the meager history: a thick rag quilt that kept her warm through Montana winters; a black cat named Horse; a white Ford that fishtailed in the snow. Inside the family homestead she had an Air King radio to keep her company, and outside it she tended a garden of flowers. In these historical accounts, the garden got more mention than her parents.

To this verbal history were added three extant photographs of her life before his birth, enigmatic and uncommunicative. Charlie initially found them packed away in a shoebox of documents in her sock drawer. He later rediscovered them in the kitchen drawer and still later in a box of Christmas ornaments. Then they finally disappeared permanently, like his mother, from the material world.

In the first, George and Sadie were standing outside a clapboard church. His grandfather wore a brown suit, his grandmother a spare, lacey wedding dress. The picture was overexposed, and their faces washed out to the gray-white of the sky behind the church. Charlie passed by the photo quickly each time, avoiding the wan smiles they offered, trying to conceal the desperation settled in around the corners of their eyes.

The second, a baby picture of his mother. In it, she appeared as a plump child, with a wisp of blond steam rising off her head. Though he loved the photo, no amount of scrutiny could bring his mother out from the round infancy of the baby's face.

The last picture was also of his mother, taken sometime in her mid-teens. She was posed at the front door in a white living room, school books in one hand, the other reaching limply for the doorknob. She was round-legged in a way Charlie had never seen, full through the hips and belly. By the time he became aware of her body, she had flattened out, begun to dry up. He could see his mother in this girl, in her eyes, mainly, the only tangible evidence he had that she existed before he was born.

The biography Charlie knew began on a late May evening when she was 26.

Spring had been creeping up slowly to the plains, but after two days of warm sunshine, winter returned. By three in the afternoon, spits of snow were streaking the rain. Most of the midday crowd had taken to their pick-ups; only Art Pendleton nursed a beer. He sat and drank, and Mary smoked and watched the sky grow black while she plugged nickels into the juke box.

"You don't mind if I leave the lights on bright, do you, Art? Just feels warmer that way."

"Anyway you like it, Mary."

"I don't think we're gonna have much traffic tonight, anyway."

At about five the sole customer of the evening walked in, a man in beige slacks, shiny cowboy boots, and a sky-colored hunting shirt. Jerry Fearl, Charlie's biological father.

"Well it's a hell of a night out there," he said.

"Yep, mister, it sure is."

"Snow in *May*; I've never seen anything like it."

"We get a few of these every year. I like it though, all cozy one night, but the next day the sun shines and the snow's gone."

Jerry sat at the bar next to Art and ordered a cup of coffee and a burger.

"Still pretty sloppy, the snow?" Art to Jerry.

"Hell no, it's sticking now. Maybe a half inch."

Art looked at his watch, his two fingers of beer. Began counting out money.

"Mary," he called into the kitchen, "this feller says the snow's startin' to stick. Think I'll head on home before Joanne starts worryin'. You give me a call tonight if this gets bad and you need a ride."

Mary's voice rose over the sizzle of beef and pop of deep fryer: "Art, when the hell have I *ever* needed a ride? Man alive, it's just a little ol' Spring drizzle."

Jerry, alone, sipping his coffee, listened to the last of "Chances Are." Then silence, until his ears became attuned to the sound of wind rounding the northeast corner of the building like rushing water.

Charlie's mother returned with a plate and deposited it in front of his father. A thud in the quiet as it hit the thick walnut bar.

"There you go, mister. Lord, it sure is quiet in here." To which Jerry responded by putting mustard on his bun with a tinny scrape of knife. She hit "no sale" on the register and whisked a handful of change out from the till.

At the jukebox, she asked "What do you like, Perry Como or Dean Martin? Or do you like country? I got some Johnny Cash on here."

Jerry daubed a fry in a pile of salt. "It doesn't matter to me." He listened to silver cascading down metal chutes, a pause and then "Five Feet High and Rising" started.

"I like Johnny Cash. You can't dance to him, but he's nice to listen to."

She sat at the end of the bar, fairly near him, and picked up a newspaper crossword. He ate slowly, sipping his coffee meditatively between bites. Mary, used to hiding in the kitchen to avoid men's stares, peeked.

Top-heavy, short, like Popeye. He had thinning sandy hair with a razor part, face and neck and hands red from exposure, skin lined, bubbled, and burned, sausage fingers, eyes faded blue. Despite the weathering, he was quiet and mannered, with his shoulders drawn in. When he picked up half of his neatly-cut burger the word that came into Mary's mind was gentleman. Like hold-your-elbow-on-icy-ground gentleman. She watched him eat fries off his plate one at time like they were chocolates.

Jerry finished his meal. "Ring of Fire" was playing, and Mary came down from the end of the bar to fill up his coffee cup.

"Just halfway," he told her. "And maybe you could put a little Jim Beam in there to warm it up."

When she turned back around with the bottle of bourbon, Charlie's father was standing at the jukebox. Hand in one pocket, feeling for change. "Let's see," he said. "What do you have on this thing that we *can* dance to?"

When she related the story, Charlie's mother remembered every song on that jukebox. Jerry started out with "I Left My Heart in San Francisco" and then came and took her hand and led her out in front of the bar. Until that moment, Mary had never met a man who actually enjoyed dancing or was any good at it. Dancing was something to be endured for her sake. But gentleman Jerry was a dancer; he enjoyed the movement of bodies, the orchestration, the subtle contact of hands on hips and shoulders.

After an hour, she turned off the neon Bar X Bar light and put the Closed sign in the window. She got some more change from the cash register and they worked their way through the danceable songs a second time. Then a third. In between songs they sipped toddies and listened to the storm. Finally they had listened to the songs so much that Mary started playing the ones that weren't much good for dancing, and they danced anyway.

Late that night, under a clearing sky, Jerry drove Mary through the still, snowy streets of Lima to her house. He held her elbow and escorted her to her front door and then followed her right on in and sat down at the kitchen table on the side next to the Air King. Horse jumped into his lap, settled, and started purring when Jerry stroked his belly.

Charlie heard the Jerry Fearl story in several variations. But it wasn't actually the *Jerry Fearl* story, it was the opening scene to Mary's autobiography. Fearl, Charlie's father, a missing chapter in the narrative of his own life, was only a symbol in Mary's.

"Jerry Fearl was a first for me, that's all. He was different. He didn't want a family, didn't just want sex. He just liked me, liked to talk and spend time. He was an easy man to be around."

"Why didn't you go after him?"

"You know, I did like Jerry a great deal. But it wasn't Jerry so much that I was after, I don't think. Before him, I just assumed every place was like Lima, with the same set of losers. But when I met him, I thought—well, if a traveling *feed* salesman liked to dance, maybe there was more out there after all. It must be Lima that's the problem."

Fearl's arrival was, for Mary, a metaphor of birth. The moment when the events in her life started to happen because of her, rather than to her, when she became aware of the world, the possibilities beyond the 234 people of Lima.

But Fearl, something more to Charlie than a metaphor, never reached full stature as a person. Mary knew too little.

"Where was he from?"

"Yakima."

"Originally?"

"I didn't ask."

"What is Fearl—is that German? Was he a German?"

"I don't know."

"Did he have brothers, sisters?"

"Charlie hon, I've told you everything I know."

"What did he look like?"

"Subtract the me from you and add thirty years." She looked at the top of his head. "Jerry's hair was lighter."

"Do you think he's still there?"

"When you were born I tried to contact him, let him know he was a father. You know, as a courtesy. He wasn't at the number he gave me, though. And directory assistance said there was no one in Yakima by that name." Not a word of Fearl's history, casting a long shadow over Charlie's.

Jerry loitered in Lima for two weeks, dancing with Mary, among other undiscussed, but self-evident things. When he finally decided he'd used up the story he'd been telling the feed company about a cracked engine block, he gave Mary his phone number in Washington and told her he'd be back through in a year if he didn't hear from her sooner.

A week after he left, she gave notice at the bar. She traded her white Ford for a pick-up, loaded everything she wanted into it, and then sold the rest at a garage sale. Took Horse and pointed the truck west.

She drove toward the Pacific because there were more towns in that direction. First through the dry irrigated farmlands of Southern Idaho, stopping off in Pocatello and Twin Falls. She liked Twin and considered staying there, but it seemed like an awfully short trip, so she got back in the truck and kept driving. She thought about the turn at Highway 75 that led to Sun Valley to the north, but decided the jet set was not for her. Instead went south on 93 toward Nevada. It was hot and dry and by the time she hit I-80, she decided to go west because east only led back toward Salt Lake City, and Mary didn't care for the Mormons she'd known. Horse was hot and cranky and paced next to her all the way to Reno, which seemed good enough and so she stopped. Again, Mary's autobiography emphasized the journey more than the destination.

"Reno was neither here nor there," she told Charlie. "It was big enough for a start, good as anyplace to land. Horse liked it."

She found a place to stay with Mrs. Hugh Maguire, a widow with a room to let, and employment at the Red Spot Tavern. Mrs. Maguire was a retired nurse with varicose veins and a fierce caffeine addiction. Tall and rangy and used to giving orders, she took pregnant, solo Mary on as well as in. During the pregnancy, she was constantly waving food under Mary's nose, trying to fatten her up. She tried to make her new charge stop smoking as well, enacting a no-cigarette rule in the house. Mary took her addiction outside, and Mrs. Maguire extended the no-smoking rule to the porch. So then Mary started spending her time in the garden, adding flowers to the yard or taking frequent smoking walks, working off Mrs. Maguire's bacon and pie. Her landlord eventually relented and Mary was allowed to smoke indoors.

The Red Spot was a tavern for locals, the den of Dottie Hensher, a singer who had worked the casinos in the 30s. Finished in red — velvet wallpaper, wool carpet, felt on the pool tables — it was an homage to the real Red of the Red Spot, Dottie herself. Once a blondish-red redhead and later a dyed flame redhead, she was the main attraction. From time to time, she still sang when the crowd was in the mood. The Red Spot was off the casino track, and most of the patrons — construction workers, cops, and bikers — knew Dottie by name.

Charlie's own biography began the following February. For the first years of his life, the three women shared him equally. Mary worked swing, from the time the tavern opened until 8 or 9 at night. Most days she took Charlie in with her and watched him until midafternoon, when it started to get busy. At first she left him in his little cradle on the bar where she (and Dottie and the other waitresses) could keep an eye on him. The lunch crowd adopted him as their mascot, and by the time he was crawling, the entire tavern watched him scuttle around. At three or four, Mrs. Maguire picked him up and watched him until Mary got back from work.

This continued until Charlie was about three. The three moms, the dozens of uncles, the bar. Mary had no particular interest in men, and Charlie's presence on the bar eliminated any need for her to invent children and husbands. There were men at the bar, men to give her a ride home on occasion, but no romance.

Victor di Paulo entered the story in 1967. A young lawyer with a defunct marriage, he fled the East Coast to put some distance between his past and his future. Cleaving to the American mythology, Vic went west after his marriage went south. Starting fresh. Twenty-eight, ambitious, ready for adventure.

Yet Reno was more west than he had hoped, and his early months as an assistant district attorney were lonely and bleak. He actually felt as though he'd been transported into a cowboy-booted Western, something like Ava would have admired where silent, armed men stood stoically quiet, a six-shooter presumably at their side. Vic kept his eyes closely on the Lee Marvin types.

It was December, Vic having put a few months of loneliness under his belt, and the tavern was sporting a holly necklace and bowls of candy canes. It was just after work, and the red warmth of the bar lured him in. The happy hour regulars had already gathered. He sat at a corner booth, ordered a ham sandwich and a beer and observed that stocism left the men of Reno after a few beers. He left without speaking to anyone, but nevertheless buoyed by a social contact high.

The next night he walked by the bar again, hesitating before he went in, still feeling like an outsider among the cozy crowd. A few quick drinks while he ate a sandwich and then he decided to join the men at the bar. Getting beat up by a Lee Marvin type at this point seemed preferable to sitting alone. He was regarded suspiciously for his suit but was offered boozy companionship. It wasn't ideal, but pleasant enough to encourage him to return the next four days in a row.

At first the thick-necked men of the bar were wary of his uniform—he lacked the boots and jeans they used to identify social appropriateness. But other indicators were more positive: he gambled on football, swore, told earthy jokes, and played pretty fair pool, and so eventually they started to come around.

He officially became one of the guys when he received his name, from Bug Johnson, while paying off a bet. "Thanks a lot, Mister," Bug said, smoothing the lapels of Vic's blue jacket, "it's a pleasure doin' business with ya." He emphasized the word "mister" so that it seemed like a name. Thereafter he was Mister or Mister Vic.

As the Red Spot increasingly became his home, he developed the habit of sitting at a booth and eating his dinner before joining the crowd. Sometimes he brought someone from work, sometimes one of the guys would join him, sometimes he ate alone. Always the same thing, a ham sandwich and a beer.

Dottie and the waitresses noticed him right away and giggled and elbowed each other when they took his order. His suits, the black hair that flopped down over one eye, his smile, and his ease made him stand out from the other men. His charisma was not internal, as with most Nevadans. He was chatty, his body was on the move, his hands provided punctuation. But in a state of unmoving faces, it was Vic's eyebrows that seemed most exotic. They moved on their own, rising, falling, doing little tangos all by themselves.

He was relatively short but barrel-chested. He wore fashionable suits that fit snuggly and came to a point at his patent-leather shoes. In Nevada, when men did wear suits, the legs were roomier to accommodate Tony Lama uppers. They waitress pretended to be unimpressed by his singularity, but nevertheless hastened to his table to see how they could put his eyebrows on the move.

Mary noticed him too, but unlike her co-workers, she noticed other things as well. That he had many ties, but only two suits, blue and brown, and two pairs of heavily-polished shoes. That when he arrived after six he generally "skipped" the discounted happy hour ham sandwich. That when he bought beer for the boys, he paid for pitchers instead of single bottles.

After a couple of weeks, two of the three waitresses began strafing him at his back corner booth, asking as they breezed by: "The usual?" They saved their flirting for when they brought the sandwich out. But the third always came and took his order. For months she pulled up next to his booth, pad and pen in hand, and asked, "So, you know what you'd like tonight?" Whether she had taken his order a week ago or three nights in a row, "So, you know what you'd like tonight?" The options stretched out before him. What *would* he like tonight? Each time he stopped short to consider. He imagined infinite possibility.

The waitress was Mary, who was in a Holly Golightly phase with her hair. Vic, who at the time was also not looking for a woman, looked at its ascending height reluctantly. She seemed older than the other waitresses, though she must have been about his age. Partly the way she dressed, he decided. Jackets, cardigans. Large top layers that gave her the effect of a lab technician or a doctor. This neutrality, combined with the openness of her question, allowed for the possibility that he might have changed since the previous day. Eventually, he started to pay closer attention to her.

After weeks — months? — she started adding, "How are you tonight?" to her verbal repertoire. A slight acknowledgement of connection.

He took her at her word, a woman checking in on her regular, and let the possible answers stretch out before him like he did the menu. "Fantastic day — couldn't ask for anything more," or "One of those days, you know," or, "I don't really know."

And then she would nod. "So, you know what you'd like tonight?"

The Red Spot became his professional as well as recreational destination. In addition to after-work dinner, he occasionally came during lunch, in the afternoon, with clients or colleagues. When he discovered Charlie, he became one of the uncles of the extended Red Spot family. Although Charlie was still a toddler, Vic sat on the floor in his suit and talked to him about baseball. On his fourth birthday, Vic gave Charlie a Yankees cap that covered his whole head.

His relationship with Mary developed more slowly. Four months in and they were still at the "How are you tonight" stage.

Then, one night in March they moved to the third question. Instead of how he was, she asked, "What do you do for a living, then?"

"Lawyer." He pondered whether to tell her that he worked at the D.A.'s. Didn't.

"You like it?"

"I do. It's all right."

He remembered her pausing for a moment before she nodded and asked him what he'd like to order.

After that, she'd ask a new question about once a week. He answered carefully, trying to keep up their bond of complete openness: Divorced. Two girls. They live with their mother. Jennifer and Theresa. New Jersey, originally. One brother. No, don't really like Reno. Came here because the District Attorney was hiring. No, no plans to move — not yet anyway. Sixty-four Ford. Vic di Paulo.

On the nights when she didn't ask about his life, she reverted to "How are you doing tonight?"

Their relationship developed at barely more than an idle. At first he thought about her only when she was standing in front of him. Yet over time, she laid claim to a territory of his thoughts that grew by minutes on either end of their encounters. Soon he was thinking about her as he walked to and from the Red Spot. Then while he checked the clock in the office, before getting up to go to the Red Spot. Then without warning, at times not associated temporally or spatially with the Red Spot.

One particular May evening she added, "Must be hot out there, you're sweating." She made a move with her hand to touch his head and then caught herself, startled.

He pretended not to notice, but his eyebrows ran up his forehead. "It is—start of summer, I guess. I stood out on the sidewalk for a few minutes, soaking it in. You never know what tomorrow will be like."

She looked down at her receipt pad. "True."

"I love the sun. It never gets too hot for me."

She nodded, waited to see if he'd add anything. Then, "So, you know what you'd like tonight?"

Vic paused back, considering his options. His right eyebrow rose. He looked at the small menu of choices, then at Mary's hands, poised at eye level. Her fingernails were clipped short but painted plum, matching the buttons on her cardigan. He was having the same difficulty not reaching out to touch her. Finally he looked up at her, eyebrows dancing.

"You."

Round trip to Phoenix, $319. He calculated the cost of driving: gas $250, food (en route) $30, cost overrun contingency $30. Total $310. Combined with wear and tear on the cab, it was no contest. With no ground transportation, he would be stuck at Vic's the whole time, but it was a fair trade-off.

"Can I go, too?" Janie.

"No."

"I'd pay for my own ticket."

"It's not that. I'm just going for such a short time—in Tuesday and out Thursday morning."

"I don't care, it's long enough for me to meet him."

"Next time."

"You mean in three years when you visit again?" She looked at him; he looked at the ground. "Why not?"

"Because Vic's an asshole and even I don't want to go see him."

"He's not an asshole."

"No, he's not really an asshole. We just don't have a lot in common."

"Well anyway, it wouldn't matter if he was an asshole. He's your father."

"He's not."

"Don't get semantic."

"I'd prefer to go alone. Really."

"Okay, why are *you* going?"

"I need to have a talk with him. Father-son kind of thing."

"Why are you being so evasive?"

"Why can't we just drop this?"

"Fine."

"Good." He smiled; she scowled.

"You're still the doghouse, buddy."

"I know."

Janie dressed for the part. She had her hair pulled back into a ponytail and wore a tight white T-shirt with the number 30 in black letters. Jeans, tennis shoes. She had a cigarette between her lips and both hands on the wheel, a no-nonsense pose. While they sped down the highway, she checked the rear-view with furtive glances. The whole performance, channeling Spencer Tracy.

"You make a hell of a cabbie."

"You're just sayin' that because I'm so hot behind the wheel."

"Matter of fact, I *am* saying that that because you're so hot behind the wheel."

She took a theatrical drag and blew the smoke right at him. She had mostly given up the habit, but would miss its theatric offensive uses. "Well, you still have explaining to do."

He leaned over to her, removed the cigarette, threw it out the window and kissed her. "I know. I'll tell you all about it when I get back."

He kissed her again and got out of the cab.

"Hey Shorty, what do you think about me picking up a fare back into town?"

"You're packing, right?"

"Of course."

"All right then."

She shot off at 30 mph, merging into traffic and disappearing down the ramp away from the terminal, trying to jockey around another slow-moving Broadway Cab. He wondered: would she actually try to pick up a fare?

Gate 7, Concourse B. Clustered around the entrance to the walkway, his fellow travelers divided into easily observed camps based on skin quality: luminous or pallid. Two groups were going away or home, desert or rain people. The former looked comfortable in bright colors, short sleeves and gold jewelry, the latter like British colonists bound for Injah, shuffling and squinting, preparing for the sun's attack.

The batting of clouds extended from Portland south to Eugene, after which the blue skies remained unblemished to Arizona. From overhead, the sun glinted occasionally on water or metal, little of the latter as they flew over long uninhabited stretches of first forest, then high prairie, and finally desert. Phoenix finally, stretching out flat, with squat buildings spread like spores out toward the horizon.

Next to him, an old woman placed her hands over a pumpkin-colored handbag and waited while the plane emptied out. Congenial cabbie at the ready, he offered to carry her cloth shopping tote off the plane for her.

The first assault was the shockingly bright airport, chilled to sixty degrees. At his gate were two families, a flight attendant, and Vic di Paulo, charging with a smile—assault number two.

"Charlie! Last one off the plane—I thought I had the wrong flight." Pumping his hand, clapping him on the back, words crashing like fists. "A hundred and four yesterday but only 95 today—how about that? Don't say I didn't put out the red carpet for you. A hell of a heat this late in the year. I checked the weather in Portland, 62. Not too bad for up there, I guess. This won't be too bad, then. So how was the flight? Did you get lunch? I guess it doesn't much matter with the cardboard they feed you. We'll get you something to eat, something cool to drink."

They rolled down the concourse in single file, Vic at a near sprint, sending pedestrians dodging from their path.

"Long time since you've been back to Phoenix, hasn't it? I was thinking about it after you called to say you were coming down. Three years, I think—wasn't it '89?"

Charlie considered the math, noted his muscles braced against the town. Maybe it had been three years—he thought Janie had been exaggerating. It felt like three months.

"Fall when you came, too—well, that's easy to remember. Same time your mother . . . ." Vic looked down at his shoes for a moment. Or at his hand, where his wedding ring still glimmered—Charlie couldn't tell which. They had come to the top of the escalator. "No checked luggage, I take it?" Vic, looking up and forward, sent a thick, furry arm toward Charlie's neck, where his hand rested a moment. Then patted. "Good to have you back."

Into the crushing desert sun and to the parking lot. It wasn't the heat so much as the dry air that sent Charlie's head spinning. He slowed to an amble and trailed Vic by a larger and larger gap. When he finally caught up, Vic was standing next to a cobalt assault vehicle.

"Well?" Vic gave a head shake toward the car.

"Hmm? Oh, this thing? New car?" It was so exclusive that there was no evidence of the manufacturer. Connoisseurs could identify it from its shape as surely as they could a silhouette of Marilyn Monroe. Vic's eyebrows were raised in glee. He reached into his pocket and then the lock pins popped up in the vehicle.

"Cool, huh?" More from the eyebrows.

"All I care is that the damn thing has air con."

"Air con? This baby will make you a tossed salad if you want it."

They drove through a city crystalline with sun, ricocheting, refracting, reflecting on facets of glass from buildings and cars. Each time Charlie came back to Arizona, it felt more remote from his experience. When he lived here, he had the sense of being out of place. Unlike his fellow Phoenicians—most of whom, like Vic and Mary, were immigrants—he couldn't identify personally with the city. He spent his time there like an expatriate. In the nearly ten years that he had been gone, the city had passed from his consciousness and now had the quality of a dream.

Charlie's genes, the liquid genes of Jerry Fearl—O'Faerghail before Ellis Island—linked him through generations to a Northern, cloud-dwelling people, people of water. Water that lapped the shores and fell from the sky, of invisible water suspended in air, trapped in clothes and hair, water that soothed lungs and moistened skin. His genes came from people who liked salty, bland foods, ale, the scratch of wool. The memory in Charlie's genes rejected this city, kept it from becoming a part of his being.

"Scotch and water for me. Whatcha drinking, Charlie?" Vic, whose people had basked on baking rocks by the Mediterranean, had a different relationship to Phoenix. It connected to the taproot of his family's sun-dwelling past.

They were inside a restored, turn-of-the-century bar, a cross between western saloon and wood-paneled pub. It was dark and cool, which Charlie appreciated. "Just a tall glass of ice water for starters."

"We have some homemade lemonade. It's good—not too sweet."

"Great, I'll have that."

Vic's eyebrows dove. "Lemonade? Bring him a scotch, too."

After the waitress left, "Lemonade?"

Charlie looked around. "What is this place? I don't remember it."

"Oh, it's been here forever—it had just gone to hell. Ol' Moose Johnson bought it a couple of years back and fixed it up. You remember Moose."

"Moose? No."

"Ah sure you do. Moose's Chevrolet?"

A pause and then Vic's thick fingers drummed out "Fly Me to the Moon" on the table. Charlie watched him fidget, smiling. "Anyway, he did a fine job."

Vic hated dead air, dead spaces. Vic wasn't a sitter. In the back of the cab, Charlie never had to say a word to guys like Vic. They segued from one tangent to the next without prompting. But silence, even companionable silence, unnerved him. After an excruciating six seconds, Charlie asked. "So whatcha been up to?— how's your golf game?"

"Hey, I was just about to say. Not about golf"—a shake of the head—"too hot for that until November. I've been looking into investments. Pretty seriously. I mean, maybe as something to do as a kind of post-retirement job. Well, maybe that's saying too much. Premature. Anyway, I've begun to take a serious interest in the market." A pause and he lowered his head. "Greve." Eyebrows up. "Have you heard of it?"

"Greve? No."

"They're a land developer. Behind a lot of the building projects down in Yuma—I thought you might have remembered the name.

- 84 -

Anyway, forget retirement: theme casinos. That's the new thing in Vegas, theme casinos. You build an entire complex that has a casino, hotel, and theme park rolled up into one. It's the new Vegas. Family Vegas. Greve's going through the permit process for a project called The Amazon. A long building with an atrium kind of thing down the middle that an actual river flows through. Right down the middle of everything—the hotel, restaurants and casino. They'll put in real palm trees, vines, spider monkeys, tropical fish— the whole deal. This way you bring the kids along and throw them into some scuba gear while you go off to gamble. The whole thing's a wholesome family vacation, so the customer pays for everything. One hundred dollar rooms, $20 alligator fettuccini, $5 drinks and because they're all part of the show, no more comps!"

"A tropical river in the middle of a desert."

"Amazing, isn't it?"

"Open-air?"

"Nah, they can't do it that way. The city has some kind of problem with the water use." Charlie was about to say something, but Vic kept going, waving down a waitress while he talked. "Greve's stock is trading at twelve bucks right now, but in five years it will be ten times that. . . ."

Charlie polished off the scotch and ordered a beer, letting the late afternoon slide into a hazy evening on Vic's alcohol. After a couple of hours they came back out onto the street, blinking in the light of sunset.

"What do you think? You want a good steak, maybe some barbeque? Saint's is just a couple blocks over. You like Saint's, if I remember."

They stood for a moment and watched the sun crawl up the tips of the tallest buildings. The bright violence had given way to a radiant heat, coming up from the sidewalk and off brick and cement. A nurturing, hot bread warmth that Charlie had forgotten. A touch of breeze stirred the air slightly. This was the moment that kept thousands pouring into the Valley of the Sun every day.

"You know, the thing I really miss is Mexican, I mean the kind you get here. We get decent Mexican, but not like here. What about Chilango's or Café Del Toro, one of those places?"

"I know just the one. It's in Mesa, but it's worth the trip. Chilango's burned down in a grease fire and Café Del Toro isn't as good as it used to be. We'll go to Casa Azul; it's fantastic."

Vic kept up a constant stream of commentary as they sped east. He toggled CDs in his right hand, popping them in and out of plastic slip covers until he found one he liked, left hand occasionally sweeping across a section of the city that had changed, a flow of information on the political background, the players, the hidden agendas that all the locals knew.

A 20-minute drive, and in the nineteenth, Vic made his first inquiry about Charlie. "So what does bring you down? I assume it's not just to see your old man?"

"Ha. The old man could visit me, if he wanted to, you know."

"With that nasty weather up there — are you kidding?"

"You're not going to believe it, but I have a business proposal for you."

"No kidding? Okay, here's the place."

The were pulling into a converted filling station. Every inch of it painted milky blue, including the pavement of the parking lot. The name of the restaurant was written in yellow cursive on the front and side.

"Everything's good, but the *chile rejenos* are —" he paused for emphasis as he pulled in next to a wounded Caprice. "Mmmmmm."

Vic lived in a condo in Scottsdale. Due to residual aesthetics from his youth, he liked tall buildings — one of the few incompatibilities about living in Arizona. The condo, then, a compromise: it was on the top, or fourth, floor, which was tall enough to look out over the roofs of adjacent buildings. There were no higher roosts. It was a corner apartment, sporting a wrap-around balcony and views of Phoenix on the horizon.

Charlie, standing in the living room in shorts, stretched and watched Vic, who simultaneously surveyed his kingdom out on the balcony. He was ignoring a pile of papers in front of him and sipping his morning coffee. A scratch of his knee and then Charlie went to the kitchen — separated from the living room by an island bar — and poured himself a cup of coffee. Still watching Vic.

The move to Phoenix came in 1971, a month before Charlie's 6th birthday. It was the first major decision in Vic and Mary's three-year relationship, a prototype for all that followed. Vic wanted out of Nevada and Mary wanted to get to Arizona. Their desires fit together like gears, moving the mechanism of their relationship forward. Unlike some couples, whose desires merged, Vic and Mary continued to pursue separate paths that happened to travel parallel courses. The walls between them didn't dissolve but rather snuggled up against each other. A love duplex: together, but not.

Vic's motivation to leave arose from his growing dissatisfaction with Reno. In the first place, he didn't like the people, whose interests domestic, recreational, and professional he did not share. They still believed in the Wild West. In business, they were oriented toward quick killings, big scores in the short term. A predisposition that came not from gambling (as he first guessed), but the more ancient Nevada business of mining, which appealed as a get-rich quick opportunity equally to the industrial captain and weekend prospector. They wanted to live alone, away from neighbors, even when they were in the city. For fun they hunted or fished or talked about hunting or fishing, always in the company of alcohol. And on Sunday they went to church. At first, all of this had the virtue of novelty, but as the years wore on, Vic felt isolated.

In the second place, his job. He had taken the assistant D.A. position because it was available and distant from his ex-wife, not because he wanted to be a D.A. The work was hard—which he didn't mind—but the wages were low and fixed, no matter how hard you worked. He didn't want to shift jobs in Reno and lock himself into more years there. Anyplace seemed better than Nevada, but his preference was toward the sun and cities. He wondered about California.

While Vic languished, Mary blossomed. On advice from Dottie ("You don't wanna be tendin' bar your whole life, darlin'—why don't you go down and learn shorthand at the business college?"), Mary went back to school. Though not for shorthand.

She took up the arts. Her latent interest, expressed thus far in canvasses of leaf and petal, expanded to paint, clay, and camera. First she took a watercolor course just for fun, then sculpture, photography, and drawing. She had some facility in each one, but it was when she took a class in painting that she found her medium. The swirl of colors—more solid than watercolor, more suggestive than line—was like discovering a new language.

During the first months after she started taking the course, she went through a period of intense activity, painting whenever she had free time. In order to save money, she was painting on salvaged material—doors, plywood, scrap metal—with watercolors, house paint, whatever she could get on the cheap. During this time her mind became recalibrated, musing over images and colors in all its free moments. She saw the world reflected through a canvas.

Eventually, she developed a palate of bruised purples, black, and gray. Her images were generally landscapes, midnight or stormy. Though the locations she depicted were spacious, her style was crowded and intensely active. Night skies pulsed, fields writhed with bush and tree. Many had roads cutting through the picture; at a severe angle or almost invisible at the edge of the canvas, disappearing toward the horizon. They were like release valves to ease the mind of the viewer. Sometimes she added an occasional building or two, taverns, gas stations, or derelict structures on the outskirts of small towns, lurking like thieves in the dark. She worked with small canvasses, some no bigger than a sheet of paper, that compressed the action down to a point of volatility.

For her, Reno was too small. There were precious few serious artists, fewer art galleries, and precious few who ever got near an art gallery or museum. In Reno, art meant a sentimental oil landscape of Lake Tahoe that you bought at the Holiday Inn. It didn't occur to her to think of moving until one of her teachers recommended Arizona. A serious but supportive group there, a few galleries, and lots of light. Add Vic's desire to get out and she was convinced.

One of his mother's pictures hung on the wall of Vic's condo. Placed prominently, over the back of his sofa. Charlie took his coffee and studied it. It was an uncharacteristic Shaver, something she might have done especially for Vic. He couldn't recall. A city street at night, Hopperesque in blacks, uninhabited except for a single yellow window in the upper left foreground. But in the shadows, bricks roiled, drainpipes curled and twisted, and black doorways and windows gaped like silent screams.

"Your mother hated that picture." Vic, still sitting on the balcony, hollered over his shoulder. "I found it a couple of years ago in a big crate full of other paintings she hated. Most of those were her rejects, but this is a nice one."

"Do you like it?" Charlie was studying a pipe that ran up the side of a building.

"A lot."

"Yeah, me too. She never painted cities."

Charlie backed up to the opposite wall. "You know, that's one thing you and me have in common, we like cities."

Vic glanced at the picture over his shoulder. "I didn't know you liked cities. You've never really lived in one. Not a real city—a big city."

Charlie joined Vic on the brilliant balcony. He squinted, regretting it. "Yeah, it's true. Maybe it's the cabbie thing—I like the aesthetic of cities. Portland's an aesthetic town."

"So what's your plan for today? I have two meetings—I'll be tied up from about ten thirty to two. "

"Just my proposal. It ought to take an hour or so—I was thinking this evening."

Vic stood, stretched. "Good. Are you hungry?"

"I could eat."

"Well I'm starved. I thought you were going to sleep all morning."

As Vic cooked, Charlie bathed. When he came out, a plate of sausage links and scrambled eggs awaited.

"So there is some news," Charlie offered.

"Yeah?" Vic stopped to look at Charlie.

"I have a new girlfriend."

Back to his breakfast. "Is that right?"

"Janie."

His jaw worked a sausage. He was smacking noisily as he chewed. "How long have you been dating her?"

"I don't know—a couple months, I guess."

Another pause. "What's she do?"

"Tech writer."

He looked up. "Really? That's a good job. With all the computer stuff these days."

"Probably so."

"How'd you meet her?"

"Cab. She was a fare."

"You picked a professional woman up in a cab?"

Charlie laughed. "I said she was a tech writer, not the president. Actually, it was a selling point."

"Why's that—slummin' it with the cabbie?"

"Pretty much."

In dramatic voice, "The seamy underbelly of urban life."

"Well you know, I let her roll drunks with me for fun." Vic stood to rinse off his plate. "She just moved from Minnesota and I guess all the people she works with are pretty, ah, conventional. Programmers and engineers."

"I gotcha. Contrast is good that way. That's how I landed your mother. You have a picture of her?"

"Hmm. You'd think I would have thought of that, wouldn't you? Sorry."

"But she's a cutie?"

"Did you have to ask? Of course."

"What color is her hair?"

"Almost black."

"Janie, huh?" He passed by Charlie and clapped him on the back. "Good man," he said on his way to the bedroom.

Charlie sat at the island, chasing a glob of egg around the plate. After a few minutes, he poured himself another cup of coffee, took it back to his plate and watched the steam. Loitering in gentle morning catatonia. Vic was in the bedroom for a long time. When he came out, Charlie was tapping his plate with a fork. It was after ten.

"I'll leave you the keys to the Passat in case you want to go out. Like I said, my meeting will be done around two, so I should be home at two-thirty or three." He was roaming the room, collecting wallet, keys, sunglasses, file folders, and a writing pad. "Think about what you want to do tonight." He stopped and looked at Charlie. "Anything you want, all right?"

"Yeah, absolutely." They looked at each other. "Thanks for the car."

"Yes sir." Then, on his way out, "All right, see you soon."

Once they got to Phoenix, Vic and Mary's lives continued on independent, complimentary tracks. For a year they lived apart— Vic in a rented house and Mary and Charlie in an apartment complex that Mary managed. It was a tough year for both of them. Vic struggled to find work, watching his confidence and funds dwindle as the months passed. Mary, who with Charlie in school for the first time had large swaths of time to paint, struggled with her art. In the spaciousness of the day she was having difficulty turning the colors into her crowded landscapes. Yet weekends, which they spent mostly together, took on the calm aspect of their Nevada lives.

They returned to Reno in the summer of 1972 to get married in the Red Spot. Dottie took all the tables out and packed the people in—the regulars on one side, the waitresses and Mary's artist friends on the other. Mrs. Maguire gave Mary away and Bug Johnson stood as Vic's best man. Charlie, dressed to match Vic and Bug in a blue, ruffley tux, bore the ring on a silvery-pink pillow. Which he hated. Afterward the crowd passed around easily-pilfered bar glasses full of champagne, so he considered it fair trade.

It was 11:30 as he drove toward town. After fifteen minutes, he took a left into the middle of a vast residential tract. When they moved into their house in 1973, it had been on the far edge of development. Their back yard had overlooked a field of weeds. Now that field was just a layer of suburban sediment, blocks and blocks from the far edge of new development on the new outskirt of the much larger town. The ring from the early 70s was enclosed by subsequent developments in the late 70s and mid-80s and then joined to the neighborhoods moving south in the past couple years.

He took another left and drove half way down the block, parking opposite a dingy white house. The model of 1971 modernity looked cheap 20 years later. A trampled lawn dotted by broken toys and candy wrappers. Near the driveway, a little girl was digging into the dirt with the claw of a hammer. When she looked up, he waved.

They moved into the house when it was brand-new the fall following the wedding. By then, Vic was employed and Mary's painting was back on track. The next four years were the "happy family" years, though it was a strange happy.

Vic and Mary's lives diverged more sharply and they became even more independent. Vic's time with working-class barflies was done; he was on to a full wardrobe and upward mobility. Although Mary went to Arizona for the community and support, she instead withdrew into her painting. Her pieces continued to shrink, some now postcard-sized works that looked all the more active and dense for their size. Yet they still spent most evenings together, still looked forward to each other's company, still loved and liked each other, even as the directions of their lives drifted. Gears fitting together, married and single.

Then came the cancer year. It began with a flu bug that left Mary with a chronic cough. As the months went by, she collected new symptoms — fatigue, loss of appetite, weight loss, insomnia, nausea, constipation, pain. Some waned as others waxed. The doctors diagnosed it relatively late, but Mary told Charlie that she had known since she developed the cough that cancer had taken hold of her body. She believed she could feel it spreading, feel the cells revolting and growing, cellular fire burning through her tissues.

Mary chose to let the cancer kill her naturally, without a fight. She accepted her death and put it, along with all her energy, into her canvases. In the last months of her life, their home became a workshop on death. Mary painted and coughed and wheezed, Vic prepared documents and made arrangements, and Charlie held his breath, trying to stop time. Toward the end, there was more resting and less painting. It was summer and Charlie spent it in the dark, air-conditioned house, watching Mary.

She died in September. Vic had rearranged her studio space and installed a hospital bed. Mary couldn't breathe well enough to lie back, and so she sat in her bed, coming in and out of consciousness. Charlie put an easy chair in the room off to the side of the bed and sat with his mother. She had a canvas near her bed that she had been working on. She asked Charlie to prepare it with a layer of white. She only had the energy to work on it once, about a week before she died.

Although her paintings were tiny, they took weeks to complete. She managed just the skeleton of a picture, a series of strokes that outlined a room, empty except for a chair. After a half hour, a fit of coughing wracked her body and she dropped the paint. By the time it left her body still, she was exhausted and had to lie back down. The canvas had a spray of tiny blood droplets from that coughing fit, strangely consistent with the tiny strokes that were the components of all her paintings. After her death, Charlie put the painting away in a box that he kept under his bed. To him, it wasn't ghoulish, but the most potent reminder he had of her. When his anguish over her loss was most profound, it gave him the sense of some connection to her. He was twelve years old when she died.

The little girl looked at him for a long time without waving, and then went back to her digging. He put the car in drive, went around the block, and headed for the cemetery.

Charlie made Vic buy a black granite tombstone. The words were painfully white in the sunlight: Mary Shaver 1938-1977. Vic had wanted a lighter stone, something that would seem more in keeping with the faded desert, but Charlie was adamant.

"She liked dark colors."

"I know," he had conceded.

It was a flat stone like all the others in the cemetery. An unimpeded green carpet in the middle of the desert, unnerving to Charlie, but something he guessed she would have liked. He crouched down in front of the stone, which like the others had two cement holes recessed into the ground like golf cups, on either side. Into the one to the right he placed a paint brush, handle down. His ritual, buying a brush and dipping it into paint, letting it dry, then putting it into the flower container. Always a dark color she would have liked. Today's was Cadmium Red Deep.

After they removed the bed from her studio, Vic and Charlie left it like it was. Charlie spent hours in the room, sitting in the chair, looking at her art. Twice he tried his hand at painting, thinking maybe he could take these to her grave. A way of sharing something. He prepared palettes and dipped a brush in the paint, but the colors weren't like words to him. His hand didn't know what to do. After one of these efforts, he forgot to clean the brush and found it, days later, crusted with paint.

"Hey Mom," he said, still crouched over the flower cup. She seemed to exist more in the granite than under his feet in a box in the earth. "Red today. A little bit of brightness in it, like a tail light, maybe."

When he was younger, he couldn't talk at her grave site, stricken with the experience of her absence. Her funeral had been open-casket, which Vic preferred. Charlie hadn't objected. She was gone; the body wasn't important to him. Yet on the day of her funeral, he was shocked at how the body affected him. A plastic mask, it was similar to hers, but strangely off. The skin around her mouth was pulled back unnaturally, her normally sun-damaged forehead smooth and white. Seeing her corpse was the moment he recognized what the future would be like. Never her again, in the tangible, unpredictable present, but almost-her, a fixed imposter of thought and memory.

After her funeral, the idea of talking at a grave seemed stupid, so obviously a game of pretend. But later, when he was near the end of high school, he developed a relationship with her memory. She became a little sprite living at the cemetery, his own creation but independent, a character possessing his mother's enigmatic personality. Someone else to lean on, not unlike, he imagined, other people's relationship to God. The sprite only visited her at her grave, though—he couldn't feel her presence in Portland. It seemed to live in the black granite.

"I see they've been keeping things in better shape. Grass is green—none of that patchiness like the last time I was here." He put his hands on the stone, fingers splayed. Then lifted them off until they were just brushing the rough surface. Eleven a.m. and it was already sizzling hot. "I'm down this time to try to convince Vic to finance a movie I'm working on. We did pretty good raising money, but I'm still short. How do you like my odds? I made up a pretty snappy promotional video, so we'll see. I give it about a 50% chance."

At the far side of the cemetery, a middle-aged woman was walking her dog. A car was just pulling out of the cemetery and onto the street. Otherwise, no movement. A fat drop of sweat rolled off his cheek and splattered the stone, evaporating in seconds.

"How do you feel about brunettes? I have one. Janie Prescott. She's an Amazon—I only come up to her nose." He had no idea what his mother's reaction would have been to Janie. When she died, he was pre-sexual. "She's a good egg."

He stood up. "Well, it's hotter than hell, Mom. I think I'm going to go. I wanted to let you know that life is pretty good right now. The movie's in good shape, even if Vic doesn't come through. I've raised enough money to at least begin shooting. I got lucky with Janie—she's special. Cab driving's good, too. Everything's going well. Keep your fingers crossed and don't worry." He reached down and picked up a fleck of paper from the grass. Another drop of sweat ran down his nose but hung there. "I love you, Mom."

Evening. Charlie and Vic were back on the balcony, digesting. They had decided on Saint's and were full of steak and ribs.

"Well." Charlie said.

"Yes sir, we have some business to attend to." He stood up. "Tell you what, why don't I go make us a couple of drinks—a bit of a digestive—before we start."

"Yeah, that's good, I've got to get some stuff ready. Rendezvous in the living room?"

When he came out of the bedroom, Vic was sitting in the easy chair diagonal from the television.

"Why don't you come over here? This is a multimedia proposal."

"Ooooh, excellent." Vic went to the couch, Charlie to the VCR.

"Before the proposal, a bit of video. Please sit back and enjoy yourself."

Vic's promotional video was the same as the others, except for the ending. This time, it didn't end after the camera swung around to the front of the cab. Instead, it went to black, waited a beat, then came back to the same shot. This time Lapierre was absent, and Charlie was leaning on the hood holding a blackboard with words in chalk:

> A film by Charlie di Paulo
>
> Produced by Victor di Paulo

The screen went black. Charlie rewound to the final shot and paused the video.

Vic sat a moment and then turned to Charlie, eyebrows flat. "Interesting."

"I have a business proposal for you."

"Let me guess—producing your film?" Chuckling.

"See, sharp as a tack, that's what I need in a good producer."

"All right, I'll bite. What's a producer do?"

"There are actually a lot of different roles. I had you pegged as the executive producer, the guy responsible for mounting the production." He paused and studied Vic's eyebrows for activity. None. "The person responsible for the financial piece. I'm not exactly sure how it plays out in Hollywood, but what I'm offering is that, in exchange for some financial backing, I'll give you 100% of gross. Anything I make from it, I'll give to you. Also, I'll give you the first right of refusal to produce my second film. This movie's already gotten some attention, and I think I can use it to finance a feature. So anyway, that's the proposal." He paused and then added awkwardly, "I would love to have your long-term support in this."

Again, Vic gave him an inconclusive "Interesting." He looked at the television. "Let's keep talking. How much do you need?"

"Five thousand."

"Okay, that's not too bad. But what are the chances you'll make anything from it—I mean, it's a hell of a long shot that this brings in a dime, isn't it?"

"No, it'll definitely make something. Actually, it already has. I showed it at the Zale in its current Super 8 form and it made about $100. I'll be able to show it there again at least a few more times, and Ava always shares the box. I'll try to get it shown at film festivals, which could lead to either placement with a traveling festival or possibly a video. Local TV, PBS. There are several options. And it's a pretty small investment."

"All right. Let's say, best case I break even, worst case I'm in the hole for forty-five hundred. What you're saying is that the real return comes when I back your second movie."

"Right."

"Okay. So what's it going to be about?"

"I'm not sure. I haven't written it yet."

"What *kind* of movie will it be?" Charlie started to talk, but Vic raised his hand. "I mean, is it going to be a regular movie, with a real plot, talking characters, two hours long, that kind of thing?"

"Yes, a feature."

"Good." Thinking. "So what's something like that cost? You've got professional actors, a crew, equipment, and what? Film, I guess—is film expensive?"

"Oh yeah. Film's really expensive."

"Actors, crew, equipment, film—what's all that cost?"

"If you're very careful, you can make a pretty decent feature for a hundred thousand."

Vic laughed—not cynically, but at Charlie's boldness. He leaned back and settled into the couch, put his glass to his lips, but didn't drink.

"You understand that I wouldn't be looking for all that money from you."

He lowered the glass, right eyebrow raised in skepticism. "Oh really? And where does Charlie the cab driver come up with a hundred K?"

"From investors who have seen the script and 'Taxicab Triptych' and think it's a good investment. That's what I'm talking about.

'Taxicab Triptych' is good, Vic, and it's going to be better once I get it on 16mm. People will want to invest. That's how movies get made."

"Do you want another drink?"

"Do you have any beer?"

"Sure, hang on." While Vic was in the kitchen area, Charlie rewound and ejected his video tape.

"Let me clarify the offer. If we were to write this down as a contract, you would get $5,000 and I would get 100% of all income earned—"

"And a credit as producer."

"Yeah, and credit as producer. Then I would get the chance to invest in your second movie. By the way, what are we talking about there—ten thousand, twenty, fifty? What were you thinking?"

"I didn't have a number in mind. The offer I'm making kind of hinges on the idea that you believe in the film. Since you said ten thousand, let's use that. We call it a $100,000 movie, and you invest ten, so I would offer you 10% of gross. I wouldn't offer everyone that kind of deal, but because you're helping me out on the first one, I would want to make sure you were the first one paid on the second one."

He looked at Charlie and worked a molar with his tongue. "Since you brought this to me as a business deal, let's look at it that way." He stood, paced. His eyebrows had been and remained mostly inactive, which Charlie took as a bad omen. "And then I'm going to offer you a counter proposal."

This caught Charlie by surprise, but he liked the sound of it. "All right."

"As a business opportunity, what you've offered is weak. I *could* make money in the long run, but it's a huge risk. Here's why. First off, this short you made about the cab driver—it has no appeal. Maybe it's good filmmaking, I don't know, but it's very slow and has no plot. Most people with think it's boring. I think you know that, which is why you're offering me every nickel you'll make on it."

"To make up for the fact that this movie's DOA, you offer me a second deal, which is smart. But I have to calculate whether the second movie has any better chance of making money than the first. You tell me you're talented, so I'll take your word for it. That little promotional video you did was very clever. That's the plus side. On the debit, we have a guy with no education, no contacts, no equipment, and no money. And a really weird first movie. So that's a lot on the other side."

"I look at it and I think that the odds are very, very long that there will ever be a second movie, let alone one that makes money."

Vic stopped pacing and rubbed his chin. Charlie said, "Which means no. To clarify."

He looked up. "That's right. But I have the counter offer."

"Okay."

"You want to be a film director, right?"

"Actually, I *am* a director."

"Sorry, no offense. But I mean, you want make a career out of it, make movies for a living, right?"

"Yes."

"Because this is an important point. Maybe you want to make movies in your spare time. But you want a career, right?"

"Right."

"Okay. Let me tell you how I see it, then. If you want to do something, there are usually many ways to do it, but only ever one *best* way. You've got to consider all the options and then select the best one, right? You want to be a filmmaker. There are a lot of ways to do that—you're going one route, but there's also, what, film school? What else?"

"You can try to work your way up from the bottom, but I think that's only good for the crew."

"Yeah. Anything else?"

"I don't know. Where are you headed with this?"

Vic hovered over his slouching step-son, eyebrows finally on the move. "How about an internship?"

"I don't know."

"I even know a guy at Fox—he works in contracts but I bet I could give him a call."

Charlie sat up. "I appreciate it, but I don't really want to go to L.A."

"What do you mean—L.A.'s where you make movies."

"Look, Vic, I—"

"Because you may have to make a sacrifice here, bud."

"Really, I've thought about this. I've already made the plan—it's to get this film finished."

"You don't *ever* want to go to L.A.?"

"I'm not thinking that far out—but not anytime soon."

"Fair enough. What about the idea of interning, though? Living there temporarily?"

"It's a good idea, Vic, it's just not for me."

He was back to pacing. "Fair enough." After a moment, he stopped to loom over Charlie again. "All right, what about film school?"

Charlie didn't immediately answer.

"What if I put you through film school?"

He hadn't expected that. Vic was hopping around the living room, which he hadn't expected, either. Just a "not interested" and then on to bed was more what he had prepared for.

"Man, that's generous. Why would you put me through film school instead of producing my film?"

Vic bounded toward the chair. "I want you to succeed. You came to me with a business proposal — an *investment* opportunity. If I'm going to invest in something, I want it to succeed. Sending you to film school seems like the way to go. Actually, I think the internship is the way to go — get in there with the actual film guys and mix it up. But that's more my approach, and anyway, I probably can't help you much on that front. You want my financial help, though, so film school, that's a good bet. A good investment, something I can do."

Charlie exhaled. "So here's the thing. What you've just offered me is really nice. You caught me off guard, so I'm in shock a little bit. It's a generous offer and I really appreciate it. But it's not actually what I'm looking for."

"You don't want to go to film school?" He was genuinely surprised.

"No, I don't, really. I mean, it's a good idea, but it's a left turn. I've already got this film going; I know how to make films. I just want to *finish* it." He stopped a moment to think. "My goal here is different. I'm not trying to make a successful career out of filmmaking, I'm trying to figure out how to get my films made. I'm not looking at it like a job. But I will consider it."

"Hmm." Vic rattled the ice in his glass and started toward the balcony, stopped, went back to the kitchen.

"So then you're not interested in producing the short?"

"I don't think so."

"Okay. I thought I'd make the offer."

"You understand that it's because it doesn't make sense as an investment."

"I guess so."

"You brought it to me as a business opportunity."

"I did."

"I didn't want you to think I was just being unsupportive."

"I did consider asking you for the money outright, but I figured you wouldn't have gone for that."

Vic had a fresh drink. He came in and sat down on the couch. "That's probably true." He sat for a moment and then reached for the remote control. "Either way it's a bad deal. It's either charity — which doesn't do you any favors — or a bad business deal." He looked at Charlie, eyebrows flat. "But you made a good pitch. I'm proud of you for that."

"Thanks."

Vic turned on the television.

Reel Two

| 6.

"Well?" Lapierre.

"Close." Charlie.

Speeding down I-205 from the airport, top down. Charlie was hunched and huddled over a heating vent in the dash.

"Damn."

The sky was a low ceiling of clouds, cooling the air to the low fifties. Yet Clay was in shirt sleeves, the top of his aerodynamic head poking up into the wind.

"Ah, what the hell, we knew it was a long shot."

"You think there's any chance he'll kick in later? After we get some of it done?"

"No, I don't think so. He's a man of decision, ol' Vic. He'll stick to his guns." Clay jockeyed with a van for an open space in the left lane. The cabbie admired his moves.

As the car dodged, Charlie dug into a canvas pack at his feet for a spiral notebook. "All right. You don't have any plans today, do you?"

"I have—"

"I mean real plans. Appointments or something."

"Hey, there are thousands of yuppies in this city depending on my $75 handmade *Poniedzialeks*. They don't make themselves, you know."

Charlie thrust a script into his field of vision. "Check *this* out." The front page said, "Taxicab Triptych, a screenplay."

"Whoa, let me see that thing." He made a swipe for the script, but Charlie snatched it away.

"The road, if you don't mind." Back in his heater-crouching position, holding the script down at the floorboards. "I bombed out with Vic, but I did get this finished when I was down there. After the rejection, I had a little time. Socially awkward to just pal around, you know? I also have the shot list set, a preliminary list of locations, and a shooting schedule. We'll try to get as many scenes from part one done as we can before we run out of money."

Lapierre grinned. "So we're going ahead anyway?"

"Absolutely."

"Good. I wasn't sure you had the stones to forge on."

"Pssh. Because of *Vic*?" He frowned. "Come *on*."

"This is going to be a hell of a thing. Lines, man, I can't believe it!" Lapierre let out a whoop and poked his head up fully into the wind.

"Then let's go to the Film Center and talk to October, see how we get equipment and so on *if* you can squeeze it into your schedule."

"Today?"

"Sure, why not?"

"Now you're talking."

"That way, I'll have two sets of ears. It'd be nice to have someone else there." He felt a cold prick on his neck and looked up at the sky. "I'm thinking of promoting you to Assistant Director."

"Promoting?"

"Yeah. Being behind the camera's where the action's at. Acting is for suckers."

Clay eyed him. "Actually I'm thinking of backing out altogether."

"Damn talent."

"Or maybe I'll demand a bigger piece of the action. What were you going to offer Vic—100% of gross?"

"Okay, okay, I admit it, acting's the best."

"That's more like it, camera jockey."

Pinpoints of rain were starting to polka-dot the windshield. "Hey, it's raining," Charlie noted, indicating the lack of roof.

Lapierre responded by mashing the gas. "Well then, I better pick it up."

"It looks abandoned." At the Film Institute, Lapierre looked dubiously at the stairs leading down.

"Come on." Charlie led him down to the foyer, looking for a yellow head. The front desk was unattended, and a quick survey of the rooms also failed to turn up bodies.

"It *is* abandoned."

It wasn't. The desks were still there, the computers, the film stock. "Everyone's just off somewhere. Let's poke around; we'll find her." First into October's office. Or the room, anyway, where Charlie had first discovered her. There didn't appear to be name tags on any of the doors. He looked into each one, in turn, walking in to make sure someone wasn't just out of sight. Finally in the equipment room, they found a hipster in Buddy Holly glasses bouncing a rubber ball off the wall.

"We're looking for October."

He didn't take his eye off the ball. "I think she's editing." They didn't move. "Do you know where the sound room is?" And then, without putting down the ball, he described how to get there.

The second floor was a little more lively. A woman in an Indian-print dress threaded a projector in one of the screening rooms; two people chatted outside the bathroom. And in the room Buddy Holly described, October Moore, sitting at a sound station with earphones on.

Charlie flapped his arms to get her attention. She raised her eyebrows and waved, then held up her index finger. It was past tube-top weather, but Charlie was still disappointed to see that she had on a rather pedestrian wool sweater and jeans. Clay would have admired the tube top.

"Charlie!" She took off her headphones and stood up.

"This is my friend Clay—"

"Yeah, I recognize you—the cabbie." She put out a hand and shook Lapierre, who outweighed her by 100 pounds, all the way to the shoulder. "Nice to meet you. So what brings you down?"

"Well, we're starting to think about shooting."

"Oh, outstanding." She clapped him on the back and guided him toward the door. "Come on, I'll take you on a tour."

"There's still a lot left to do in pre-production, but I wanted to get the lay of the land here so I'd know how much I have to prepare for on the technical side."

"No problem. I'll show you what we've got."

She took them into the screening room, where the India-print woman was now watching a Super 8 rough cut, and through it to a hallway that led out the back. It terminated at a vast wooden cell that looked like it was once a storeroom. Thirty feet long, with a ceiling rising fifteen feet before hitting a bank of fluorescent lights, it was unfinished fir: rough floor planks, six by ten support beams, and a wall of tongue and groove, mounted on every surface with film stock, editing tools and equipment, stills, and posters.

Charlie and Clay, simultaneously: "Cool."

"This is the 16mm editing room. It always looks like this." She ran her fingers through a tassel of film. "This is all left-over stock. People leave it for the students to cobble together in editing class. Found footage." She turned to Charlie. "Do you know how to edit 16mm?"

"No."

"Well, a class is a good way to go. In fact, you can start editing your own movie there. Filming is relatively easy, but editing will take you a little time to master." She walked around the room, identifying pieces of equipment. "I know you won't remember any of this, but anyway, this is the editing room."

She took them through the rest of the building, room by room, introducing them to people as they went. (Buddy Holly was named Shawn.) In the equipment room, October quizzed them about cameras.

"Okay, you want crystal sync, right?"

"That's sound-synched, right?"

"Yeah. So let me ask you—have you shot anything on 16mm before?"

"No, but I've worked on sets with them. Actually, so has Clay."

She nodded, started back in on the camera, and then stopped. "I'll show you how this works and let you get used to it. Maybe I'll come to the first shoot, too, in case anything out of the ordinary happens."

"Are you serious?"

"Yeah. I like helping out on projects like this. As long as we work when I'm free."

"No problem. Thanks."

"Anyway, it's pretty straightforward; I'm sure we'll have you up to speed before you shoot. Why don't you leave me a script and I'll look at your shot list?"

As she was talking, Shawn was bringing lights and light stands out. October had a tendency to speak elliptically; getting distracted by the lights, making a comment or two, and then coming back to the camera. Then the sound recorder and microphones started appearing, which were similarly folded into the explanation at random moments. Technical terms were hovering in the air: aperture, boom, tungsten, cardioid. Charlie tried his best to follow, wishing he had a notebook. He was happy Lapierre was there to listen with him

Clay yawned, bored. It was about time for his afternoon coffee, and he was thinking of the closest place they might get one after October quit talking. He looked at Charlie: he appeared to be catching the important bits.

That evening, Charlie arriving at the pods.

A steady flow of knit-shirted, balding men scurried to the parking lot. He checked the clock on the radio: 5:02. Janie would have been gone at least seven minutes. He sped toward the train, making it to within a block of the stop before hitting a red light. While he watched, the train pulled up in front of the large clump of commuters, among whom, as subtly as crow on a snowy roof, blended in Janie. He laid on the horn. Everyone except the crow turned to look. The train pulled up and they boarded — still watching the frantic cabbie blow his horn. Janie was in the middle of a clump of men just getting on when the light turned green.

He pulled up next to the train as it started to move, trying the horn again. A bored teenager sitting next to Janie watched him. She played with her gum while Charlie pointed aggressively. Finally, listlessly, the girl tapped her on the shoulder and pointed back at Charlie.

At the next stop Janie got off the train, working like a salmon against another group of boarding workers, arms up and forward. As she jogged toward the cab, he hollered out the window, "I've been honking at you since the last stop!"

"Oh, that was *you*." Arriving, greeting him with a smooch. "I don't like to give honking maniacs the satisfaction of my attention. What are you doing here? I was totally trying to zip home so I could be there when you came by." She looped his head with arms clasped at the hands.

"I thought you might need a ride. Come on, hop in."

"Shouldn't you be working tonight?"

"I should, but I thought I'd pick you up first. 'Cause I'm such a sweetheart. But I'll never get to work if you don't *get in the damn cab*." She pacified him with another kiss.

On the drive to her apartment, her hands were not far from his body; they brushed a shoulder, poked a rib, tickled a thigh. He smiled.

"So how *was* it?"

"Oh, fine I guess."

"How's Vic?"

"Same old."

"Hmm. Well, was it sunny?"

"Whoo. And hot." He thought for a moment. "Dry."

"Did you have your big chat?"

"We did."

"I see. And how did it go?"

"As expected, more or less."

She looked at him. "Thanks. Thanks a lot, Mister Information." On the "may" of information, she delivered a punch to his biceps.

He began his account again. "Oh my *God*, it was such a good time. First, Vic and I went to have a drink. Oh, well, actually, I *should* say, first Vic showed me his new car. It was beautiful. Blue! Well, we just talked and talked and talked—" He glanced at her, smile spoiling his smooth delivery. Another punch, this one with some pepper.

"Just for that, buddy boy, you're going to tell me what the hell it was you went down there for, and if you don't, I'm gonna squash you."

He smiled at her. "I planned on it."

"What?"

"A squashing."

On the way down the freeway, Charlie passed the Lloyd Center exit, Janie's.

"Where are you taking me?"

"I have something cool to show you."

"Ooooh, goody."

In his usual space outside the VMC was a Honda. Old. Might someone new in the building now be driving? He pulled into a space across the street, mildly irritated.

They waited in the hall for Oti, hearing a banging and thudding coming down the shaft. The push buttons, like the elevator, were historical pieces of technology. Metal, the type that didn't light up. Once the button was depressed, there was nothing to do but wait, listening up the shaft for information about the lift. Eventually it came thumping down, filled with two men and a couch.

"This happens about 50% of the time. Someone's always moving in or out," he told her.

Eventually Oti was free and in they went and up.

"HI." Laura was standing in front of her open door, back to them, smoking and looking down the empty hall. Clad in lime green sweatshirt and pants.

"Hi Laura. How are you?" he asked to the back of her head. They waited. A curl of smoke was the only activity. Janie's face expressed curiosity, but Charlie shrugged. He opened his door.

"I'M OKAY." Without movement.

"Good to hear. See you later." And into his apartment.

She started to query him about Laura but in the center of the room was a tripod and 16mm movie camera.

"Is this *yours*?"

"No, Clay and I went to the film center today after he picked me up from the airport. October lent it to me overnight. Pretty cool, eh?"

She circled it, looking at it from different angles. "It's so much bigger than your super 8—it looks like a real camera." She turned. "I mean—"

"No, it's fine. The super 8 doesn't look like much." He went to the lens and removed the cap. "Look through here."

"Are you renting it? It's out of focus."

"The dial closest to you. I'll have to after today. Don't knock it over though—I'm liable for it."

"Okay, I got it now. Wow. So wait a minute—does this mean we're ready to start filming?"

"Is that an offer of assistance?"

She looked up. "Well for one thing, I thought I was one of your stars. And yes, I'll pitch in on the set. Maybe you need a gofer."

"Hmm, no. How about a gaffer? Or maybe a grip. Best boy?" He winked. "No, it'll be a little while. I've still got a lot of stuff to line up."

They loitered. She looked through the lens, circled the camera, looked back through the lens and tested the tripod arm. While she was trying out a slow pan, Charlie sidled up. He led with his nose, diving through dark curls for the nape of her neck. She abandoned the camera and straightened up to facilitate his burrowing. Then pulled down a red collar to offer greater access.

Events escalated, time took flight. Charlie guessed that he wouldn't be getting to work after all. As expected.

Around two and Janie's eyes were red and droopy. They had relocated to her apartment so she could get up without waking Charlie in the morning. He should have been more alert—if he had gone to work, he'd still be driving for another few hours—but he was fading, too.

"So tell me what you really went down there for."

"Now? It's kind of late—"

She was on her side, face next to Charlie's shoulder. He could only see the top of her head and the tip of her nose. "Now."

"All right." He decided to go right into it, no fooling around. "I was hitting Vic up for money. For the movie."

She sat up. "Money?" She said it as if it were a question she had just asked herself, not one posed to Charlie, and so he didn't answer. "How much money?"

"Five thousand."

She put both her hands on his chest. "Did he give it to you?"

"No."

"Really? Hmm. I thought the film place was going to give you the money."

"Well, they're giving me some. Not enough for the whole project."

"So how come you didn't—" She stopped and drummed her hands on his chest while she thought. "How come you didn't tell me? Her mouth drew in and she gave him a good thump on his sternum. "Huh?"

He caught her fists and sat up. "You mean, why didn't I tell you about Vic?"

"Okay, let's start there."

"Me and Vic don't really see eye-to-eye on a number of things. Well, I mean, I wasn't trying to keep that from you—I just knew we'd have to talk about the money thing first, and I was just trying to put that off."

"What are you talking about?"

"I didn't want to ask you for money."

"Why not?"

"We haven't been going out that long, you know. I don't know."

She was sitting in front of him, cross-legged, an index finger at her lower lip.

"But you asked Clay."

"Well, of course."

"That friend of yours in grad school?"

He paused.

"Yeah—"

"Who else?" Janie had leaned in toward him, but at the same time they saw that a person-by-person inventory would be unpleasant. She leaned back and squeezed his hand gently.

"I want to get back to this—you're not off the hook yet. But tell me what happened in Arizona first."

"Oh, you know. I told Vic I needed money, and he told me to piss off."

"Seriously."

"Actually, I asked him to produce the movie. I told him what a producer was and made him a business offer. He passed."

"Really?" She put her hand on his knee. "He just said no?"

He pursed his lips and leaned back against the wall, pondering how to put it. "No, he actually offered to put me through film school instead. *Then* he passed."

"Are you kidding?"

"Nope."

"And that was no good?"

"No, it was cool. It shocked me, to tell you the truth. It's classic Vic though, when I think about it. But I don't want to go to film school." He thought for a moment. "And he didn't want to be a producer. So there you have it, the classic father-son bond in action."

"He's not your father."

Charlie smiled.

"Okay, so now about this money thing."

He groaned, slid down the wall and put the covers up to his nose. "Yes."

"Why didn't you ask me for money?"

"It's a complex issue."

"What are you talking about?"

"I didn't want to bring that into the mix, hitting you up for money."

"But what about just telling me what was going on?"

He thought for a minute. "If I had told you I was short of money, would you have tried to give me some?"

"Probably."

"See, I know, that's part of the problem. How much would you have given?"

She thought for a second. "Whatever you wanted. Charlie, I have a great job."

"I know, see. It puts too much weight on the relationship, that kind of thing. And it would have been weird *not* to take your money. So I decided not to ask."

"Ah."

He was holding her hand, but it had gone limp in his lap. He had no idea what her objection was. He thought it had gone pretty well. He'd been clear. He hadn't tried to soften things or disguise the situation. This was exactly the kind of thing he'd hoped to avoid.

She got up and went to the bathroom. After a moment, he heard her run the tap.

"I'm trying not to make a big deal out of this." When she returned, she was carrying a Mason jar full of water. "It's not that you didn't ask for money, exactly. You were very sweet to try not to sully things that way." She touched his shoulder with her index finger.

"It's that you're so secretive. You don't let me in on things. It just makes me feel weird."

"I . . . hmm."

"I mean, I didn't even know you needed money. God, everyone else must know you're trying to raise money. And then this whole Vic thing."

"Well yes, I guess I see your point. I hadn't really thought of it in those terms."

"I *know*. That's what I'm pissed off about. You were so busy worrying that I would lose it because you wouldn't take my money that it never occurred to you that I could be a supportive, normal girlfriend."

"Ah." He picked up her finger and kissed it. "I was being stupid. I'm sorry."

She let him kiss her finger for a moment and then said "idiot," but gently. Then in a fluid predatory maneuver, she jumped on him, straddling his body and pinning his arms. "So you asked everyone but me for money then?"

He squirmed.

"Answer."

"Yes."

But now you're going to ask me for money, aren't you?"

"Yes."

"Well?"

"Please, ma'am, spare some change for a poor movie man."

"What was the most you got from someone?"

"Friends?"

"Why?"

"Well, the most I got from friends was a hundred. The Film Institute gave me a thousand."

"I'm giving you two hundred then."

"Hey—" A quick jerk with his pelvis, but she stayed astride him and pinned him more forcefully.

"Nope! Two hundred it is. An extra hundred for punish-ment."

Preparations to begin shooting the film involved three general domains: casting, equipment, and coordination.

For obvious reasons, they began with casting. Whereas in the Super 8 version ("Eight," as they had taken to calling it) Charlie had been able to take advantage of actual fares and an all-amateur cast, the 16mm re-shoot, with its use of sound and line readings, could not. In Eight, he had Clay drive and they pretended that they were documentary filmmakers. They told the fares to pretty much behave as if it were any ordinary fare, to talk or not about the things people talked about in a cab. Each shot was done in a single take, and when they got to the destination, they shook the fare's hand and said thanks.

But with sound the discussion wasn't for show. Because the actors would be miked, they couldn't take a chance on a fare's inappropriate or boring comments. So the friends who had played major roles in Eight were bumped down to non-speaking parts, and in their place went actual actors. Save Clay, who was himself an actual actor.

The pivotal roles were SINISTER MAN (previously Carlos's role) and KINDLY OLD WOMAN (a friend's grandmother). The KINDLY OLD WOMAN section of the film would be shot later, budget permitting, so they put that off and started casting for a SINISTER MAN.

Two weeks of advertisements at the film center and in a local theater newsletter yielded only two candidates: a youngish actor seeking to build his resume (and who could therefore be persuaded to work for free) and a middle-aged professional who had done occasional work on student films.

The young actor—Roger—read first. He was short and preppy, with thick, floppy, apparently moussed hair, wire-rim glasses, and a checked shirt. Not sinister. Perhaps with makeup. They had arranged two chairs in a line to simulate the cab. Roger was supposed to sit in the rear chair with covert menace and mumble his lines thuggishly. Instead, he skipped toward the chairs merrily and plopped down behind Lapierre.

"Where to?" Lapierre began.

"Oh," Roger said offhandedly, "just drive."

"Wait a second guys." Charlie interrupted. "The thing about this role is that you're supposed to project danger, Roger."

"Oh, all right."

"You're the SINISTER MAN, right? So you should seem dangerous. Maybe Clay there wonders if you're packing."

"Packing?"

"A gun."

"Right...*right*, dangerous. I got it."

He didn't. They tried it several more times and the best he could muster was aggrieved.

"Okay, I think you're getting it, Roger. Good, good. I tell you what, we have one more guy reading for it, and I'll give you a call after we see him."

After he'd left, Clay said, "Wow. Thank God we have another one."

However, when Al, the older, more sinister-looking, actor showed up, there was a catch.

"What's he doin' in the driver's seat?"

"He's the cabbie."

"*He's* the cabbie? I thought I was reading for the cabbie."

"No, he's the cabbie. Look, it's all right, though." Charlie imagined that the actor was concerned about having memorized the wrong lines. "You don't have to do a line reading—the scene's mainly nuance anyway. Just ad lib it."

"But the cabbie's the lead, right?"

"Well, sort of. The cabbie, the SINISTER MAN and the KINDLY OLD WOMAN."

"Look, kid, I got a career. If I'm workin' for free, I play the lead. Only reason I do this is in case one of you little shits gets lucky and makes it big. I could have been in *Mala Noche* but I pissed it away."

"So you're not interested in the SINISTER MAN part? It's pretty good. . . ."

Al was looking Clay over. "What about him? He's pretty damn sinister, if you want my opinion."

"He's the cabbie." He waited a moment and then added, "He's familiar with the role."

Al dropped his copy of the script on the chair. "All right. You guys wanna quit fucking around and let me play the lead, give me a call." He took one more look at Clay and muttered, "Pretty damn sinister, all right."

Roger got the part.

After the casting, preparations split into the two tracks of coordination and equipment. Coordination, of course, being the principle difficulty.

In order to shoot, Charlie needed a fair-sized crew (fair-sized, anyway, in comparison to what was required for Eight): actors, a cameraman, a sound person, and at least one other person to fill in with the slate, booms, and lights. Behind the shoots were more people—location owners, other equipment renters, random people on sets, and friends, families, and employers of the cast and crew. Aligning all of them to schedule even one shoot was an act of supreme organization.

An example. In one of the scenes he needed to use a dilapidated house, which he located (a regular client of Clay's). They could use it any weekday when it was vacant. But his actors, inconveniently, could shoot pretty much any time—except weekdays when they were at work.

And so it went, juggling bodies here, locations there. Balls went up into the air but didn't come down; they just caused other balls to move around. Money too, in limited supply—spend too much on costuming and there wasn't enough for equipment, but spend too little and the talent became unhappy. The free talent.

And then there was Roger. Rehearsals that should have taken a couple days were stretching into weeks. Even in the new talkie version, the roles should have been a snap: Roger just needed to portray a shady character, acting mainly with his body. Lines were minimal and were to be delivered almost affectlessly, with just a hint of malice to communicate danger. It was an understated role.

But Roger was a stage actor, or thought himself to be. He strode around purposefully, projected his voice. His version of malice, when he could manage it, was raging and psychotic. Charlie thought he could get Roger to focus his intensity down to a point, to swallow it so that it burned in his eyes. Three weeks in, however, and he hadn't gotten it.

So on regular days—Tuesday evenings and Saturday mornings—they met to rehearse. A familiar routine now: gathering at Lapierre's, pushing the couch and chair into cab-like arrangement, taking their positions and starting. After an hour or so, a break for coffee or food, then back to the couch and chair.

Charlie, each day, offered novel direction, hoping to say something that would resonate: "You're a wary guy. To you everything is dangerous, so you keep your cards to your chest. Slink. Make your eyes go shifty. Slinking and shifty. And mumbly. You're a shifty, mumbling slinker."

If Roger was responsive, he managed to get to a kind of Shatner-level of reserve and intensity—which was worse.

"You're halting again, Rog. Your voice needs to be lower, more fluid. I like the restraint you've got going on there. It's good. But your voice is still too dramatic. You don't want to draw attention to yourself."

"Settle into the chair, Roger. Like you're trying to hide in it. No, that's no good—let's try the walking again."

"Don't sit up so straight, Roger, slouch."

"Okay, that's good sinister, Roger, but maybe a bit too much. Why don't you ease back off the throttle a bit. All right, good. Good. Well, maybe not *that* much."

"Roger, let's see, why don't you. . . . . Well, why don't we take a break, instead."

It got so bad that Roger's inability to play sinister started having a bad effect on Clay, who increasingly had a tendency to go shifty himself. He'd hunch forward and sneak glances back over his shoulder at Roger.

"Okay, Lapierre, now *you're* looking shifty. You're no slinker, you're in command, right? You're inscrutable, but in command. The cab is your sovereign domain. What I want from you is Yojimbo. Right? Like Mifune." Clay relaxed, Yojimbo-ed up. "That's it."

Three weeks from the projected shoot and he had Peter Lorre driving the cab and Greg Kinnear riding in it. Flashes from Roger could not be recaptured. Clay's performances swung with Roger's, better when he was just inadequate, worse when he was bad.

But working on the equipment was frosting. Charlie allowed himself that pleasure when the whole process had gotten tediously gummed up with scheduling or rehearsals.

Some directors were technology geeks, film mechanics who approached a scene like an open hood, admiring the equipment as much as what they could put on the screen. Others had no connection to the equipment: all they saw were the final images on the screen. For them, the tools were largely invisible; they depended on cinematographers, sound recordists, and set designers to accomplish the vision through their craft.

Charlie fell somewhere between the two. The pieces of equipment shaped the film in particular ways. Like the strengths and limitations of an actor, each piece of equipment had its own character. Different tools to shape the clay in different ways. Studying the pieces was akin to training the hand; as he wheeled the camera on a tripod dolly, adjusted the focus, set the aperture, he was learning how to pinch and pull and roll the film in his hands.

The new 16mm camera, for example, was more complex than his Super 8, but not substantially different. The process was still the same: light and shadows captured on celluloid, repeated hundreds of time and juxtaposed to create motion. The way he shot the film, the way it behaved—these were the same. But 16mm film was brighter and had more depth. Where before he had to learn how to enliven his image, now he had to learn how to darken the 16mm, to turn it bleak and empty. He learned its functions quickly, but how it would make his film look, that took longer.

October was generous with her time and advice, but she didn't like to speculate about how to achieve a particular look. "Buy a 200 foot magazine of film and practice. Get used to the way it looks in different light," she told him.

It was the same with the sound recorder and microphones. She was equally enthusiastic to show him how they worked. But again, at the end of the lesson, she told him to take the equipment and go practice on his own.

The experimentation suited him; he liked the idea of using the equipment in privacy first, to get used to it. On evenings the Film Institute still had cameras and microphones and light stands at closing time, she let Charlie take them home with him for free, under the stipulation that he returned them before the Institute opened the next morning. October tried to cut him deals whenever she could. Regular rental rates for the camera, recorder, and a set of mikes and booms ran $100 a day, cheap compared commercial rentals, but stiff for Charlie. So she offered him a deal whereby if he would rent on days when the equipment was not reserved, he'd get it for half price. Due to scheduling, he could rarely capitalize on this.

To begin with, he took the camera home and shot static scenes of his kitchen or slightly less static scenes off his balcony. This served to familiarize him with the way the camera operated, the way it handled light and so on. His next step was to find someone to stand in front of the camera and speak into a microphone.

He might have chosen Lapierre, who would have been willing, if not delighted. He could also have asked for a hand from Janie, who would have been both willing and delighted, but mostly just for the fun of hanging out with him. Instead, he decided to call someone he imagined would enjoy the work itself and who, uniquely, had also used a camera before.

"Ava, it's Charlie." He called at just after 11 p.m., in the period of vodka martinis.

"Charles, what a nice surprise. I hope everything is going well with your film."

"Actually, that's the reason I'm calling you."

"There's no difficulty?"

"No, no. I'm just getting everything together for the first shoot. October is lending me the equipment while I learn how to use it and I was wondering if you'd like to help out."

"But Charles, my schedule is so full. Surely you have some other assistants?"

"No one with your experience."

"If it would help you, then."

They agreed to meet at the Zale, late evening, after the last show. Charlie arrived before Ava and began to unload the equipment. He took it into the lobby, not certain where they planned to do the actual shooting. In a neat pile in the very center, by loads: camera and tripod, recorder and mikes, wires and cords. On his third trip, he found Ava squatting over the camera.

"So much smaller," she said without looking up. "This is how you date technology—by its size." The person in the lobby wasn't any of the Ava Zales Charlie knew. This Ava was dressed in jeans, a nylon rain jacket, and tennis shoes, and her hair was pulled back into a businesslike ponytail. She looked up at him. "And probably, it is a much better camera, this little thing."

"I don't know." He thought about the classic black and whites she showed at the Zale. "Newer isn't always better."

"You're right about that, Charlie di Paulo."

He wasn't entirely sure how to interact with this new Ava, so he just treated her like the one he knew. "So what were you thinking, the parking lot?"

"No, let's go up onto the roof. No one will know to interrupt us there."

Although she had a great deal more experience with film than Charlie, all the equipment was new and so she spent the night working at his level, learning the new conventions. Nodding occasionally or commenting, "Oh yes, I see; good."

They shot about half the film, working in fifteen or thirty second bursts, each taking turns in front of and behind the camera. Mostly it was to fiddle with light and sound, with varying apertures and microphone placements and lighting choices. Ava let Charlie orchestrate the shots, adding input only when he appeared to be overlooking something.

They'd been just standing in front of the camera reciting the alphabet when Charlie decided to ham it up. He did a piece from *Dog Day Afternoon*, the part where Pacino asks the anchorman what he earns—"You're going to see our brains on the sidewalk, they're going to spill our guts out. Now are you going to show that on television? Have all your housewives look at that? Instead of *As The World Turns*? I mean, what do you got for me? I want something for that."

Ava followed up with a deliciously campy version of the Gloria Swanson speech from *Sunset Boulevard*: "You see, this is my life! It always will be! Nothing else! Just us, the cameras, and those wonderful people out there in the dark! ...All right, Mr. DeMille, I'm ready for my close-up." After Charlie called "Cut," she came back to the camera very matter-of-factly. "Well, which one did you expect me to do?"

This led Charlie to do a Travis Bickle (poorly), and Ava responded with a (passable) Scarlett O'Hara.

They were both tired by that time and they called it a night. As expected, the footage was a mixed bag—over- or under-exposed, too loud or too quiet. It was a learning exercise, after all. But the four impressions in the middle of the reel were worth hanging onto. Charlie had a private viewing at the Zale with the cast and crew of "Taxicab Triptych" to get them excited about the project, and when Ava came on the screen, they gave her belly laughs and applause. She was in the office at the time, but he brought her out for another round of applause.

Finally, after weeks of rehearsal, they caught a break on the Roger situation: a Saturday morning and he turned up hung over. Walking slowly, hunched. "Hey guys, sorry I'm late." Got to the couch, collapsed. "Anyway, I think I'm late. Am I late?"

Clay, noting the posture, cocked an eyebrow. Roger was mumbling something. Mumbling!

"What?"

"I said, did you make coffee?"

Roger marginally caffeinated, they decided to try the scene where the SINISTER MAN first gets in the cab. He started at the far end of the living room, walking slowly, shoulders drawn in. When he got to the chair, he slid into it delicately (which could be read as *warily*).

Lapierre: "Where to?"

Roger: (slight groan) "Just drive, I'll tell you where to go."

Charlie jumped in. "Roger, try that line again, but see if you can muster a little anger, like you're pissed off this cabbie is prying into your life."

They tried it again and this time Roger leaned forward when he said "Just drive." There was a bit of fire in his eyes.

They went through all the scenes in fifteen minutes, Roger nailing each one. "Roger man, this is *exactly* what we've been looking for. Do you think you can remember what you're doing now?"

He was wobbling to his feet, lurching up. "I don't know. Maybe." And then he ran to the bathroom.

At the following Tuesday evening rehearsal, Roger was sober and manic and slid quickly into the old routine.

"Remember, Rog, go for hung over."

They tried it again and he played it like he was sick, without menace. His performance wavered: Shatner, lighthearted, sick, raging, Shatner.

"It's hard to remember what I was doing."

"That's all right, let's give it another shot. Channel that hung-over feeling; I know you can do it." By this time he'd honed it back down into the sick portrayal. It was a new variation, but it wasn't what they were looking for. Possibly better than he had done in the past, but now that they had seen him nail it, unacceptable.

And of course, Lapierre slid down with him.

"Okay, okay, let's just call it a day."

"What are you talking about, we've only been doing it a half hour." Roger said.

"We're not going to make any headway this way." Charlie started for the kitchen. "Come here." He rooted around in the refrigerator. "You guys know your parts backwards and forwards. We've done enough rehearsal. Beer?"

"But we're not there yet." Lapierre took one of his own beers from Charlie, eyebrows raised.

"Actually, I think we are." Roger had declined the offering, but Charlie handed him a bottle anyway. "Here."

"So you think it's good enough."

"Roger can totally nail this thing; we saw him do it this weekend."

"Yeah, but I was hung over."

"Exactly." He clinked his bottle to Roger's. "We just need to get you liquored up before the shoot."

"Are you serious?"

"Absolutely."

"I don't know about that."

"You were perfect when you were hung over, Rog. I think you just get a little too amped. You're a good actor, you just need something to put you in a shifty mood. I bet after you do it the first time, you'll be in the groove."

"I think it's a bad idea."

"It could work." Lapierre said, considering.

"And I really think it's unprofessional."

"Oh, come on. Those actors in the fifties were always hung over. Or actively tanked. It's a long-standing tradition in film."

"Well, I guess you're the director."

"That's right."

And that was the last rehearsal. He scheduled the first shoot for the following Sunday, despite feeling unprepared. Not just Roger but everything. Everything he could control and everything he couldn't control, and most gnawingly, everything he didn't know about. Yet there wasn't much he could do. He knew from experience that you always felt unprepared going in.

You were always right, too.

| 7.

A slate ceiling at mid-oak, impressive in light-blocking, sound-muffling density, sealing off the world as tightly as a skin of plastic. It hadn't rained, yet surfaces were beaded with water drops; cars labored to wear the wet off the streets. Puffs of breath hung in the air like cigar smoke, refusing to evaporate. It was too wet to rain—they were inside a cloud.

In front of Lapierre's shaggy house, three figures tinkered with movie equipment. October was stationed behind a bushy rose. She had on earphones and spun dials. Clay's girlfriend Jen, a gangly redhead, was writing on a wooden board with chalk. And eight feet into the street, Charlie, gazing through the peephole of a camera.

"Set ready?" he called. October continued to spin the dials, but Jen gave the thumbs up. A few seconds and then October offered a thumb. Eyes moved to the living room window. "Roger?" A pause. "Jen, why don't you go tell Roger we're ready." Inside the house, the star was slumped on a chair dozing, properly poisoned after a night with his director.

Again. "Set ready?" Another round of thumbs and this time Roger's hand appeared in the window, feebly.

"Sound," he called to October, who responded by pushing a button on the sound deck. Once it started humming, she hollered back, "Speed."

He shouted back, "Camera!" He started filming, listening for a moment to the whir and flit, and then called, "Rolling."

A serious Jen positioned the board and read what was written in chalk. "Scene two, take one," her voice was captured by a mike they had attached to a cherry tree. She gave a brief, enigmatic smile and a wave to Lapierre, two blocks down the street.

"Action!"

Through the camera's eye: a cab, approaching from down the street. When he was a half block away, the cabbie came into view, scanning the addresses and decelerating. Slower and slower until at a crawl it came to a stop just in front of, and slightly below, the camera. The cabbie gave two politely-short honks and then consulted a trip sheet. Now at a medium close up, the camera scrutinized the driver's face, Lapierre nailing a spot-on Yojimbo-level cool.

Pan to the house, two beats, three, then Roger peered through living room window (shiftily) before coming out. On the landing, he stopped to study the cab and look up and down the street before locking the door. In order to prepare for the shoot he hadn't washed his hair in three days. That morning he combed it, leaving it a wavy, oily mass. While descending the steps, a clot of black broke away from the mound and fell onto his forehead. As he slunk toward the cab, he tossed his head but the clump stuck to his skin.

Approaching the cab, he hesitated to look around once more. The frame was a two-shot—Lapierre in the foreground, Roger a medium shot on the other side of the cab. Liquor circles under his eyes, pale, sinister. The cherry-tree microphone picked up the door as it opened, the scrape of shoes pushing off cement, finally the crack of the closing door in the cottony air.

Roger out of the frame, attention was drawn back to the cabbie, who was nearly motionless save for lips mouthing "Where to?" and eyes that rolled up to the rear view mirror and then back down.

He put the car into drive and pulled past the camera and out of the frame.

"And, cut!" The director stopped the camera. "We're clear."

| 8.

A paved gorge glittering in weak sunlight with six lanes of traffic, flowing at the feet of brick and metal mountains. Di Paulo, rounding a looping curve, coming up suddenly on the prone rear end of Barney Heater's year-old Mercedes. Too wide to fit comfortably on the shoulder, cars passing within inches. Charlie pumped the brake and swerved from the flow of traffic, hoping to avoid contact as he skidded in behind Heater. Did.

Under the rain of grit and noise, they made rough acquaintance. "Goddamn it! It's about time you showed up. Right in the middle of downtown and I've been sitting here watching these idiots try to smash my car for a half hour! I've called every fucking taxi in the city." Traffic had no effect on the range of his voice. "What the hell did you park *behind* me for? Get your skinny ass in the cab and bring it over here. I'm not going to walk into traffic for a goddamn cab ride."

Heater, looking Las Vegas in short sleeves and oversized sunglasses, thick South-East Asian tattoos blurred blue across massive forearms, worked a ball of gum in his cheek, jaw muscles flexing. Orders dispatched, he lifted a cellular phone to his ear and turned away from the din.

Charlie thought for a moment, considered saying "what? – I can't hear you!" just to see what would happen. Instead, he nodded, got back into the cab, and put it in reverse. When he was thirty feet behind Heater's car, he waited until a brief cavity opened in the traffic and jammed the gas pedal to the floor. A long horn blast erupted behind him as he swerved into traffic. As he swerved back to the shoulder in front of the Mercedes, the horn made a Doppler effect as the car passed, while the driver flipped the bird as violently as time and space permitted. Backing up again, protected now by the Mercedes.

He leaned over and opened front door, waiting while Heater finished his call.

"God Damn!" he said. "I know you boys are busy, but my God, a *half* hour?" Charlie was watching the road, edging forward along the shoulder.

"Yeah, you managed not only to break down in a bad place, but a pretty bad time. A lot of day-trippers headed back to the airport, that's why no one's downtown." He used all of the V-8 and surged in front of a tow truck. "So where am I headed?"

"Flamingo. You've got about two minutes to get me to the first race." He sent a wad of gum sailing out the window, even while digging around his pocket for a replacement.

"That car's a real piece of shit. Bought it a year ago out at Sid Jones' and there hasn't been a month gone by that it hasn't broken down. Sid's a friend of mine—or was anyway—but I'm through with it. It's his car now." He scanned the cab. "Hey, you got receipts in this cab don't you?"

Underneath the sun visor, battened by braided cords of rubber bands, were the cabbie's toolkit—receipts, pen, lighter. "Yep. Right here."

"Hold on to 'em. By the way, my name's Barney Heater."

The exchange of names happened with the majority of fares. The interior space of the cab distinguished the ride from other service transactions. Charlie viewed it as an offering of sorts, an acknowledgement—while inside the cab, at least—of his position. And, though it was not true in many cities, in Portland, most fares felt it impolite to sit down without making that connection.

Heater reached out to shake Charlie's hand. He had thick fingers, blunt ended and muscular. The cabbie gave his hand and his name, but kept his attention on the thick traffic. Negotiating four lanes of cars, he zipped toward the 6th Avenue exit.

Heater lifted his beige, imitation-leather attaché from the floor and rested it on his knees. While the cab bucked, he dialed his phone, then opened the briefcase while it rang, trapped in the crook of his neck. Inside were a small stack of concert-like programs, two manila envelopes, a calculator, two pencils and a pen. They began their ascent up the exit ramp.

"Ray, Barney. Whatta we got—they started the first race, yet? Okay, good." Rocketing now up the exit ramp, Charlie hit the break too late—the car in front of them looked unavoidable. Rubber gripped asphalt, sending the briefcase forward at the cab's previous speed. Heater, with the quick dart of his free hand, flicked the top shut as it shot out for his feet. Guided it to the floor, neatly closed. "The cab got here about five minutes ago and I'm—" the car skidded slightly, nestling up to within three or four inches of a silver sedan "—coming off the freeway now. I'll be there pretty quick. It gets too close to the first race, bet the first race. But *only* the first. You got 'em written down? Good."

Traffic was now moving through the intersection. Heater scooped the attaché back up onto his knees, opened it, dropped the phone in, snapped the fasteners, put it down by his feet. The cab was creeping along at a safe 20 miles an hour. Barney looked at him.

"What the hell are you slowing down for?"

Charlie tuned in the Blazers. As a special favor for getting him there by the first race, Heater gave instructions to wait outside the Flamingo, meter running. "We're billin' it to ol' Sid Jones."

He was eating phad Thai from a paper carton, wishing he had a fork. Negotiating a precarious bite up an inch to his waiting mouth with the chopsticks, then sucking, cheeks wet from snapping noodles.

The Blazers were playing the Jazz and getting thumped. Malone was hammering them inside, and the Blazers' shooters were tossing bricks. Ten minutes into the first quarter and they were already down by twelve. By the end of the quarter, he'd reached the bottom of the paper box where a few noodles swam beyond the grasp of his chopsticks. He gave up on them and the game, switching to music.

From his parking place, he had a clear view of the front door of the Flamingo. It was a relatively new business, but the space was decades old. On the street level was an open area studded with pool tables. The walls were paneled in mahogany, worn at torso level, the floor ancient linoleum, checked in black and white. A steady stream of younger men in jeans and flannel shirts poured in for an after-work game of pool and a pitcher of beer.

After an hour, Charlie noticed a second, distinct group of patrons. These invariably passed through the pool hall and descended an ornate staircase to the basement. There were far fewer of these men, but they were unmistakable: older—mid-forties and up—dressed in slacks and ties. They reminded Charlie of Tom the Priest in *Drugstore Cowboy*. One man even wore a fedora. As the evening progressed, the crowd was mostly younger men until just before nine, when the older guys started filtering out again.

Heater emerged with this crowd. Charlie was listening to the post-game show with one ear and reading an old *People* magazine he had scavenged from a bus stop a block away.

"All right, kid, let's go." Heater was with another man. Indeterminately younger—forty five, give or take ten years—a thin redhead in a tan, short-sleeve shirt and orange tie. Poking out from under the tan shirt were the slightly longer sleeves of a white undershirt.

"Ray, this is Charlie. He's the cabbie's about to have a hell of a payday. Whatta we at, Charlie?"

The meter was up to $78. Charlie figured he'd knock some of that off the final tab—thanks for the fat fare. He'd have a pretty good night going with even half that.

"Well, seventy-eight right now, but I won't make you pay all of it."

"The hell you won't. Sid Jones needs to learn a little lesson about selling piece-of-shit cars. Won't do any good if you cut me a deal."

"All right." Charlie hid his glee behind a stoic nod.

"Montavilla, 74th and Stark," Heater told him.

In the back seat, they conferred about gambling. Charlie turned the radio up loud enough so that he couldn't hear them. Some privacy in a small place.

After a few minutes. "Who won?" Charlie told him. "See, I told you the Jazz would beat the line. Hell, they beat the Blazers." Heater smacked the back of his right hand into the palm of his left. "Easy money."

When they approached the corner of 74th and Stark, Heater reached into the front seat and pointed. "You see that bar, the Ace High? Turn left and go around to the parking lot behind it."

There were no free parking spaces. "Just pull up by the back door." Then, to Ray, "Go and see if you see Jimmy in the bar. Come back and let me know where he is."

After Ray got out of the cab, Heater leaned forward, resting his tattooed forearms on the back of Charlie's seat. "Okay, I owe you eighty five for the fare, right?" He nodded at the meter. "This'll cover that." He gave Charlie a $100 bill. "Now, how late do you work tonight?"

"Four or five, whenever it really slows down."

"All right. What do you make in a night, a hundred, hundred and fifty?"

"Yeah, about that."

"All right. Here's the thing: I'm giving you another hundred right now." He placed a second bill on top of the first. "Now, I want you to go home, get a good night's rest and be back here seven o'clock tomorrow morning. We're gonna see how far we can push ol' Sid." He stopped and leaned back into the seat. "What do you think? We have a deal?"

"Absolutely."

"Good." Heater got out of the cab, reached in for his briefcase, and then shut the door with both hands, solidly. Leaning into Charlie's window, he said, "Now, you can keep workin' tonight if you want, Charlie. That money's yours. But if you're late tomorrow morning or nodding off, we're done, you got me? I'm paying you good money so I want good service. You understand me?"

"Yes sir."

"All right."

While Heater was talking, Ray came back out.

"He there?"

"Yeah, back table, north side."

Okay, go around to the front door and hold it." He ambled toward the back door while Ray scooted around the side of the building. He didn't look back at Charlie, who was backing the cab out of the parking lot. As Charlie started down 74th, Heater flitted into the building.

He switched the light off the top of the cab and considered Barney Heater. He couldn't remember the last time he'd called someone "Sir."

At a quarter to seven, Charlie pulled into the Ace High's empty parking lot. He turned off the motor and sat, sipping a potent cup of coffee and studying the tavern. A squat square of brownish bricks with a flat top, street-facing windows boarded up and painted green, the color of the trim. There was no way to guess how old it might be. However, an addition—a wood-paneled structure perched on the western third of the roof—could be dated to within a few years of 1970. An office?

At five to seven he went to the back door. He considered knocking, but then he checked the knob. It was unlocked. "Hello. Mister Heater?"

When there was no answer, he went in. The back door led to a hallway with pay phones and bathrooms and then opened up into the tavern. He was surprised by how light and clean it seemed. The windows were boarded up to within a foot of the ceiling, leaving a ring of glass, like a continuous transom, around the top of three walls. A golden glow of natural light filtered in: a bar with a halo, he thought. Fresh pine tables and a clean blue floor, white walls.

Preceded by a thumping of feet, Heater came clomping down the stairs and into the room. "Charlie. Thought I heard something." He looked at his watch. "All right." He passed Charlie and veered toward the bar where he busied himself. He poured coffee and started collecting the remains of what looked to be a T-bone steak and eggs into a pile. T-bone for sure; the eggs might have been potatoes.

"Coffee?" Heater was holding the glass pot, mostly full, over a clean cup. Charlie shook his head no, and Heater took it along with the breakfast dishes to the kitchen.

The dishes crashed and Heater appeared again, going back behind the bar. "Here's the thing. I've got a full day today, but I don't want you on the meter. Sid's not *that* bad a guy—he's also not an idiot. So, I figure I'll need you all day long. Maybe until as late as last night. That's a hell of a day. What's it going to take to keep you behind the wheel?"

Charlie had only ever had three $200 nights, and one of them had come from Heater. He thought a moment. "Is it just for today, or are you going to need me tomorrow?"

Heater came out from behind the bar, and put his coffee on a table next to Charlie. Dressed today in black slacks and a cream shirt. He paused to remove a pack of Juicy Fruit from his pocket. After he had the gum trapped between massive jaws, he took Charlie by the shoulder with his free hand, and held him there like he was an apple he was considering buying.

"All right." He nodded and didn't say anything more. Charlie didn't know what this might mean. Then again, "All right." He let go of Charlie and turned away. "I tell you what we'll do. What are your shifts, twelve hours?"

"Yeah, round about, depending on business."

"I'm gonna give you $150 for the whole day. But if we go over 12 hours, you can put me on the meter." He was back behind the bar now, leaning over and looking at something. "Now, I *may* need you after today. I don't know. Before you leave tonight, give Ray your home phone. That way I can reach you if you're not at work." He didn't look up. "Deal?"

Charlie nodded, then verbalized when the hunched Heater failed to look up. "It sounds good to me."

Heater looked up at him, paused a moment, then nodded. "You can go out to the car. I'll be there in a minute."

It turned out that Heater had a number of businesses in the Montavilla neighborhood. Their first stop was three blocks away, a towing business. "I usually walk, but what the hell, you're already on the clock."

Montavilla was a downtown-like strip of stores running six blocks. All in the style of the Ace High, single stories, brick and glass. A style of the 40s or 50s, Charlie was beginning to think. Architecture as statement of purpose: clean lines, sharp edges, efficient, and straightforward — ready for business.

Heater got out of the cab without providing instructions and sauntered ten feet where he stopped to refresh his gum. Old wad on the concrete, two fresh sticks from a pack in the front pocket. Charlie stayed put, tuning the radio in to the morning news.

When he got inside the building, Heater started talking to a fish-eyed employee. Thick, convex glasses magnified his gray pupils, a nimbus of fuzz atop a balding head. Heater said something to make him laugh and his eyes became slits.

As they continued to talk, Charlie looked up from time to time to monitor Heater. A shrill voice spilled out of the radio as it went to commercial break, and he shut it off. Inside the building, the employee retrieved a brown vinyl bank envelope from a locked cabinet and put it up on the counter. Heater ignored the envelope and spoke to the man, moving slowly around the counter. Than a clap on the shoulder from Heater, a shake of his bald head, and the man reluctantly withdrew wallet. Eyes googly now and wide.

While Heater hung on to his shoulder, the employee pulled out a fan of bills, putting these on top of the bank deposit envelope. A few more words from Heater, a nod, and they both smiled. Heater took the cash and slipped it into his front pocket; the bank envelope went under his right arm, like a newspaper. Another nod and smile and then he went through a doorway to the garage and out of Charlie's sight.

Fifteen minutes later, Heater strolled out of the garage and got into the cab. He didn't say anything, so Charlie sat silently, watching him through the rear-view mirror. He went through a methodical accounting of his money. First, a careful count of the towing deposit, comparing his count to the total written on a slip of paper. Then he took out a small notebook from his breast pocket, making notations next to columns of words (which Charlie took to be names, although he couldn't actually read them). Finally, he took the bills from his front pants pocket, counted them, checked his notebook again, and then put the money in a paper envelope. Both paper and vinyl envelopes went into the beige briefcase, which went on the floor.

He looked at Charlie. "Go up another block and hang a right; we'll go another block and then you'll see a roofing place on the right."

For three hours they roamed Heater's fiefdom. Each step, the same routine; back-slapping, jokes, the exchange of money. Rarely, Heater paid someone else; usually they paid him. And then occasionally (generally following a Heater pay-out), words caused Heater to pull out his little notebook and jot something down.

After their last stop: "If you don't mind my asking, why is everyone giving you money?" His eyes flitted to the rear-view mirror, but he didn't want to appear invasive; Heater didn't look up.

"I make book."

"Ah."

"They usually pick the wrong team."

And then they were off to the bank, to make a deposit.

They returned a little past eleven and the Ace High was humming. A clientele of retirees, mostly bullshitting at the bar, and neighborhood workers eating lunch at the tables. Heater instructed Angelo, the cook, to fry up a steak for Charlie, brought him a beer ("you drink beer, don't you?" as he dropped it on the table), then disappeared up the stairs.

An hour passed and then two and no sign of Heater. Charlie strolled down the hall and found Angelo smoking a cigarette near the back door.

"Heater always up there this long?"

"Oh yeah, man. Sometimes three, four hours."

"I might go sit in the cab and wait. You want to tell him when he comes down?"

"No problem, man."

Heater emerged a half-hour later, at a trot. Charlie was dozing, listening to a talk radio program. All cab drivers ended up listening to talk radio. This show was a local guy Charlie liked, but he wasn't particularly provocative. Today's topic was a fight in the state legislature over light rail.

Heater climbed into the front seat this time. "All right, Charlie, I finally got Sid on the horn—let's go pay him a visit. It's on 122nd and Washington." As they were driving, Heater told him, "I want you to come in with me, all right?"

"Really?"

"Yep. Just come in there and stand next to me."

"Okay."

A young salesman about Charlie's age took them past gleaming new cars smelling of rubber, then began steering them toward a wall painted like a Jamaican beach. Just a few feet before the wall, a door materialized, hidden in a thicket of palm trees. This aperture led to a cramped warren of dingy halls and rooms. As he walked, Heater flipped a coin in his right hand.

Sid Jones was an older, skinnier version of Heater. More the appearance of a retiree than auto magnate, in a blue polyester blazer. At the V of Jones's open collar was a nest of white chest hairs.

"Barn, you're a sight for sore goddam eyes!—come on in and sit down."

"Your eyes are gonna *be* sore when I'm done with you, you son of a bitch." Heater hunched slightly, a fighter going in for a jab. He stopped in the center of the office, eight feet away from Jones.

Jones turned to Charlie. "Look at how he treats his old friend. Like I screwed his wife." Charlie wondered about laughing, looked at Barney, didn't. They waited a beat and Jones came around to the front of his desk. "How you doin', young man. I'm Sid Jones."

"I'm Charlie di Paulo."

"He's the cabbie who finally picked me up last night on the goddam 405. You owe him a lot of money, Sid."

"Barn, sit down for God's sake. We're all friends here. I'm going to make this right by you, so why don't you just sit down? There, Charlie, pull up that chair over there, will you? Can I get you anything—a glass of water, coffee, a soda?"

Heater made a conciliatory move, thumping his thick body onto the chair. "Yeah, get us some coffee, Sid. Bring a cup for the kid." Legs apart, ready for action, but at least he sat.

"Good. Sit and relax and I'll be right back."

They sat for another moment in silence and then Heater turned his head slightly to Charlie and gave him a wink. He leaned back into the chair and started whistling a big band tune. The moment he heard the door, his body hunched, his legs spread, and he leaned forward, ready again for action.

Sid put two chipped teacups on the edge of his desk in front of them. "All right, Barney, let's talk about your car."

"It's not my car, Sid, it's yours. You bought it from me last night."

For the next hour they played a game of reverse car-selling, with Heater trying to un-buy his new Mercedes. Sid maintained a staunch deal's-a-deal position, and they circled endlessly. Heater emphasized the word "lemon" while Sid relied on "friends." Periodically, Barney would ask Charlie a question about the circumstances of the breakdown, the unreliability of cabs, or the escalating cost of cab fare.

The conversation wore on past interest to Charlie until, unpredictably, Heater offered an alternative demand—a trade-in for a red and white Nash Cosmopolitan Jones had in the used lot.

"You want the Nash?"

"I want the Nash and ten grand in cash for the lemon."

"You don't want the Nash."

"I'm takin' the Nash, Sid. Obviously you won't take your lemon back, so I'm takin' the Nash."

"Come on, Barn, the Nash is a novelty car. It's a woman's car— hell, it's a *small* woman's car. A co-ed or something. I don't even think you'd fit in it."

"I'll fit."

"I got a whole lot full of classics. Bigger, more stylish. You know what I got out on the lot right now? A fully-restored Hudson Commodore. Now *that's* a Barney Heater ride."

"Charlie, you ever buy a car, don't come to this swindler."

"For Pete's sake, Barn. You thought that Mercedes was unreliable? Hell, that's the best there is. You'll spend your *life* in the garage with the Nash."

"Well hell, Sid, I spend my life in the garage with your brand-new cars. Might as well have a classic. If it breaks down, I'll call a cab." He grinned and elbowed Charlie.

Heater got the Nash. Once Sid was convinced Heater really wanted the car, he was happy to make the trade. Another hour negotiating the trade-in value of the Mercedes, and then for the first time Heater went out to look at his new car.

It was a nice car—mostly restored, but the paint job was a little chipped and there was a tear in the upholstery on the driver's side seat. Down down down went Heater as he climbed in, toppling from an awkward squat. Once in, he filled up two-thirds of the width of the car, but had a couple inches to spare over the top of his head.

"Keys," he said to Sid, arm out like a plane's wing. The tiny engine turned over and Heater revved it gleefully.

"See, Barn, everyone's happy."

Heater might not have heard Sid; he was speeding off toward the back of the parking lot.

As he drove, Sid told Charlie, "He's an SOB." Heater banked at the corner, car listing inelegantly. "But what are you going to do?"

Heater made two passes before pulling up next to them. "Sid, I don't care what your mother says about you, I like you. It's a hell of a car."

He started waving his arm out the window, which Sid took to be a handshake offer. Heater continued talking while Sid shook his hand. "Charlie, go get the cab and follow me—we'll take this out to a guy I know does auto-body work."

Then he was off for another spin around the lot.

| 9.

Verticality. To communicate the quality of "sinister," he needed a looming environment. One of the oldest parts of town was the neighborhood surrounding North Russell Street, a few blocks of apartment houses and taverns, built on a small bluff on the east side of the Willamette. Founded by Germans in the 1870s, it was a long-forgotten island stranded by a rail yard and tied off by highways that looped and rose a hundred feet overhead. The massive cement supports, the rise in elevation, and the narrowness of the 19th-century streets, sent the eyes up, gave the location height and danger. A cab passing along Russell looked marginal, a bug at the whim of this oversized landscape.

The location of the second shoot.

Charlie arrived first, an hour before the designated 9:30 a.m. start time. To check the equipment, prepare for the shoot. He parked in front of the White Eagle, the neighborhood's signature establishment — a dive bar of notorious history — and studied the shot list. He planned three components: an interior cab shoot with line readings, a side shoot of the actors in the cab (similar to the promo), and exterior long shots of the cab driving through the neighborhood. Externals first, to get in the swing of things, followed by the side-by-side. Unless they were really on a roll earlier in the day, they would finish with the interiors, which were going to be a trick.

The Caddy rolled up behind him at 9:15. Lapierre was the first in a procession of cast and crew, all arriving at one- or two-minute intervals. By 9:22, everyone but Roger had arrived. An auspicious start.

The crew was larger for the second shoot than it had been for the first. He had recruited volunteers from among his current and growing contacts in Portland's film community. From Ava's group of screeners, Tony and David had lighting. They were offering their sweat in exchange for the use of the camera after Charlie's shoot ended (hypothetically in the afternoon). They had a night shoot and this way saved rental fees.

Andrea and Amy, students at the film institute, had sound. They were helping on a barter relationship for his own help on their production—a typical Institute arrangement. Rounding out the crew were Jen and Katie. Katie, a high schooler who also came through the Institute, was a PA. Jen had no title, and was afforded Clay-level respect, but she was also essentially a PA.

In preparation for the day, Charlie had brewed two thermoses of coffee and purchased two dozen doughnuts. He directed the arrivals to the cab's open trunk, where the goodies were displayed. Not exactly *Home and Gardens*, but no one turned him down. Once Roger arrived (9:28), he went through the shooting schedule and shot list.

"Okay?" Nods. "Questions?" None. "All right then, let's get ready."

While the crew started prepping the set, Roger and Lapierre did a quick run-through of their lines. After fifteen minutes, everything was ready. Charlie told them to take their places. He waved to Jen, positioned at one end of the street, then to Katie. They waved back—signaling the all-clear on traffic. He was about to holler at the actors, but stopped. Lapierre was sitting on the back of the Caddy, Roger pacing in front of him. From where Charlie stood, he seemed a little jumpy. Perhaps not fully hung over.

He strolled over. "How we doing, here?"

"Great," Roger chirped. Lapierre frowned.

"Let me see a run-through."

They read the scene—a tension-builder wherein the fare goes from suspicious to sinister. Roger started as innocuous and worked his way almost to suspicious. Lapierre's performance, playing off Roger's, started well but deteriorated.

"Good. Hey Clay, come with me for a second, will you? I need to figure something out about the first scene. Hang tight, Rog."

Out of earshot, Charlie inquired, "He's sober?"

"Not completely, but he's not as hung as he should be. Partly he's just amped."

"Okay, we've got a couple-three hours before we'll be doing the line reading. Why don't we see what he's looking like after an hour. Maybe he'll settled down."

"And if not, we go to plan B?"

"Yeah, but let's give him a little while."

Plan B involved a bottle of gin in Lapierre's glove box.

The first shoot was nothing—street shots of the cab driving down Russell, turning, disappearing down Interstate Avenue. While he filmed Roger and Clay, the sound and lighting folks started unpacking equipment.

The second shoot would be nearly nothing—at least, once the cab was properly lighted. It was not the easiest task, but Tony figured out how to attach lights to the seat next to each actor. That way light came in at a sharp angle on their passenger side. Charlie was going for a noir look here, high contrast, light and shadows.

He planned to shoot the scene from three different angles: once as an establishing two-shot, and in separate close-ups of each of the actors. Although it was slightly different from the way he shot the promo, it was logistically the same kind of shot, so Charlie expected an easy go.

But an unexpected problem emerged. Although the day was overcast, the cover was light, and the clouds formed a massive diffuser overhead. The effect through the camera lens was glare—and windows that were like mirrors. They minimized the glare slightly when they tried going the opposite direction on the road, but the reflections still spoiled the shot. When he and Lapierre had tested the shot out earlier (without film), they shot on the shadow-side of the cab. They moved the production a block and tried going west and then east, trying to find shadows. Glare. The interior lighting helped and when they traveled east the light was the best, but the images were still muddy. They had to scrap it.

"We'll shoot the interiors instead, and see if the light changes after that. Sorry, folks."

He sent Katie off with a $20 bill for snacks, ignoring the 17-year-old disdain she directed at his food budget. The crew dispersed to their own cars, and the actors retired to the Caddy for more rehearsal.

Charlie went to the trunk, scrounged three swallows of coffee from the thermoses, ate a maple bar, and pondered the next shoot.

Katie returned with respectable provisions — starch, sugar, fat, all cheapo off-brands. A large quantity for a small price. After the doughnut breakfast, this offering was met with more guarded delight, but everything was gone within five minutes.

By request, Katie also brought back a large coffee for Roger, who started slurping hungrily. During the deliberations over glare, Charlie and Clay agreed to implement Plan B, forcing a healthy slug of gin down Roger. Their efforts had been largely successful — Roger got an initial bump from the gin but was now crashing into fatigue and surliness. Charlie eyed the coffee sliding down Roger's throat in gulps, but he was distracted by Katie, who gave him fifty-two cents in change and started asking about the lighting. Roger eyed Charlie eyeing his coffee and scuttled back to Lapierre. By the time Charlie arrived, they were back into a scene.

Roger was mid-sentence: ". . . up here; yeah, turn right there."

"Where'd you say you were going, again?"

"I didn't."

Roger was trying to shield the coffee from Charlie's view with his body. He took a surreptitious sip.

"Hey." Charlie was grabbing for the cup.

"Come on, Rog."

"Man, I need this coffee. I'm really tired."

"I know, but you're better tired."

He slouched and considered the coffee before giving it up. "This sucks."

He had done all right, though — the cup was more than half-empty. He patted Roger's shoulder. "Good man."

They returned to rehearsing, and Charlie took the crew to study the logistics of the next scene. Katie was right — lighting was going to be a problem. If they wanted the actors lit at all, it wasn't possible to position the cameraman on the seat next to either actor — the lights took up most of the seat. The cameraman would have to sit in the seat next to the other actor and shoot over the seat. Using Tony and David as stand-ins for the actors, Charlie took his place in the cab and Andrea adjusted the lights. First they would shoot Lapierre and then shift things to shoot Roger. Once the coffee boost had worn off.

The vagaries of filmmaking work both ways: if sometimes the easiest shoots are ambushed by inexplicable obstacles like the wrong kinds of clouds, at other times expected obstacles fail to arise and a complex shoot can also go off relatively smoothly. The difficulties for the afternoon shoot were of the molehill variety—botched line readings, a bumped camera, a delivery truck in the middle of the road. In two hours following a trouble-free shoot, the director called it a wrap.

As they were boxing up lights and mikes and lenses, swaggering around like a seasoned L.A. crew, Lapierre handed out bottles of beer. Then Charlie held up a $100 bill and asked, "What do you want Ulysses to buy you, booze or food?" The choice was almost unanimous—booze—and they walked across the street to the White Eagle to spend it. To the dissenting voter, slightly green Roger, Charlie promised a cheeseburger and Coke.

"Nice and greasy, to sop up the bile," he said, grinning.

He sent Lapierre in with the money and then went to finish labeling and recording his footage. After each canister was labeled, he made a notation in the spiral Steno. In a right-hand column was the amount he had allocated for the shoot. Next to it he entered the amount of footage he had actually shot. For the second time, he had shot more than he predicted—even without the side-by-side shoot they had yet to complete. Overage two times in a row. A pattern? He frowned and put the Steno in the glove box.

He tried not to think about it and went in for a beer.

10.

Charlie and Janie, standing next to a wall of frozen turkey carcasses. Shrink-wrapped in yellow and red, fitted together like stones. Janie, sporting a Santa Claus beard, leaned on a shopping cart filled with provisions for the annual Holiday Feast: two cans yams, one can cranberry sauce, one sack potatoes, one box stuffing, two onions.

"No, I think frozen is the best."

"What are you talking about?" She moved to the wall and tapped a turkey with her fingernail. It made a sharp, flinty click. "Look at these — they're probably four years old."

"That's what you'd think, but I've made fresh and I've made frozen, and the frozen is always superior."

She tapped again, absently. "Here, you try it." She spun around and pulled off the beard.

"What do you think, a fifteen pounder?"

"We're not getting frozen. You made me get the canned cranberry. We're not getting a frozen turkey, too."

"Listen, missy, how many turkeys have you cooked in your day?"

"It's not *me*, it's my mother; she wouldn't consider buying a frozen."

"And how are her turkeys?"

"You know, they're not actually very good, now that I think about it."

"Dry?"

"Yes!"

"Yep, that's a fresh turkey for you. Better get the frozen."

While he adjusted his beard and patted the mustache onto his lip, Janie perused the birds. She found one and held it up for perspective. "This one's sixteen; what do you think?"

"Small. Maybe eighteen."

She returned the turkey to the top of the wall, but poorly. It came down, bouncing once on the edge of the refrigeration case and thudding like a cinder block on the floor.

"Ho, ho, ho!" Charlie said, bearded and pointing.

"Shit. Should we buy this one now? It's probably bruised."

"Nah, we'll just take this one up with us and let them know what happened. They shouldn't have piled them so high." She was looking at him and so he asked, "What do you think?"

"It's a bit leprechaunish on you."

"Ho, ho, ho!" said Charlie Claus.

A spitting drizzle had begun while they shopped for turkeys; heavy drops with a hint of ice, snapping as they hit the pavement, yet broadly spaced—which seemed to Janie an act of spite. Standing next to the cab, she let out a long Laura-like shriek.

In the two months since the clouds had settled permanently over the city, Janie's mood had steadily darkened. A malaise that crept up like illness, sapping her energy, then progressing to a dull melancholy and a more profound depression before arriving, most recently, at active pissiness. Which, Charlie was alarmed to discover, she seemed to direct most often at him, with remarks like "Your city is a hell hole!"

She had taken to jumping him, wrestling him to the ground, and demanding change. "Why do you like this shit hole so much? It's like one of those half-witted lap-dogs, drooling all the time. Make it stop raining!" He'd grunt and flail and she'd lock his head under her arm and make demands: "Will you make it stop? Tell me you'll bring me the sun for *one day*." And he'd grunt and she'd let him go and then she'd collapse back into depression and fall asleep.

Thus he was on a mission of mood rehabilitation, trying to put her in holiday spirits. Though shopping for the annual Holiday Feast was properly the purview of the host, Lapierre, Charlie commandeered the task for Janie's sake. For the familiarity of it. Then he'd planned a trip to B. Moloch's—an airy wine bar—and perhaps an impromptu, sappy holiday movie. But she was having none of it. Even the seasonal beard failed to provide the expected lift.

"Goddamn rain!" she raged, looking up, ready to beat it down with her hands.

It was time to bring out the big guns. Foregoing the afternoon's activities, he took her straight home, ignoring the groceries in the trunk. He closed all the curtains and turned on every light in the apartment, then set the heat to 75. Light and warmth. While she sat on the couch listening to Garrison Keillor, he went to the kitchen for additional aids. He started with Kalhua and bourbon hot cocoas and then prepared a plate of fatty treats, both savory and sweet. He would restock as the need required.

She was puddled on the couch when he returned, already glistening around the neck from the heat pouring out of the vents.

"A tonic for the lady. No argument; drink it right down."

While she sipped, he began peeling, working from the shoes up. When there was nothing more to remove, he demanded that she drain her mug, then laid her out on the couch. Again, he started with her feet, kneading and rolling muscles, working his way up. Periodic breaks were given for food and hooch, but he didn't let her speak until, at seven thirty-two, she propped herself up on one elbow.

"I feel better."

"Good."

"Your town is still a horrible, nasty place, but you're all right."

"Thank you."

"Probably though, you'll have to do this at least once a week— how do you feel about that?"

"There are worse ways to spend an afternoon."

"Well, if you keep this up, I promise not to move away."

"Deal."

She reclined; exhaled. "Carry on."

Charlie awoke to a particularly violent, but brief, thrashing. Midday, mid-December. He yawned. The thrashing resumed for a more sustained burst, then stopped. A pause of several seconds, and then there were three sharp raps at the door. It was Mr. Booth, holding a battered package he was unable to force through the mail slot. "Wouldn't quite go," he explained, unrepentant.

Charlie blinked and his head spun. "Well, looks like you gave it a good try, anyway."

Booth studied him through greasy spectacles, before handing the package over. "Yes." Then left, thumping with one bad leg down the hall.

The package Charlie held was wrapped in brown paper, addressed by hand in even, block letters. He recognized the return address and smiled.

In Ames, Iowa lived an 83-year-old man named George Pinsky who, since the spring of 1947, had operated a small store called Pinsky's Lenses. He sold principally new and reconditioned camera equipment, but also did a small mail-order film development business on the side at prices he hadn't updated for 20 years. October tipped Charlie off, but swore him to secrecy.

"We can't overtax him, you know. He's old." Charlie promised not to tell.

Along with the recommendation, October had offered a caveat: Pinsky always returned the film, and it was always well-developed, but response rates varied. If Charlie needed it done quickly, Pinsky was not his man. She'd estimated two weeks, though six wasn't out of the question.

The nameless address on the upper left corner contained only a street address and the town of origin, which in this case was adequate. He stopped to calculate. Over a month since he sent the first two rolls of "Cab Driver," but not quite six weeks. Five and change. But then, he was in no hurry.

They were the first of three shipments Charlie had sent to Pinsky and the most promising. He shucked off the creased and torn cardboard and was pleased to see that the film itself was protected by individual plastic containers. He recalled the gleaming plastic cases at the Film Institute, and placed his own on the dinette table to admire. Then left them while he went to prepare a cup of coffee, keeping near enough so that he could glance up from time to time and keep admiring.

He sat, put the cup in aesthetic proximity to the film (black plastic, black coffee, white flecked Formica top, white cup), and selected the left canister. He spooled out a dozen frames and held them up to the light. There was his cab, driving down the street, Lapierre at the wheel.

Due to the Booth delivery, the day was relatively young; due to the film's arrival, Charlie was energized. H decided on a brief constitutional. Afterwards, perhaps a trip to the Film Institute to find a 16mm projector.

Down Oti and out onto the street, mind on the film. The cab, displaced again by the rogue Honda, was parked across the street and merited no look from its owner, who watched the toes of his shoes appear briefly at the south edge of a concrete canvas in his field of vision.

He was halfway down the block when he heard a bellow. "Hey mister!" He lurched with surprise, then looked toward the cab, dubiously.

"Hey mister, nice cab you got here, wanna sell it?"

And there was Carlos Munro, sitting on the hood. Carlos the philosopher, letter-writer, and erstwhile SINISTER MAN, back in town.

Charlie sized him up. "It'll cost you."

He was wearing a pea jacket and a felt hat, and was lounging in comfort on three duffel bags. "I just got in." He slid down the hood and continued at a moderate holler. "I had this weird idea that I'd walk right up to the cabbie line and there you'd be." When Charlie arrived, Carlos met him with arms—something between a handshake and hug—and continued with the story. "But when I got there, I decided, 'What the hell, I might as well take a cab anyway.' I got some old bastard named Carlyle—I don't know if that was his first name or last name. He knew you."

"Well goddamn, welcome back! Good to see you. Where you stayin'—with your folks aren't you?" he said, looking at the luggage.

"Yeah, I don't know, the whole cabbie experience inspired me to come see you first."

"Carlyle'll do that for you. Inspiring. Well, come on in, I'll get you a cup of coffee."

They gathered up the luggage and went back toward Oti. The bag Charlie carried was smallish, but predictably dense; sharp corners and planes poked through the fabric. "Books," he said. It wasn't a question.

In 1983, Vic put Charlie on a plane in Phoenix, gave him a meaty hand and a nugget of advice: "You don't have to *like* your roommate, remember, but you do have to *live* with him, so go easy." Charlie was off to college, already filled with more dread than anticipation. Vic had predictably made it worse: now he feared the person he'd be sleeping next to.

By the time he arrived on the fourth floor of Harrison Dorm, he was sick to his stomach from it. Down the hall he went, reading names written in a childish hand on sheets of construction paper. Outside room 421: Carlos Monroe and Charles Depaul. Each sheet was accompanied by a cut-out of a photo from a magazine. For Monroe the artist had selected a yellow rose, and for Depaul a Saguaro cactus. Charlie assumed Depaul and he were one, so he poked his head into the room to clarify. It was empty.

A cinderblock cell, 15 feet long by a dozen wide, with a bed, closet, and desk on either side, and a single window, looking out toward another dorm, opposite the door. The left half of the room was barren, but the right half looked fully inhabited. The bed was neatly made, the closet full of clothes, an electric typewriter on the desk, and a sweater draped over the chair. And lining the walls were hundreds of books. On book cases, in milk crates, and along shelves of questionable construction.

Charlie had pulled his trunk and suitcases into the room and was reading the spines of books when Carlos came in.

"Hello." Charlie turned around. "Are you Charles Depaul? My name's Carlos Munro." He was wearing brown corduroy pants, a black turtleneck, and brown leather shoes with a tassel. Charlie, by contrast, was dressed like a college freshman: Sex Pistols t-shirt, jeans, sneakers.

"I don't know. I'm actually Charlie di Paulo, but this is the closest I could find."

"This is probably it. My name's Munro—M, U, N, R, O—not Monroe. Apparently our R.A. is illiterate." He paused and scratched his cheek. "Which probably doesn't augur well for the education, does it?"

(Later, when Charlie had installed his own dorm accoutrements, he revealed himself to be equally enigmatic. A single poster of

Coppola's *The Conversation*, with Gene Hackman looking paranoid as he listened to a headphone. Carlos called it iconic.)

Whereas most college students had a variety of material enthusiasms, for Carlos, books met every need. They functioned as entertainment, information, art, companionship, furniture. On Saturdays he spent the day at Powell's, a cavernous bookstore in a seedy part of downtown Portland, and during the week, he read through his new purchases. This, of course, was in addition to the books he read for classes.

Charlie, on the other hand, didn't much go in for books in college. Not even the ones he was supposed to buy for his classes. (In fine symmetry, he soon had no classes for which it was necessary to buy books.)

Despite Vic's advice, and despite the differences between Carlos and him, he did like his roommate. In fact, when June (and the end of Charlie's college career) rolled around, Carlos was the only serious friend he had made at college.

They weren't very good roommates, however: Carlos like to sit and read, while Charlie preferred chatting or listening to music or drinking Rainier pounders, or (most commonly) all three. The two lifestyles being incompatible, they divided the time in the room between reading and non-reading periods. Charlie continued his self-education in film during the reading periods. In the nonreading ones, he pushed beer.

"Well, it worked out; you may have missed your calling as a filmmaker if I hadn't driven you away," Carlos noted later.

"That's a fine way to justify your antisocial behavior. You didn't care what I was doing, as long as I was doing it away from your books. You'd have liked it as well if I was selling my blood."

"You did, sometimes."

"See."

"So how long you here for?"

"That's an interesting question. All I'm working on is my dissertation. They had low enrollment this year so they cancelled one of the sections of Intro to Philosophy. I've got seniority, so I *could* teach it if I wanted to. But I wouldn't mind hanging around here through the summer. I might be able to pick up a little work down at Swan Island. Do an honest day's work."

Carlos would have been a third-generation dock worker. Following the jobs, his grandfather had moved from Ohio in the forties, when the Portland shipyards were turning out 1,000 ships a year for the war effort. His father Harold followed in the sixties and seventies, and Carlos started when he was 16, non-union grunt work, in the eighties. He enjoyed manual labor, and would have been happy upholding the family tradition. But by that time the economy was in the toilet, and there were no new union jobs for him to move into.

The economy eventually recovered, but not soon enough for Carlos; by the late 1980s, he was already in graduate school. But he continued to pick up odd jobs down at Terminal 4 for the occasional summer work—Harold's name was always good enough to scare up something.

Charlie studied him. "That'd be great." He considered whether Carlos would perhaps be a good replacement for Roger. Too much footage had been shot, he concluded, sadly. "How's the dissertation?" Carlos was working on something to do with class and economics. It wasn't clear to Charlie where the philosophy came in.

"I'm ahead of schedule."

"No way."

"Absolutely."

They were sitting at Charlie's little dinette table; Carlos was studying something out the window and didn't look up as he talked. "Are you working tonight?"

"Planned to."

"Blow it off. Let's go shoot some pool."

"Ah, I could squeeze in an hour."

"When I'm gone, I sure miss this green. Look at it: it's luminous." He stood up. "An hour? Well, all right. I 'spose the folks would appreciate an evening with me. Come on, let's get my shit over to the house. The folks will be happy to see you."

"How's the old town looking to you?" Charlie was taking Stark to the Munro residence.

"About the same." Southeast Stark always looked the same. Leafy and residential, houses and yards nicely kempt. Except for the cars, it might as easily have been 1954 as 1994. "So, Janie?"

"Yes?"

"Are you going to tell me about her?"

"What are you saying?"

"You're about as forthcoming as a brick wall."

"Hey, all you have to do is ask."

"Tell me about her. How's things?"

"See, how hard was that?" He waited a beat. "She's fine."

"Very nice. Thanks."

"Things are good. She's good. I mean, she's great. She's a little different from other girlfriends I've had, but she's fantastic."

"Not the usual di Paulo hipster chick?"

"Well, no."

"Or oldster French woman?"

He glanced at Carlos, who grinned. "She's hip in her own way, though. She's elegant hip. A vast wardrobe, dozens of shoes. But she doesn't really take it seriously. More like a game of dress up. I think she likes to go to the places that she'll most stand out in her clothes. She's cool."

"So what about Ava?"

"Done."

"Very good. The ending?"

"Not a problem. She essentially denied that anything was happening and then she gave me a thousand bucks for the film."

"Are you kidding me?"

"Nope."

"Did you take it?"

"Absolutely. She cares more about me making movies."

"Wow. You have pretty good luck with women, Charlie boy. Stay away from cards."

Carlos watched Laurelhurst Park pass by on Charlie's side of the car. "Elegant," he said. "I could make a crack here."

"What? You don't think a cabbie can be elegant, college boy?"

"Don't drag your fine profession into it. You were a meager bastard long before you started the hack gig." Charlie started to respond, but decided to concede the point.

They were crossing 60th, beginning the ascent of what was optimistically called Mount Tabor, on the back down-slope of which the Munros lived. Harold had wanted a larger house, commensurate with his union salary, something closer in, but Carlos's mother, Inez, demanded elevation. She had come to Oregon as a child from the coffee-producing town of Vulcán, which clung to the side of mighty Barú Volcano in Western Panama. She lived for the next ten years in the flat valleys of Western Oregon and so when she agreed to marry Harold, he had to promise to take her to a mountain. Although Mount Tabor was just a high spot in the city, it did look toward Mt. Hood, which satisfied her.

"So how's the film going?"

"It's a mixed bag. Some days are good, some days are bad. Seems to be completely random—it has nothing to do with how hard the shoot is."

"Are you satisfied so far?"

Charlie held up a paper bag. "This is the first of the developed footage. We'll know soon enough."

"I'm sure it's fine," Carlos said, his head craned forward as they neared home.

The house was a little butter-colored cottage. Harold was smoking a cigar on the porch as they drove up. Charlie honked, sending Harold into a run. The cab was still rolling when he reached it, and he slapped the rear as Charlie brought it to a stop. By that time Inez was on the porch and the screen door snapped like a firecracker as it slammed behind her.

"Hey! Hola, look who's here—my son, Plato the philo-sopher!" Harold was partly greeting and partly hauling his son out of the car with his lanky steel arms. "Ah, my son."

Inez made it around the car, but Harold still had Carlos in a bear hug. "Kah, Harold, let go of my son."

After he turned Carlos loose, Harold turned to Charlie. "And look who brought my son, Charlie di Paulo. Get over here and say hello." A tear was threatening to breach Harold's lower eyelid.

A few minutes later and Carlos had extricated himself and gotten his luggage as far as the porch. The Munros were pumping both of them for information, playing tag team questioners and moving on to a new query before the last had been answered.

"What do you need, bathroom?"

"How's the dissertation going, son?"

"You look thin, have you been eating well? Do you have enough money—don't tell us you're not eating well because of money!"

"When you going to give up this cab driving thing and come work for me?"

"Would you like something to drink? Coffee?—it's just perking."

"I heard you're working on a new movie project?"

"Would you like something to eat?"

"How long are you staying?"

By the time Charlie checked the time, it was a quarter after six. He was full of coffee and pound cake and an hour late for his shift. He didn't mind.

11.

Darkness was well-established, though it was only 5:15. Rain descended in explosive shrapnel, lit briefly in the headlights of passing cars. Charlie, looking like he was dressed for a funeral in coal suit and hat, stepped from the cab and collected three paper sacks from the back seat. A short trot to the front of the theater and he juggled his packages while trying to locate the correct key. Written on a piece of paper at eye level in pink maker: NOTICE: MONDAY DECEMBER 19. 7:30 SHOWING CANCELLED FOR A PRIVATE EVENT. THE MANAGEMENT REGRETS ANY INCON-VENIENCE.

He took the bags to the concessions counter where they shed water into little puddles. Ava had left the lobby lights on for him and in the dreary winter night, the theater took on a cheery aspect, or at least a cozy and warm one. From one bag Charlie produced two reels of film and a video cassette; the other two bags he put in the soda refrigerator behind the counter.

From the initial conceit of a screening party had emerged a grander vision: a kind of cinematic holiday event. Guests had been invited by mail and encouraged to RSVP. The affair was to be a formal one, jackets mandatory, ties in colors as available. Refreshments would be served. The formality for Janie.

The "staff" arrived while he was in the projection booth. Eliot, Jen's little brother, who aspired to film, and his girlfriend Julie, standing awkwardly in the center of the lobby. Eliot he positioned near the front door with a camera and a very large flash; Julie manned a bank of wine under the starburst at the entrance to the theater.

Advice to the teens: "Eliot, as fast as the camera will go, just keep it flashing. If your film runs out and people are coming through the door, keep the flash going. Don't be shy, either—get right up on them. Julie, you're going to have to watch the flow of wine—what you have there is all there is. So if you see someone perpetually filling up—like Lapierre, you gotta watch him—start short-filling them."

At twenty to six, he heard a banging on the front door. Janie, in black, looming even larger in heels. He took her arm and led her into the theater. "Welcome. May I take your coat?"

"Why thank you."

"You look gorgeous."

"Yes," she said, handing him an overcoat.

She looked around at the theater, finding it unchanged. "How's it going? Are you ready?"

"Yep, just about. I need to attend to the food and wine next, but the film's ready to go."

"And me?"

"You can join me in the lobby and greet guests if you wish."

"Am I co-hosting?"

"I didn't want to be presumptuous. Yes."

"And what if I don't want to?"

"But you do."

She frowned and, after a pause, swept past him on her way back to the lobby. "Maybe. But it *was* presumptuous."

They were ready by five to six. Charlie and Janie were stationed somewhere near the middle of the lobby—far enough from the door to draw people past the camera, but close enough for them to see if they looked through the window. Eliot was fighting the creep of his jacket, his size 42 shoulders scrunched into his father's size 40 blazer. He kept scratching the back of his calf with the toe of his shoe. Julie was rearranging a pile of cheese, trying to look busy so Charlie wouldn't catch her sneaking slugs of Riesling from the bottle.

The first arrival was Roger, at 6:01. He stood outside the theater and peered in, catching sight of Eliot, whom he did not know, and who, Charlie immediately understood, looked something like a theater employee. Roger froze, looked up at the sign in the door, and then peered through cupped hands back at Eliot. He did not look toward the center of the lobby.

To Janie, "Good lord." Then to Eliot, "Wave him in, Eliot." Janie and Charlie started waving as well, and Roger opened the door, tentatively, before finally looking around and catching sight of the hosts. "Camera, Eliot, let's go!"

He sprang into action, charging the befuddled Roger, flash flashing. "Roger Kreske, folks," Charlie hollered at the startled actor. "One of the stars of our show and an honored guest." Rapid applause from the hosts, joined a moment later by Julie. Then Roger got it. He lit up and made a showy walk across the floor, giving the camera little smiles and flashes of teeth. "All right folks, let's give it up for Mr. Kreske!"

Of course, no one else arrived until 6:20, when they started coming in clots, fashionably late. Charlie had invited everyone associated with the production, everyone who had given money, and for good measure, everyone who hadn't but might. A second group of invitees included a cohort of filmmakers who had screened at the Zale, and several from the Film Institute, where he was starting to make friends.

As the fashionably-late arrived, the welcome was increasingly robust. Lapierre came toward the end, around a quarter of seven, to a Hollywood reception. Cheers and hoots, reaching a crescendo with Charlie's description, "The star of the picture . . . ."

Fidgeting next to Charlie, Roger mumbled, "If I had known you were going to do this I would have come in late."

For another quarter hour, they milled around the lobby, taking in wine, dispensing small talk. Charlie worked the room, pushing alcohol on the timid or dour, stoking the fires of festivity. Just at the moment he had completed his circuit and was about to start herding people toward the theater, he spied a skulking Ava making for the office. Eliot was standing next to Julie, surreptitiously sipping from one of the glasses on the tray when the host pssst'ed him. "Eliot, camera!"

"Ladies and Gentlemen, please." Scuttling Ava, keeping to the back wall, ducked her head when she heard his voice and sped to a trot. She had a clear lead on Eliot. "Thank you. We have an unexpected surprise tonight. The owner of this theater, Ava Zale—" there was a smattering of applause—"that's right, most of you know her. She's a huge supporter of film in Portland, and she's offered up her theater for our screening tonight." Eliot, young and uninhibited, had sprinted along the hypotenuse between the theater door and office, cornering Ava with a flurry of flashes. "I see her trying to sneak in along the back wall there, so before she gets away, why don't you all give her a big hand." Then pointing. "Ava Zale!"

After the last cheer, Charlie gave Eliot a signal to begin shepherding people into the theater. As this had not been prearranged, Charlie had to gesticulate rather broadly, finally mouthing out to Eliot, "Get. Them. Into. The. Theater." With Janie's help, the crowd began to spill slowly out of the lobby.

Once the last of the stragglers had been herded into the theater, he surveyed the wine and snacks. Cheese holding its own, crackers low, wine running out quickly. He gave instructions to Julie to ration as she poured—and not to worry about the food. A quick sprint up the stairs to the projection booth where he consulted with Ava, and then back down to begin the screening.

As he was jogging back through the lobby, a figure slipped quietly in the front door. Carlos, in a newsboy cap and fingerless gloves, lurking like a thief.

"Hey, nice work. Everyone's already inside."

"Ah, good."

"I thought you were blowing me off."

"What are you talking about? I have to check out this new guy you have in *my* role."

"He can't hold a candle to you."

He moved in closer, maintaining his shady demeanor. "Janie here? You should introduce us."

"You should have come during the social part of our evening— that's when I was making introductions."

"You know my ways."

"Well, come on. You can sit in the back of the theater—I've got everyone down in the middle. You can hide here away from everyone."

By that time the group had settled comfortably in a nest of seats in the middle of the theater, wine glasses refilled. He began with a short clip from Eight to contextualize the new footage. A brief introduction of what they were about to watch, instructions about what to look and listen for, and then he screened his raw footage.

It was the scene where Lapierre picked up Roger—the introduction of Sinister Man into the narrative. Contrasting the faraway, cramped look of Eight, the image that appeared on the screen was luminous and spacious. With the first moment of movement—the creamy skin of the cab floating into the frame—the guests hooted and applauded. For the duration of the footage, audible commentary competed with exhortations for silence. Excellent turns from the actors—a gritty scowl, a good line reading, a furtive glance—garnered bursts of applause.

After the first viewing, the proponents of silence demanded a second viewing and after that, there were calls for a full showing Eight. And once there was nothing left to watch, they demanded bows from the cast and crew.

Charlie joined Janie and signaled to Carlos to move up and join them. He sat on the aisle, dissecting the footage and the reaction it received. As they watched the second section of Eight—the Kindly Old Lady section—the crowd had gone relatively quiet, trying to take in the oblique narrative, and Ava came in to join them. It was her heavy, sweet perfume that Charlie noticed first: she was standing in the aisle slightly behind him, watching the screen.

"Ava," he whispered. "Hello. Please, sit." He stood up to make room.

Janie looked up, then absently started to rise, still watching the screen. Ava passed under her chin—way under—and Janie's attention was drawn away from the screen.

Once she was sitting, Charlie leaned over and said, "Ava, this is Janie Prescott, my . . . friend. And you know Carlos."

"Janie, Ava Zale. I've told Janie a lot about you, Ava."

Janie, who until that moment had given no thought to the older woman, now scrutinized her. Tipped off by Charlie's funny tone, his use of the word "friend."

"What do you think of the footage, Janie?" The first syllable came out soft, with a slow zha: Zha-nee.

"I like it."

Ava looked at the screen, then turned slowly to Janie. She paused a moment, and then offered "It is a pleasure to meet you" before slipping out.

It took a half hour after the lights went up before people began filing out. Discussions were tethered to the topic of film. Those immediately involved in the production spoke of their roles, brushing off the difficulties with the last two shoots: the film was progressing splendidly. In other conversations, the footage was judged (favorably) against classics of film—Bergman (pacing), Truffaut (characterization), Kurosawa (visuals). The booze ran out soon after and people continued their conversations while donning coats and hats and moving toward the exit.

Ava, standing next to Janie, watched the trio of Roger, Lapierre, and Jen leave to a final round of applause. She said to Charlie, at just more than a whisper. "This week would be a good opportunity for another round of fundraising. Very well done, Mr. di Paulo."

"There's someone in the cab." Janie, pulling up short in the vestibule in front of the Zale. It was by then just after nine and a small line had formed for the evening's sole showing of *Psycho*. Charlie, following too close, crashed into her.

"What?"

"In the cab. There's someone *sitting* in the back seat of the cab."

Despite a film of condensation on the inside of the cab, Charlie could indeed make out a figure in the back seat. Blotches of unmoving brown and camel. The rain had subsided and left just a few beads of water on the window. A wind whistled from the north. He started for the cab.

"Charlie!"

"It's all right," he said, tapping the window with a single knuckle. "It's Carlos." Inside, the figure turned, rubbed off the condensation, waved.

"Sorry. He knows I don't usually lock the car. Sitting in the back seat—I figured it had to be him." He opened the passenger-side door and poked his head into the cab. "Hey there."

From behind him: "You don't keep it locked?"

He moved aside for her to climb in. "Who's going to steal a cab?" Before he closed the door, he noticed a fold of Janie's raincoat hanging out the car and bundled it in.

While he was scuttling around the cab, she turned to the back seat and offered a conciliatory, "Hello, Carlos."

"Hello, Janie." Then, after Charlie climbed in the cab, "That was no introduction. I thought we'd go out and get to know each other a little."

"Each other?"

"You can tag along, of course."

"Thanks."

"What do you think, Janie? A game of pool, piece of pie, cup of coffee?"

Charlie, thinking Janie might be uncomfortable by the situation, tried to jump in. But too slowly.

"Absolutely." She smiled brightly, suspicion transformed to anticipation.

"Good."

She climbed up onto the seat back and leaned toward Carlos with characteristic brio.

"Where should we go?"

"Lady's choice. What are you in the mood for?"

"Hmm. I do have to work in the morning."

"Coffee then?"

"Oh no. That will just keep me up. Better a place with good whisky sours."

Carlos smiled. "Whisky sours. All right. What's that call to mind, cabbie?"

"Carolina Café?"

"No, that's no good—too loud, too much of a scene." He leaned back. "I think maybe Shanghai's. It'll be quiet."

Charlie turned around. "Let's see, don't they also have pool?"

"That's right, if the mood should strike."

"Carlos is a pool fiend."

"Shanghai's it is, then," Janie agreed.

"To Shanghai's, cabbie!"

When the Bowman Bakery was built on NW 12th, the owner, Hollis Bowman, had to clear the land of Douglas fir. Built on a parcel west of what was then Portland, an early example of sprawl. Years and fires and collapsed economies had changed the building and its ownership. It grew and shrank and moved a block and grew again and, for the past six decades, sat and decayed. Its second and third stories had been converted to cheap storage, the spaces now mostly filled with forgotten, moldering wares.

But in the southeast corner of the basement was the hibernating building's heart, a lively tavern that had been there since the move to 13th Avenue in 1896. Compared to the fortunes of the building, the tavern's were more stable. Six owners in just under a century — and only two since 1960, when the name was changed to capture the "romance" of earlier years. Under the current proprietorship (effective 1981), a single change: in 1990, the bar started pouring microbrews.

It was the only life for blocks. Now mired in a dead-end neighborhood by the freeway, separated by blocks of boarded, uninhabited buildings, a nook of the city abandoned even by the bums.

When they crossed Burnside at 12th, Janie studied the boarded Pella Building. "Where *is* this place?"

"Not too far," Carlos said.

"It's cool," Charlie said. "You'll like it. Trust us."

Janie looked out the window dubiously. There were no cars, no stores, just silent, dark buildings. But then, at the corner of 12th and Irving, three cars parked in a line and a neon sign in long, narrow letters.

Charlie coasted along the edge of 12th, through empty parking places, until he was across the street from the bar. "This remains weird, guys," Janie observed, not neutrally. "Those are the first cars we've seen since Burnside." Charlie and Carlos climbed out of the cab, but Janie sat and watched. Outside, the streets were glossy under the streetlights. A blond woman in a wool hat was standing outside the building, smoking. Everything seemed to be in sharp focus.

Charlie stopped in the middle of the street and looked back at Janie. She finally climbed out.

Sounds seemed louder, clearer — a crack from the car door, snaps from heels, ricocheting off dead buildings. The woman underneath the neon light smiled as they passed and Carlos tipped his hat. The smoke from her cigarette looked like steam in the light.

Janie had the sense that she had walked onto a movie set. The abandoned town, the smiling extra on a smoke break. Even time felt artificial, as if beyond the set it might be noon — or midnight. She wondered, if she reached out and scratched the brick wall of the building, would it make the hollow noise of papier-mâché?

They descended six granite stairs, the top of which was flush with the sidewalk. Charlie reached the door first and held it open, nodding as Carlos and Janie passed by. Janie's sense that this was all artificial began to drift away when she reached the cozy, smoky dark, but it did not vanish completely. A row of windows ringed the south and east corner of the pub, and she could see the crystalline set outside.

But inside, the ambiance of the old bar started setting her mind at ease. She could tell from the furniture that the place had not been updated for decades: although the wooden tables and leather booths had a certain historic charm, they were worn, unsentimental, and small. Little blue lamps dotted the tables and at the north end of the room were two pool tables, unoccupied.

"You know, I think I'll have a whisky sour with Janie. Whatcha having, Charlie?"

"Yeah, make it three."

At the bar, two suits smoked cigars and drank industrial beer; in the front corner booth, a young couple were curled together, nose to nose. Beyond that, the choice of tables was unfettered. Janie wound through empty tables to the booths under the east windows, selecting one for its remoteness and darkness.

"This place *is* cool," she pronounced.

"I don't know why I haven't brought you here before." Charlie turned around to admire the place through Janie's fresh eyes. He watched Carlos meander among tables.

"Yeah, why *haven't* you brought me here? What else is there that you haven't shown me?"

Carlos put the drinks on the table. "Let me guess—he tends to take you to places that focus on beer?"

"Yes!"

"There's nothing wrong with that, of course. Sometimes he just gets a little single-minded."

"I don't know what you're talking about; Janie's a terrible beerhound."

She did not look at him but sent an elbow out on a policing mission. "Beer's *all right.*"

The elbow probed his upper rib cage. After the third thrust, he grunted.

"So, what did you think of the footage?" Carlos asked.

"It was pretty damn cool."

"I thought so, too. He's gotten better since the Super 8 days. What do you say? A toast to the director: May all your shoots go smoothly and may your film canisters always remain full."

"Hear hear."

Charlie bowed his head. "Thank you."

Carlos was sitting sideways—legs out on the bench seat and back against the wall. His hat, which he still wore, rode low over his brow from the contact with brick. Next to his chin, the deco lamp sent out a blue reflection across the thick shellac, looking much the same as neon on wet pavement.

"I suppose the two of you go to movies a lot, then? What kind do you like, Janie?"

She looked at him and then back at Charlie. "You know, we haven't been to a single movie together. That's totally weird—why don't we go to movies?"

"I don't know. Different schedules?"

"We have a *terrible* relationship—you don't take me to the cool places and we don't go to the movies together."

"When I first knew Charlie, he used to live at the theater."

"Mainly because Carlos never left the damn dorm. I was banished."

"He kept a little notebook—he'd write notations down in it about what he'd seen. Do you still keep one?"

Charlie moved an index finger from whisky to mouth, sucked meditatively, then said, "I do, but only for notes about my own film. Sometimes I'll make a note in there if I see something interesting in a movie, though, for future reference."

Janie turned to look at Charlie, leaning in until he could feel her breath on his neck.

"What kind of movies do you like, Janie?"

She paused a moment, and then turned to Carlos. "All of them, of course. But I guess if I were to rent a movie, say, I'd probably go for an oldie. Or start there, anyway."

"Oldies? And Charlie hasn't taken you to the Zale?"

"Not before tonight. We *should* go to the movies—you can show me what I'm missing."

"All righty, how about we quit talking about where Charlie hasn't taken Janie."

Carlos poured the last of his drink into his mouth and swished it around. He swallowed and put the empty glass on the table with a click. "Another round?"

"Here, let me buy it." Charlie, proffering a twenty.

Portland was the topic of discussion during the second round, with Carlos directing.

"It's not that there's nothing to do here or anything like that." Janie said, on the defensive. "You all just think it's so special, when in fact it's an ordinary middle-sized town."

"And?"

"And what?"

"And what else don't you like?"

She paused to think. "You know what it is, the people here are complacent. No ambition."

"What?"

"Everyone's *soooo* relaxed. It bugs me."

"They're not energetic enough for you."

"That's right. Everyone moves in slow motion. All this flannel—it's like you're in your jammies all the time."

"I think this is the clouds talking. Did she hold this opinion before the weather turned bad, Charlie?"

Janie intercepted. "Turned bad? I think we've had about five sunny days in the last three months. And then it didn't even *turn bad*—it just turned gray. I know *bad* weather, and this isn't bad. It doesn't even rain all that much. Just gray. It doesn't know what it wants to be. It's like weather purgatory."

"I think we've identified the problem."

"We did have a pretty early fall," Charlie admitted.

Outside, a freight train blasted its horn. It was loud enough that the floor seemed to vibrate. "But this place is cool." She ran a hand along the table. "I will say that Portland has an above-average number of cool places to drink." She took a swallow. "For an ordinary, middle-sized town."

Midway through the third round, Janie made an observation.

"But the actual floppy disks your software comes on—where's that made?" Carlos was asking about the company she worked for.

It was a question that had never occurred to her and she was wondering about why it had occurred to Carlos, which in turn led her to note: he had been asking all the questions.

"I'm not saying. You've been asking all the questions here, buddy, and I think it's my turn to start getting some answers."

Carlos smiled, and Charlie explained, "He always does that. He loves to ask questions. It's kind of like the way you lean in too closely when you talk to someone. Those are your idiosyncrasies."

Janie leaned in too closely and said—loudly—"And Charlie is quick to say blunt and inappropriate things."

"Well there you have it," Carlos said.

They all smiled. Carlos smiled at Charlie, thinking that he was happy for his friend. Charlie smiled at Janie, thinking that he was happy to see her happy. And Janie smiled generally, thinking she was due for another whiskey sour.

The Lapierre abode, windows cheery with yellow in the November night. Cars huddled at the curb, like policemen at a parade. Janie and Charlie arriving just after seven thirty, parked two houses down and came bearing booze and sugar.

Since early afternoon they had labored baking holiday pies, with mixed success. The results rested on the palm of each of Janie's large hands. On her right, an apple that never cooked through, burned at the crust, and sagged in the middle. On her left, a sweet potato pie of rich luster and appetizing hue and aroma.

In Charlie's hands the alcohol: a half rack of expensive beer and a bottle of cheap scotch.

"Ah, reinforcements," Clay, who happened to be near the door as they came through. "And pies!" He leaned down to inspect. "Homemade to boot. Very nice."

"The apple's no good, but thanks."

"We'll put it aside—a late night snack for when the taste buds are shot."

A run of mismatched tables extended lengthways through Lapierre's two living rooms, an undulating Chinese dragon, draped with sheets and lit with candles. Empty except for two chairs— Carlos and an unidentified woman, who had been lurking beyond the crowd. Other guests had retired, inevitably, to the party gathering-area proper: the kitchen. Charlie nodded at the woman as they passed into the noise and light.

A wave went through the kitchen as attention shifted briefly to Janie and Charlie. Greetings were offered. Then fragmentation, as conversations resumed. A hand reached out for the scotch and Charlie heard, "Oh, the good stuff." It reappeared amid a grove of bottles on the kitchen counter, along with wine and liquor, and a 2-liter bottle of soda. Clay relieved Janie of the pies, hoisted them above his head, and snaked to the refrigerator.

The room was over-hot from bodies and the baking turkey, sending Janie toward the back of the room and the open window. Charlie drifted until he found a meagerly-attended conversation between Roger and a nervous skinny girl he didn't know. She was gulping down smoke from a cigarette, nodding like a bird. Roger flashed a grateful smile, and Charlie offered an opinion on Captain Picard — the unfortunate topic of conversation.

During the evening, bodies circled like electrons around the stronger personalities, breaking off and joining other molecules of conversation. Janie, Clay, and Carlos, nuclei of different elements on the periodic chart: Janie, an unpredictable conversationalist, attracted adventure-seekers; to Carlos were drawn small numbers, but deep thinkers; and Lapierre, like an awesome big brother, offered rare, laconic opinions but frequent, booming laughs, attracting clouds of jovial drunks.

Late in the evening, after they had eaten and reassembled in the kitchen, he was standing alone at the liquor counter and turned around to survey the room. First Clay noticed him and winked, then Carlos, whose voice stopped briefly, mid-sentence. Finally, Janie, near the kitchen table at the far corner of the room, paused with a wine glass at her lips. She looked at Charlie, but didn't move. She held the gaze for a beat, two, five, then languidly swallowed and blinked and turned back to the conversation. Charlie put down the bottle of Scotch and instead went to the fridge for a beer.

12.

I was thinking we could catch that movie."

In the parking lot of the 13th Avenue Plaid Pantry conveni-ence store, trying to hear Janie through a pay phone.

"Tonight?"

"Yep. Carlos was right: it's about time we went to a movie together. I have the paper right here in front of me." He thought he heard the crinkly snap of newsprint, but it might have been the connection.

"You had Mike tell me to call you because you want to go to a movie?"

"Yep."

"Don't do that."

"How else can I get through to you?"

A homeless man had sidled up to Charlie on the pretext of checking the phones for change. He fished around the coin return, then gave a surprisingly white-toothed smile. Charlie dug into a front pocket.

"You shouldn't abuse the system."

"Mike doesn't care; he likes me."

"It's not handy for me, then."

He had a nickel and four pennies. One finger to the smiling man, and he pulled out the wad of change from his front shirt pocket. Peeled off a one and smiled back.

"Your attitude doesn't seem to bode well for my plan."

"I can't do it tonight. This is my busiest season."

"Yeah yeah, your busiest season. I'm well aware. When, then?"

"I'm off Sunday night."

"Sunday it is. But it has to be a good movie. No crap on the first one."

He leaned against the brick façade of the building and watched a young couple walking their dog down the street. A setter, stepping with dignity, sampling, occasionally, an odor in the air.

"It was nice of you to call. Nice—" He thought of her sitting in her arm chair, paper laid out on her lap.

"Yes?"

"I don't know why I was snippy."

"Psssht."

"You can call Mike any time. He doesn't mind."

"I know."

"Me either."

"I know."

A Chinook, he realized, stepping into the day. He'd been fooled by the occasional rattle of rain against the window, allowing it to send anticipatory shivers down his collar. Chinook winds blew up the ocean from California decorated in Oregon gray, but when they shook water from the clouds, the drops landed with soft warmth of the southern sun. It was a fine greeting for his fine mood.

He spent a few hours on the meter, then headed for the Film Institute to collect equipment for the evening's shoot. It would be the easiest on the schedule, and he was looking forward to it with relief. With two night scenes to film, he had a maximum of flexibility and a minimum of obstacles. He could either shoot inside or out, depending on the weather. The exterior shots required no dialogue, the interior just a few words. Mostly they were portraits. If it rained, they'd do the interior scenes; dry or spitting, exterior.

Somehow the side-by-side shoot from Russell Street, a tiny scrape of a setback, had turned gangrenous on him. Apparently glare was the norm; their test shoot had been the anomaly. Charlie decided that glare wasn't ultimately debilitating, though—it would lend a quality of realism to the shoot that might accelerate the sense of danger. So after two aborted attempts, he planned a shorter segment that would use the glare as an intentional effect.

The problem they couldn't surmount (and which Charlie hadn't foreseen) was artistic: during the cab shoots the film didn't look like what his mind saw. The close-ups weren't close enough. The performances were fine, but the shots failed to adequately capture them. Part of the problem was the distance and part was the angle—some of the shots needed to be from the front, which they couldn't achieve from another car. It ended up looking like a car safety filmstrip. To capture foreboding, close-ups were essential.

They were going to have to re-shoot most of the footage with Charlie riding on the hood, the only place he could get adequate close-up frontal shots. Of course, he couldn't crouch there when the car was moving, not without risk of dropping the camera (never mind himself), and only a few shots could be done on a stationary car. So he decided to invent a harness to strap himself in. And so, while he worked up a hood harness, he decided to opt for an easy shoot to restore equilibrium to the production and buoy the troops (and himself). Setbacks, setbacks.

As he approached the Institute, the wind had picked up sufficiently to rock the cab lightly as he turned onto Salmon. He inspected the sky. The wind was still warm but now it brought a steady drizzle and every few minutes a shower would roar through.

On the way from downtown to Lapierre's house—the rendezvous point—he noted that the rain could now not properly be called a drizzle. He shifted the wiper setting from "intermittent" to "low." Atop the arching Fremont Bridge, the cab shimmied in the wind. The exterior shots were definitely out.

At Lapierre's he found his crew and actors drinking coffee in the living room.

"This is pretty serious wind." Roger, who with no lines was sober. A mite too perky, observed Charlie.

Clay was standing nose to window, hands on his hips. "Listen. That wind's really blasting. A storm's blowing through. Could you hear it in the cab?" They sat in silence and listened to it thunder against the west wall of the house.

"It'll mellow out in a few minutes."

"I doubt it."

They waited a half hour and the wind didn't settle. It wasn't getting worse, though, either. They gave it another half hour.

"Hey Roger, you should lay off that java. You're getting jumpy."

"No I'm not."

"It's not going to matter," reported Lapierre from the window. "It's way too windy to shoot. You can't have a howling wind in a few scenes and never again."

They gave it another half hour, and then Charlie took the mikes to the cab, just to be sure. It sounded like the cab was parked in a river. The shoot was aborted.

He was home a few minutes later, wondering if he should call Janie. Just after eight, but feeling late. She'd like the spontaneity, though. He dialed. The machine picked up after six rings, and he left a long, wandering message, expecting her to climb out of the tub and answer the phone. Neither did she do that nor call him back later.

Janie was uncharacteristically jubilant for a grim January evening. She had his arm in a two-handed grip as they walked along Northeast Broadway, one arm through his, the other like a pincer on his humerus. Her long legs in full canter, dragging him along.

"Come on, we're gonna be late." They had selected Wenders's *Wings of Desire*, playing at the Hollywood. He grinned and dragged his feet. The joy and clinging pleased him, and he wasn't in a hurry for it to end.

"Let's get those little dachshund legs of yours moving."

Janie, with some ritual, had been intent on choosing a worthy movie. The big event of the season was *Unforgiven*, but she rejected Clint. Good press or no, she wasn't allowing a western to be their first movie together. Other first-runs rejected: *The Scent of a Woman, The Crying Game, Glengarry Glen Ross*. On Charlie's recommendation, they decided on the Wenders.

"You're sure this guy is good? You don't hear much about German directors, you know."

"He's good."

"Except that Nazi, what was her name?

"Leni Refenstahl."

"Yes. He's not like her, is he? A crypto-fascist or something like that?"

"He's not a crypto-fascist."

"But he is good enough, right? I don't want a second-rater from Germany, Charlie. This has got to be good. We could go to *The Crying Game* instead."

"Wenders is one of the best. Seriously."

"All right," she said, floating out a final sortie of skepticism to test him. "If you say so."

"I haven't seen this particular movie, but I'm willing to bet that you will have seen nothing like it. Wenders is unique."

Satisfied, she gave him one of her huge, guileless Janie smiles.

Seven minutes later they stood at the rear of the theater, eyeing seats. "There," she pointed to the right wing of the theater.

"What are you talking about? We're not sitting off to the side. Look, there's a whole row right there in the middle."

"I like the side. It's like you're peeking in on real life."

"Well, today we're sitting in the middle." He attempted to drag her.

"Charlie—"

"Ah!" He held up an index finger. "I'm running the show today. As requested." They smiled at each other. Different smiles, for different reasons. "No voyeurism today," he said, leading her to the center of the theater. "Today a proper viewing."

The cab glided to a stop outside a filthy Winchell's Donut Shop a few blocks from the theater. Silence between them unbroken since exiting the theater. Janie had been looking out the car's left side, past Charlie; when she turned to see where they had stopped, she smiled and nodded.

Two cups of dun-colored coffee and a pile of donuts, then lounging on molded plastic and admiring the gray of Sandy Boulevard. Janie pulled out a crumpled pack of cigarettes and removed one of the two remaining. She broke the silence: "I've been holding onto these for an emergency."

Another space of silence while they sampled their environment: caffeine, sugar, smoke, and dim fluorescence. She exhaled out of the corner of her mouth. "An emergency."

"What'd you think?" she asked.

"You first. I'm still digesting."

"Oh *man*. You're the filmie—you start."

"Oh come on, there's no wrong interpretation. *You're* the college graduate."

She dipped a cake donut into her coffee and watched crumbs separate and float out to the edges of her styrofoam cup. "It was amazing. I think it was the most hopeful movie I've ever seen."

"Yeah, that's good. Hopeful."

"It was pretty simple and straightforward, in its way. I don't know what else to say. It's the kind of movie that makes you feel more than it makes you think."

"It's interesting to say simple, because the filmmaking was, mmm—subtle, maybe. Not really sophisticated, but not straightforward like the story."

"More." She was trying to savor the smoke and coffee in the manner of the movie. "Why subtle?"

"Well, it was shot in black and white symbolically, obviously. But I think he actually had a couple of functional reasons, too. Black and white tends to seem more realistic than color. So even though the angels couldn't experience the human world, they could see it more clearly."

"Hmm." She was not immediately convinced.

"It also allowed him to introduce the fantastical elements and make them more believable. The angels, the carnival—it seemed as straightforward and naturalistic as the people."

"Ah." When she placed all her attention on the coffee, she tasted a bitter tinniness with a strange kind of pleasure.

"And that bit contrasted the images of post-war Germany, which were cold and mechanical. Humanity existed in that mechanical, hyper-real world, just like the angels."

Janie removed the last cigarette and lit it on the end of the penultimate, still smoldering at filter's edge. She nodded. "Maybe."

"It was filmed honestly. He tried to be as authentic as he could with his thoughts. He let you see everything in a frame; he held it there. Landscapes and interiors, and then he did close-ups of people in the same way. You could study the terrain of their faces. In order to really sell the idea of angels, he had to be honest. Even his special effects were old and simple—double exposures and fake wings. That was also to gain our trust. Wenders is one of my favorite directors because of that—he's very generous to his audience."

She thought a moment. "I guess you could be right." She had been peeling the chocolate off a donut, and paused to lick her thumb and finger. "So what about your film. Is it generous?"

"I hope so. What do you think?"

"I don't know."

"It's a little different in my movie. I'm trying to tell a simple story about artificiality. It's hard to be fake and real at the same time."

"Yes." Charlie waited. She was looking out the window. After a few more moments, she said, "It's starting to rain."

They both had partially-eaten donuts in their hands (Janie's the denuded chocolate). They dumped them back in the box with an unmolested maple bar.

"Come on, let's go walk around in the rain," Janie said unexpectedly. "I'm in the mood."

13.

Janie, from deep within her pod. "Come *on*. I've got to get out tonight." She was standing and surveying the fractal of cubicles as she talked.

Charlie, in front of the Safeway at Tenth and Jefferson, regretting he had called. "Tomorrow. We can go out with Carlos—he wants to get together."

"Seattle."

"Oh, right. Shit." A two-day training; he'd forgotten.

"You'll be having fun, then. In the big city."

"Sure, hanging with the engineers. She paused, changed tactics. "Just dinner?"

"I can't—lots of fares this time of year, lots of money."

Silence from the other end of the line. She was cocking an arm back to launch a paper clip at the adjacent cubicle—at Mel Tompkins, who was mocking her with a pouty face. Conversations, even at a whisper, traveled one cubicle's distance; Janie's voice broadcast to three or four, and Mel was sneering at her for her tone of voice.

"We never see each other."

"We do."

"In weird hours. We never get to do fun stuff. Dancing, for instance." Tompkins dodged right, but Janie's aim was true—he took the clip on his cheek. She stuck out her tongue.

"Well—" There was nothing to say.

"Come by tonight after work. At least I'll see you when I get up in the morning."

"Will you let me sleep, or are you going to wake me?"

"I won't wake you."

"Promise?"

"Yes!"

That night he slid in next to her late, at 4:02. The room smelled warm and sweet. He spent an idle few seconds with his face burrowed in the mass of her hair before dozing off sometime before 4:03. At 6:49, she climbed on top of him, pinning his arms under the covers. He struggled feebly.

"You said you wouldn't wake me."

"You knew I was lying."

"It's true."

"Hey Shorty."

"Hey good-lookin'. Whatcha up to?"

He was at the airport, having just dropped off a sizeable contingent of Filipinos, one of an armada of taxis they had commissioned for the journey. Three for humans, two for cargo: cardboard boxes wrapped in jute. They were bound for Manila, leaving on the redeye. Charlie got humans because he didn't mind them. Carlyle they assigned to the luggage.

"Making fudge."

"Oooooh."

"It's not for you. I'm taking it to work. It's the new thing at staff meetings—someone always has to bring a treat. My week."

"Just like that. You didn't even consider making an extra pan for the cab driver?"

"It's still possible." She had the phoned tucked under her chin while she stirred the chocolate. "I'm going to try a bribe. Fudge for a plan to go out with me on Wednesday. Wednesday's your next day off, right?"

"It is, but I had a shoot scheduled. I thought I mentioned it." Silence. "Janie?"

"You didn't."

"I think I did."

"Look. I would have remembered."

"I thought—"

"How much more do you have to shoot?"

"A few more times on the Sinister Man segment. Then I'll be out of money, so my calendar will be open."

"I thought it was hard to schedule."

"It is."

"Well? You shoot all the time." This, a trifle more plaintive than she wished. She adjusted her tone. "All right—no fudge for you."

"I felt my prospects dimming."

"You got that right."

"What about coming to the shoot?"

"Nah, it's all right. It's fairly boring, if you want the truth. A lot of standing around.""

"Yeah, I know."

She turned her attention back to the bowl; it had gotten stiff and she was really having to work it. "So how's it going tonight?"

"Good. Just made thirty bucks on an airport run."

"I thought I heard announcements in the background." She put down the bowl, wiped her hands on the apron, and picked up the phone. "Okay. Your next day off is Friday, right? After the shoot?"

"Right."

"We're going out, then."

"Is that right?"

"Yes, and there'll be no backtalk on the matter."

"What about fudge?"

"None of that, either. All that's left for you is to pine for it. But futilely."

"Hmm. I believe I'm free."

"That's better."

"What are we doing?"

"I'll investigate the possibilities. I'll call you with your instructions."

"Instructions?"

"Yes—what to wear, when to be here. Possibly more, that's why you're waiting."

"Yes ma'am."

"Drive safely."

"I will."

The day following the fourth shoot, rolls five and six arrived from Pinsky. Booth graciously knocked this time, handing Charlie the package without comment.

He yawned and took the rolls to the kitchen for visual inspection. They looked innocuous under the 60-watt bulb, but they caused him a faint dread. He tapped one of the cases, picked it up. Contained on the coils of celluloid inside was a verdict of his effort, a judgment already minted and frozen on thousands of individual frames. He put down the case and turned to prepare a cup of coffee.

So far the verdicts had been mixed. The first two rolls were pretty good. They benefited from his wonder at the new project, perhaps, and also from their relative ease. His mind's eye had seen images richer in depth and detail, but the ones Pinsky sent back were adequate.

Rolls three and four were not as good. Charlie had difficulty putting his finger on the nature of the deficiency, but one scene seemed instructive. It was a scene in which the Sinister Man chatted outside a ramshackle house to another, equally sinister-looking crony. The scene occurred late in the segment, when the cabbie has returned to pick up the Sinister Man where he had dropped him that morning. It was meant to convey imminence—danger lurking. Charlie thought the shoot had been easy. All he had to do was position the camera inside the cab so that the scene of the chatting thugs was framed by the car's window. This, to indicate the trapped claustrophobia the cabbie felt as he watched.

(The other man was played by Carlos, who joked throughout the set. "Oh sure, I get demoted from SINISTER MAN to SINISTER LACKEY." "Great, make the Latino play the shady character." But he did a great job—he *was* shady.)

When he got the film back, however, Charlie was dismayed to see that he'd failed to capture the danger. The film expressed nothing more sinister than a couple guys chatting in the rain—they might have been bank tellers. The shot's composition had great visual appeal, with the windshield framing the screen, but outside, near the house, it was neutral. The scene felt too remote. It worked as a good establishing shot, but then he needed tighter close-ups to communicate foreboding. He would have to go back and get some close-ups.

He sat at the kitchen table, clearing his mind of what he hoped to see. He focused in on what was already filmed, already printed and waiting to be seen. Although the verdict was already in, he imagined he could ensure the film's quality my imagining it hard enough. But the dread returned. They were going to be flat.

Later that afternoon, he dropped by the Institute to screen the film. October was in the hallway talking to Buddy Holly when he came in.

"New footage?"

"Yeah."

"Cool. I think room two is free; you mind if I tag along and have a look?"

"Let me look at them first. I'm not sure . . . ."

"No problem. Come flag me down when it's ready."

Room two turned out to be occupied by a class of Super 8 students. He tried room one (occupied) and three (lit and messy, empty but probably in use). Room four, the largest of the Institute's screening rooms, was dark. He would have preferred a smaller setting, but this was the only choice. The room was so large it had its own separate projection booth, up a flight of stairs at the back.

After he had threaded the film, he sat in the murky light created by the projector's bulb. A deep breath and then he flipped the projector on. The first images started to roll and he took another breath. He watched both rolls twice and then sat and pondered them until he saw a tuft of yellow pass in front of the beam of light in the room below.

"Hey," she said. "I figured you were ready." He started to talk about the film, but she held up a hand. "Let me see it, first."

She waited until the second roll spooled through the projector and started slapping its tail before she shut off the motor. In the near-dark, she started threading the film back through the camera to rewind it; just enough light reflected back off the screen from the projector's bulb for her to see what she was doing.

"It's good," she said.

Charlie cleared his throat. He had now seen the footage three times. Each time he watched, he hoped they wouldn't be as dully composed (flat, as he feared), that the actors wouldn't seem as amateurish,. Each time his stomach clenched: they were.

"Seriously, Charlie, this is good stuff. Technically, it's adequate—which is the best you could hope for with your budget. But the acting, script, and shots are really good. It's obviously an indie, but it's better than almost everything that gets made here." A sincere appraisal, benefiting Charlie not at all.

"It's nice of you to say. Thanks."

"With amateur actors and no budget, it's going to be a little rough."

"It's true. You're right."

He waited while the film rewound. October was still smiling, somehow leaving him depressed. Maybe it was that she had nothing to compare it to. It met her expectations, which were none. But next to the footage that ran through his brain, what he saw on the screen was bad. Amateurish and bad.

At seven Wednesday evening, a message from Mike to call Janie. Following his initial hello, the full conversation went like this:

"Ah, yes. Seven o'clock, casual dress, but not *too* casual."

"What are the plans?"

"For you to be here at seven, in casual dress."

"I see. So by casual, you mean Oregon formal."

"No, better than that. No jeans, no flannel."

"Oh *my*. You mean Minne*sota* formal."

"Seven."

"Sharp?"

"Of course."

"I guess I'll see you then."

"Yes."

Charlie, in gray slacks and a black shirt, arrived an hour and 22 minutes early. Earlier, in fact, than Janie: she was still traveling from the pods. She did not look across the street as she came down 17th, and thus did not see the cab parked there. He stole up behind her as she studied her mail. "Psst." She jumped.

"Bastard!" He grinned and hugged her. "What are you doing here so early?"

"I wanted to catch you before you bathed."

"Oh yeah? Why?"

"Come on upstairs and I'll show you." He leered.

It was an almost perfect night.

Janie took him to a dance performance in a tiny theater on Clinton Street. The troupe was led by an Indian woman who had created a fusion of Indian and modern dance. Charlie didn't consider himself much of a dance fan, but he was surprised by the emotion of the performance. Janie had planned to take him to a showy new restaurant downtown, but because of the intimate mood, they went instead to a cozy Italian place.

In the candlelight, they sipped wine and spoke low. Bodies hunched a little, heads down and inclined toward each other – like conspirators. Conversation had transitioned from the performance to the engineers at her office. She was envisioning an exchange with them in which she tried to describe why the dancers moved her. She held little hope that her co-workers would find it a compelling story.

Something about the exchange struck Charlie. They were speaking at a level of understanding not possible at the beginning of a relationship. Charlie knew the engineers (she was right, they weren't going to be interested); her analysis depended on that. Unlike early conversations, this wasn't investigatory. It was collaborative. They had wandered around each other's brains enough to become familiar with them. Now he felt like he'd gotten inside her consciousness and was exploring the world hand in hand with it.

She saw his mind wander away. "Well, enough of the engineers, then."

"I was listening."

She broke a crust off her bread and moistened it in her mouth with wine. "This is the good life."

"Yeah, it is great." He added, lightly, "Except for the engineers."

"Ah well, they're not so bad"

"Oh come on. Then what about the rain?"

"It's not so bad."

"You like Portland now?"

"Portland's all right. It's actually pretty cool."

"What about – "

"Okay, I'll admit, I do sort of hate the rain."

Charlie thought of his own life—Janie, cab driving, film. He felt he saw certain parallels to Janie's life—himself, the pods, and . . . what? Betrayed by his sense of shared consciousness, he said something foolish.

"What about the pods? You hate it there."

"Oh, it's fine."

He didn't understand this comment, so he tried a different tack. "Well, all right. But what do you really want to do?"

"My job's fine, really. It's what I want to do."

"You hate it."

"What are you talking about?"

"You always slag it—you never say anything positive."

"There are some things about it that suck, but it's a great job. I wouldn't have come to Portland if it wasn't."

He tried to digest this information.

"It means I can go out like this, right?" This was more a plea than an observation. She wanted to go back to the mood of five minutes ago.

"I guess so. You *like* it there?"

"It's a good company. I have really good options there. I couldn't ask for more. I mean, I just got out of college a couple years ago."

"Huh."

"What did you think?"

"I thought you hated it. I thought it was something like driving a cab was for me. You know, something you do while you work to get to do the thing you really want to do. I mean, it's a lot better job than driving a cab, but you know, a better job for someone out of college, someone more talented."

"But still grunt work."

"Well, I don't know about grunt work. But just a job."

"Isn't that what I said—it's a job?"

"But I don't want to drive a cab forever—I want to make films. I thought you were in the same boat, not wanting to be there forever. I just didn't know what you *wanted* to do."

"I don't want to be a tech writer forever, but I'll switch jobs, get to do something more creative. I'll get out of the pods before long and go to the main office downtown. You have to start at the bottom, but it'll get more fun in a couple years. It's a good company.

He paused to consider this information, this worldview. He knew that some people held it—people like the engineers he thought she hated. Or Vic, say. But they were non-people to him. Their reality was like a dog's—although he could predict how they would behave, he couldn't begin to comprehend what motivated them. Yet all the things that interested those people were as dull to Janie as they were to him. And all the things that interested him interested her. Except now that this job—which seemed to him like a realm of hell—apparently was what she *wanted*. She wasn't just biding her time. Suddenly, she seemed more inscrutable to him than the engineers. At least they fit into a category he knew.

"So you're happy now?"

"I am."

"That's wonderful." Charlie sat up and took a drink of water. He wanted it to be wonderful. He wanted his mind to join hers in the world where that was wonderful. But when he looked at her now, sitting just across the table, she seemed very far away.

14.

The false February spring. It usually lasted one week, generally at the first of the month, but this year it came two weeks late. The daffodils had burst up in surprised enthusiasm; in two weeks they would regret their haste. Clumps of melting butter swaying on soggy stalks.

Di Paulo surveyed North Albina from the idling cab.

The pavement looked rubbery in the artificial light. When cars came along, their headlamps brought a harsh clarity to the landscape. But under streetlights, surfaces appeared soft—the sidewalks a muted yellow, toes of buildings poking out in brick semicircles. Down the road, he could see a single lawn, Sendak green. He put the car in drive and pointed it toward Lapierre's house, a few blocks over.

Into the radio. "Hey Mike."

"Di Paulo."

"Whatta we got in the way of airport calls this morning? It's dead as hell out here."

"Not much. Slow night."

"I may head in, then."

"Nah, stay out. It's looking thin out there—lotta guys came in. If we get any kind of run, you'll be set."

"Yeah."

"Staying out?"

"Hard to say."

"Dammit, di Paulo."

"Cab 133 out."

The cab in park, a shudder as the engine died. Charlie took his winter coat from underneath the front seat and trudged to Lapierre's stoop. It was chilly from an objective point of view, but in relative terms it was balmy; the fresh air invigorated his body, lightened it.

On Lapierre's sloping porch, he stretched out on his back, head pointed to the street so that he could see the stars. His eyes scanned the sky for a familiar constellation, of which there were only two. Orion's belt, just over the cedar tree across the street, but no Big Dipper.

He wondered—were there people creating new constellations even now? People tired of the old ones, the strained ones, the ones based on myths they didn't know? Maybe someone had found all the symbols of NFL teams up there, or a nativity scene. What about corporate logos? Could you copyright the stars? While he pondered the marketing ramifications, his attention drifted. The stars faded and Jen's face floated into his visual consciousness. Charlie's mind, inevitably returning to his film.

He remembered her face from a recent incident. A long shoot, Charlie having gathered together all the "foreboding" shots from various scenes for a single day's shoot—mop up for failures like the Russell Street side-by-side. His idea was to put everyone in a foreboding mood and roll film.

In preparation for the shoot, Charlie had been perfecting a harness system to secure himself to the cab's hood. He wanted to get right inside the car, capture the nuances on his actors' faces as malignancy and fear rippled across them. Hitchcockian. He had devised a two-piece rigging, one for himself, one for the camera. The human component began with an old waterskiing life vest—a haute safety-yellow number from the 1970s. It had three rows of belts, and to their metal buckles Charlie attached four tow straps that anchored him in the cardinal directions to the hood of the cab.

The camera he mounted on a unipod, the bottom of which was affixed to a spring loaded shock he'd fashioned from exercise equipment. The spring offset the worst jarring, giving the turbulence a languid, rolling quality. Two straps attached the unipod front to back, and his arm stabilized its lateral swing. Once constructed, he and Lapierre practiced in the field. Idling, then barely moving, then moving just fast enough to give the camera a little swing.

A feat of cheap engineering, and a pretty good one, at that.

On the day of foreboding, Jen watched the final hood shoot (there had been three, in different locations). Charlie was pleased with his harness and his actors and was in an airy mood. The next shoot was a side-by-side. The day was darkly overcast, removing the worst of the glare. That was when Jen proposed the flying tripod.

She had been secretly working to solve the side-by-side shot, which she believed was problematic for reasons beyond reflection. The shots weren't up to par; they would be lifeless. He needed to get right up into the window, as in the hood shot. She produced a spiral notebook and explained that she had been mapping out plans for mounting a tripod to the passenger-side door of the cab.

"Look, here's a diagram. See, you open the door and rope your tripod on tightly, like so. Put a blanket behind the tripod so it doesn't scratch the paint." She pointed to a drawing. "See, that's the blanket. You gently close the door once it's all roped in and voila!"

She had four pages of sketches, each from a different angle. On the final page, she had drawn an establishing shot of the cab driving down the street, filming from the mounted camera. "See, it kind of looks like a flying buttress, doesn't it? I call it the flying tripod. It's brilliant."

It wasn't bad. Charlie admired the ingenuity and theoretical possibility of such a system—if you had a lot of money and could afford to destroy a camera or damage a car door.

"It's cool, but I don't like the idea of the camera just hanging out there."

She was nonplussed by his concern. "You just strapped yourself to the hood. That was hinkier than this." When Charlie paused skeptically, her eyes narrowed and closed the notebook. "Way fucking hinkier. You should at least let me try to strap it in."

He ultimately allowed her to try the strapping, but the result was inconclusive. She managed to get the camera positioned well enough to film Lapierre, but the door wouldn't close. There was also a little more motion to the tripod than Charlie liked, though he couldn't see how it would fall off. Too risky: veto.

Back on the stoop, he was interrupted briefly by movement in the eastern sky, activating his visual consciousness. Shooting star? He craned. No; an airplane, and by the looks of it, a small one. He continued to scan the sky until another face floated by, distracting him again. Roger, this time, in the back seat of the cab, pointing with animation at his hands.

Amid the flying tripod imbroglio, Roger contributed his own idiosyncratic help. He had an idea for a particular shot he wanted to put in the film. He'd developed a kind of white-knuckle, hand-wringing thing that he wanted to cut in to scenes of him looking sinister. Part of his shiftiness, he argued. "My face is flat, you know, no expression. But then you cut in these shots of my hands, right? Check them out." He wrung them. "You see? Good, huh?"

It wasn't good, naturally. It indicated—if anything—anxiety. Roger kept rubbing his hands, more and more vigorously, by way of convincing Charlie. A demented squirrel. He couldn't recall—what had he told Roger? The image hung there, but it didn't go forward. He couldn't recall what they'd done next.

From deep within a hole beneath his face, an echoey mumble. Like a well, although he couldn't remember why he was looking down a well. He tried to make out the words. He cocked his head and strained to hear. Then he remembered to open his eyes and there was another face. Lapierre's.

"You're alarming the neighbors," it said.

He was nudging Charlie's leg with a toe. At that moment, when he was trying to see into the well, Charlie didn't welcome the face, but it wouldn't go away—Lapierre was standing on the porch, looking down at him.

"Mumbling indecently."

It was full daylight, though the sun had not yet peeked over the maple at the end of the street. His neck was seized up, and his head boomed from the awkward position he lapsed off to sleep in. He rolled gingerly onto his side to sit up, supporting his head with a palm.

"What time is it?"

"A little after seven." Clay had two coffee cups in his hands. He sat down on the top step and put one at Charlie's side.

"I was talking in my sleep?"

"Loudly."

"Huh. I wonder how often that happens." He took a sip of the coffee—strong. "What was I saying?"

"They weren't words. Sort of shouts and groans."

"Ah." Maybe the mumbles he heard were his own. "I shouldn't be drinking this—it's after my bedtime."

"Yes, and apparently you're confused about where your bed is."

As his body slowly woke up, Charlie realized he had gotten cold in his sleep. "Let's go inside."

While he gathered himself at the kitchen table, Lapierre started mixing a bowl of pancake batter. "So what's up?"

"Not much."

"Just having a casual nap on my porch."

He smiled. "That's right."

Lapierre put a skillet on the stove to warm, then walked to the table. He poked a notebook laying next to Charlie's elbow with a deformed plastic spatula. "Then what's that?"

"Notes on the production."

"Yeah?"

"We're running out of money."

Lapierre, back at the stove. "That's not surprising."

"No. We may or may not have enough to finish this piece."

"How close are we?"

"Actually, we're not close at all. Unless some kind of miracle happens, I'm going to need another infusion."

"Uh huh." Clay held up the coffee pot.

"No thanks." Charlie watched as he began to work the spatula underneath the edge of a cake.

After he had a stack of pancakes ready, Clay sat down.

"So what's really up? Obviously we're out of money."

"Yes."

"But?"

Clay was preparing a concoction of peanut butter and corn syrup on the edge of his plate—folding the two together until he could start whipping them into an even consistency. Charlie thought: but what? The process of filming "Taxicab Triptych" had been educational. He had learned several key lessons—money and film stock evaporate more quickly than you intend. Productions are more difficult to manage the more people you have (Flying tripod!). Sound is a virtue and a curse.

Clay was spreading the loose paste onto his pancakes like frosting. Charlie watched with fascination. "That is one of the grossest things I've ever seen."

"Tasty. Wanna try some?" He held up a dripping knife.

"Absolutely not." The most important lesson remained elusive. He wasn't even sure how to discuss it. "You've seen all the footage. Let me ask you something. Is it what you expected?"

Clay waved his fork at Charlie's plate. "Eat."

"Yeah, all right." To appease his host, he began buttering.

"Yeah, pretty much. I think we've gotten some pretty good stuff."

"When you watch the footage, you see what you envisioned in your head before the shot?"

"I don't envision. It's your baby. When I watch the footage, I'm looking to see if the acting's good."

"Right, of course."

"It's not what you expected?"

"Well," he considered. He didn't know. "I don't know."

The image that came into his head was of trying to carve an object from a block of wood. A bowl, for example. But the grain of the wood wasn't tight enough, or was warped, so that as the bowl began to emerge, it was crooked. When he watched his footage, that's how he felt — like it was structurally unsound.

Lapierre reached for two more pancakes. "It's not the acting. We're doing a pretty good job. Even most of Roger's scenes are all right. Okay, *many*."

"No, it's not the acting. I can't put my finger on it."

"It's fine. Money's you're big problem. You're a pauper." He began a second preparation of pancake topping. "Oh hey — I have some good news."

"Yeah?"

"The Fire Station is doing a production of Mamet's *House of Games*."

"The movie?"

"Yeah. I got cast as George."

"No shit? That's fantastic!" Lapierre gave him a phony Hollywood smile, full of teeth. "Which one's George?"

"He's Ricky Jay's character — one of the gamblers."

"Pretty good part."

"Yeah. Not the lead, but a good one."

"When's it open?"

"September."

He had gotten to the smearing stage of his second round of pancakes. Charlie had eaten roughly four bites of his own. "I'm sorry, but I gotta go to bed. I can't eat this late. But thanks."

"No worries."

"We should go out soon and celebrate this fine news." He stood. "I'll buy the first round."

"Yes. The first round's on you."

Nineteen minutes later, Charlie was in a false night, behind blanket-draped windows. He yawned while his stomach growled; he regretted drinking even a half cup of coffee. As his lids settled over his eyes, he watched for faces to drift into view. But this time it was just darkness.

On the east wall of Charlie's bedroom hung the apartment's sole visual accoutrement: a film poster. Janie, bored, was waiting for Charlie to finish cleaning the breakfast dishes. The title read: "Un film de Francois Truffaut, *La Nuit Américaine*."

On a beige field were two enigmatic photographs. In one, a man and woman looking at each other while a second man held the woman's face. The second man's back was turned toward the camera; he held her face like a hairdresser, adjusting the angle. In the second photograph, part of the background bled into the poster's beige field, where a man—Janie presumed Truffaut—stood amid a film shoot. Flanked on one side by a man with a megaphone and the other by a woman in oversized eyeglasses, holding a clipboard. Behind the director was a cameraman, floating on a crane and manning a camera the size of a motorcycle. He was dressed in a shirt and tie and a leather jacket with a badge that lent a vaguely policeman-like quality.

Into her peripheral vision there appeared a second director, waving a cup of coffee at her.

"Finally."

"Your welcome."

"What, did you have to go to the store for beans?"

"Good thing I made decaf, Miz Hepped Up."

"Decaf?" She looked at him a little desperately.

"Kidding."

"Let's put it in a travel mug. I want to get moving."

She was headed to Minnesota for a week, her first visit back since heading West. A last night at Charlie's before she went.

"Come on. You can help me pack."

Infomercial, Steven Segal movie, football, football. She had been in the bedroom for over an hour. He wandered in to stir up some action.

She was confronting the closet, hands on hips, wearing two different shoes. On the bed behind her, she had laid out her massive molded-plastic suitcase. Charlie wondered if he would fit inside. If he ever did a mob movie, he might use it as a prop for storing bodies. She reached into the closet and pulled out two hats—a South American knit cap and a beret.

"Ah screw it. This will have to do." Into the suitcase went both hats.

"I don't know—this is fairly light packing. How many months will you be gone?"

She narrowed her eyes at him. "So when do we have to leave?"

"Forty-five minutes, an hour."

"Will you be able to pick me up from the airport?"

"Probably, when do you get back?"

"I'll have to check the ticket."

"Well, why don't we go sit and have a cup of coffee."

She smiled sweetly. "Or perhaps you prefer tea."

Janie's coffee system was the same as Charlie's—a pour-through filter. As the water was buzzing in the teapot, she tapped ground coffee into the filter from a crumpled bag. "So I was thinking about your movie."

"Yeah?"

"Can I ask you a question? I swear to God I have no agenda." She opened a cupboard. "Do you want green tea or mint?"

"All right."

"Why are you against film school?"

"Who said I was against it? Mint."

"You have to be: otherwise you'd have taken Vic up on his offer."

Charlie considered her timing. He'd been in a bit of a funk since the most recent stock had arrived from Pinsky. He wondered if it had been affecting things between them. "It's not really my kind of thing."

"How come?"

"Film schools are more about connections than making movies. You go to network."

"Really? You don't learn how to make movies?"

"Well, you do. Though mostly it's theory and craft and that kind of crap. Mostly they figure you'll hire editors and grips and gaffers and so it's a lot of sitting around talking about why Eisenstein was a genius."

She focused on filtering her coffee, thinking. Then sat down and pulled the chair up close to his.

"I've been wondering about it, though. Don't they let you make a movie in film school? I mean, isn't that your final project or something?"

"Yes, I think so."

"Well, maybe you ought to go just for that." Her voice rose slightly. "Suffer through the Eisenstein discussions for the sake of the movie. I know you've sort of hit a bump in the film, so I thought maybe this would work."

Janie's point was reasonable. He had, in fact, lately considered reconsidering Vic's offer. But each time, his stomach did a nervous little dance. Like now. He took a sip of mint. "I know, you're right. It makes obvious sense. I have thought of it."

"Well?" She leaned in, strangely manic. He wondered if she was aware of it.

"It's just ... film school's not for me."

"I don't understand."

"It's not a good fit."

"What are you talking about?" A confused squint appeared on her face. She pulled back slightly. He had a dawning sense that this discussion was one of those scenes that had already played out in Janie's mind. He was just a place-keeper holding up his end of her conversation.

"I don't know." The difficulty of communicating something you don't understand yourself. "It's pretentious."

"What the hell are you talking about?"

"Maybe not pretentious, but something. I just don't want to sit around talking about movies."

She rocked away from him. "Even if it means you could finish 'Taxicab Triptych?'"

"I'll finish it."

"With what?"

"I'll finish it."

"Okay, let's say you finish it. You could finish it a lot easier at film school. And sooner."

"I don't know about that."

"So what you're telling me is that you're against it on principle."

"Well, I don't know if I'd go that far."

"What other reason is there?"

"I guess I think of it as the opposite of that. I'm for making it on my own on principle."

Janie stood up with a dramatic lurch and scraping of the chair. His face, blank and ignorant, suddenly made her want to punch him. It was a surprise to her, but there she was, standing over him. "What good is it? For one thing, you'd have been able to make your movie for free. You would have had access to everything and it would have been free. Probably even real actors. I mean, if it's all about the fucking movie, that would have been the best way, right?"

"It's one way."

"You fucking obsess over your goddamn movie night and day, but you won't take any help. Your father's right—it's Charlie's way or the highway." He started to speak, to try to dull the force of her unexpected assault, but she kept going, her words and body driving him back in his chair. "You want help, son? Fine. Tell ya what I'll do—I'll put you through film school. Nope, not good enough for un film de Charlie di Paulo. Okay, so you want to make it yourself, I'll help you. What do you need, two grand, three? Shit, how about five grand, Charlie? I've got it in my fucking bank account right now."

Her body had coiled up like a snake above his body, spittle flying, nose to nose with him.

He waited for a few seconds, and when it seemed like she wasn't going to say anything more, he said, "Well—"

"Shut up."

These last words were a plea more than a command, spoken just before a crest of tears broke. She was still angry—she was furious—but now a part of her anger was directed at her, for allowing herself to lose her cool like this. She sat down.

"Goddamn martyr," she said between sobs. "Un fucking hairshirt de Charlie di Paulo is more like it."

She cried with her head down, batting away Charlie's hand, which appeared periodically to comfort her. She wasn't ready for him to comfort her and wasn't ready to comfort him yet, either. She could feel the arc of this little scene spread out before her and felt trapped by it: the flow of tears subsiding eventually and the subsequent relief she would feel (which made her mad); the kind words between them and the tenderness they would feel (mad); the quiet drive to the airport, the kid gloves (mad); and the aching, ill-timed goodbye with probably more tears (mad, mad, mad). The only thing that gave her comfort was the thought that she would make him leave her by the curb at the terminal so that she could go buy a fresh pack of cigarettes before her flight. The idea of standing in that little glass smokers' room with the other prisoners exhaling defiant jets of lethal smoke into their polluted little space was soothing. He reached out and she let him touch her elbow.

"I probably look like a fucking raccoon."

"No, you—"

"Shut up."

| 15.

The rhythmic waves of the telephone, splashing like water on flat rocks. Charlie regarded it neutrally from the gauze of half-sleep. The pulse had pulled him to an intermediary stage wherein he was aware that it was not water but the phone, yet he had little inclination to act on the information. A battle between forces: sleep versus phone. Eventually, the phone won.

He pulled himself off the bed and over to the couch, where he collapsed, simultaneously picking up the receiver. Dial tone.

"Shit."

He rested. On the return trip, bed calling out, it started ringing again.

"Shit."

"Goddamn Charlie, you sleep like the dead." It was Heater.

"I just went to sleep —" the clock said 7:22 " — recently."

"Time to get up. The Nash is down. I need a driver ASAP."

"Now?"

"Yes, now!"

He yawned. "I need sleep. Call the cab company."

"Charlie."

"I mean it, I'm tired."

"You're young; you'll live. Now get over here."

"Damn it, Barney." He stopped to consider a convincing argument, but it didn't matter. Heater had hung up.

From where he sat on the couch, he could see the left half of his bed in the next room, completely unrumpled. He imagined a messier bed with a lump and half a head of black hair poking out. No matter which way she lay, after a night's sleep, her hair concealed all skin. But there had been fewer mornings with Janie in his bed recently. Things a bit touchy since the return from Minnesota. Crawling back into bed—even without her in it—called to him powerfully, but instead it was to the shower and irate Heater.

Charlie drifted through the day in a half doze, sliding instantly into dreams while Heater serviced accounts of business and wager. By midafternoon they were on a return trip to the Ace High, and Charlie hoped for early release.

"All right, go get some sleep. I need you back at a quarter to seven, though."

"Tonight or tomorrow morning?"

"Tonight." He peeled a fifty off the ball of cash, then fanned through until he found a hundred. "You'll be fine."

Waking up the second time that day was a different experience than the first. Rather than a sensation of syrupy fatigue, this time he was buzzy, his skin feeling like it had lost a protective outer layer. Yet he was relatively clear-headed. The early evening air seemed heavy, thick. Clouds outside, but warm and moist.

By the time he arrived at the bar, he was more or less in his right mind. The sunlight had begun to slant horizontally underneath the clouds, creating sharp angles of shade. Heater was already in the parking lot, working a piece of gum and chatting with Ray. Charlie pulled up next to them, and without breaking conversation or looking at him, they climbed into the cab.

Moving at a crawl down 74th, waiting for the conversation to end. Midway through a thought, Heater looked up. "Eighty-four. We're going to the dog track. You know how to get there?"

"Sure."

Charlie was fond of the dogs. He and Clay had gotten into them a couple years earlier. After the local news on Channel 12, the station used to do a half-hour where they showed the dog races, one after another, with no break in-between. Before each race, the names of the dogs appeared briefly on the screen. Based on sheer impulse, they'd holler out a name and throw a quarter into a teacup. They did this until one of their dogs finished in the money. Later, they went to the track a few times, but it was extremely slow-moving by comparison and they rarely won. After the station quit running the races, they lost interest in gambling, though they still went out from time to time for the experience.

When they got onto the freeway, Heater produced a racing form from the tan briefcase and began studying it. Ray also had a form, folded lengthwise, which he removed from his back pocket. He smoothed his and joined Heater in silence.

After he had leafed through the form, Heater spoke. "All right, let's see what you got, there."

"First race: one, two, four, five, eight," Ray said.

"You like eight, huh?"

"Absolutely. Look at that, last five races, he's been in the money twice."

"Not from the outside. He likes to run from the front."

"We'll see."

Heater responded with a gurgling growl, which Charlie took to be a chuckle.

They went through the form as Charlie skimmed toward Troutdale. Rarely did they agree on the dogs, and only once did either of them seem convinced by the other's argument. In the sixth race, Ray pointed out something about a long-shot that Heater had missed.

"Well I'll be damned." he said.

The dog track was an elegant 40's-era building of heft and steel that had originally been built in the lush hills east of Portland. But now it wasn't even visible until they rounded the last thicket of pre-fab homes and turned onto 223rd. And even then, it sat in a vast black asphalt field, not gentle grass.

Charlie started toward the door to drop them off, but Heater stopped him. "Nah, go ahead and park it and come in with us. I'll buy you a beer." Charlie looked back, but Heater was bundling up the briefcase. He started to step out of the cab and said, "Come on."

On the way in, Heater asked, "You ever play the dogs?"

Charlie said, "Sure."

"You bet to win or show?"

Picking the winning dog was nearly impossible, and he and Lapierre had quickly resorted to betting show. He looked at Heater. "Show."

"Lose a lot?"

"Here and there."

Heater chuckled. "I'll bet you did."

They passed through the outside gates, Heater stopping a moment to chat with the program vendor. Charlie eyed the emerald infield lawn of the racing track, which seemed to almost glow it was such a rich green. Heater led them indoors and to a bar. A scotch and soda for himself, Budweiser for his sidekicks. It occurred to Charlie, as the tasteless fizz of industrial lager slid down his throat, that he was still at work. Cab driving had its perks.

While Heater placed his bets, Charlie wandered. Even though the first race was only fifteen minutes away, almost no one was there yet. The population that had already arrived was uniformly old and male: snow-topped, pot-bellied, and cigar-chewing. They had settled into favorite seats, colored pens and programs fanned out in front of them. A few had supporting material—binders with past performances and betting guides. These were the guys like Heater who took things seriously; he wondered if they all used the same system. Charlie imagined them budgeting the payroll in thirds: rent, liquor, gambling. He had noticed them before, but by the time he and Clay usually arrived, they were an offbeat minority. In an hour, at about the fourth race, the 20 feet between the building and track would be filled with the younger, hooting, betting-to-show crowd he knew, and the oldsters would be hardly noticeable.

He took his beer outside to the track. Although it was the cheap, watery kind of beer that tended to take on the flavor of its container (in this case plastic), he took a deep drink. Just right for the dog races.

The oval of graded dirt was about the size of a running track. On either end were the racing boxes, like at horse tracks, but miniature. A wide berm in the center of the infield was planted with flowers that spelled out the track's initials.

He had polished off about half his beer when a man came to the booth at the finish line dressed in a tuxedo and top hat. He stood at attention and then raised a trumpet to his mouth like an Army bugler and began playing some kind of British triumphal march. A moment later, handlers led a procession of the first race's dogs down the homestretch track. They waited just beyond the finish line while the announcer read each one's name, then headed back to the starting box. A young couple leaned against the rail a few feet away and commented on the dogs as they passed by.

Charlie went back in to look for Heater and Ray. The crowd had not grown appreciably; a quick count and he guessed another three or four had come in—and he saw no sign of his gambling fares. The evening light was inclining toward the golden hour. The clouds had begun to dissipate—only a few wispy shreds remained. The track building was infused with a luminosity, highlighting the vast spaces and sharp angles. The massive steel support beams, aerospace round and painted glossy blue, had an industrial-age beauty.

Charlie looked at a stocky pensioner chewing on a spit-logged cigar stub and wondered: what could I film here?

A swallow to finish his beer and then a quick jog to the bathroom before the races started. As he stood at the urinal, the announcer said the betting boxes were closed. One minute to post.

There was a big fawn Charlie liked, and lacking any other compelling interest, he hollered her number. She looked good out of the gate, but got nudged by the streaking eight and fell back into the middle of the pack. By the backstretch, she was out of the race. As the dogs came down the homestretch, he glanced back at the old men; all were expressionless. After crossing the finish line, the dogs made it to the far turn before collapsing into a canine frolic, now insensitive to the competition. The old men didn't see it; they immediately looked back down at their programs.

Heater was up in the second-floor bleachers, where Charlie found him after the fourth. The ground floor and track had begun to fill and liven up with the "show" bettors, as Charlie had expected; the bleachers, however, were still mostly empty. Heater and Ray, standing at the window, were looking down at the track.

"Charlie! Where the hell you been?" He seized Charlie in the usual, fruit-examining manner.

"How you guys doing?"

"Pretty good," Ray said.

"Ray's doing pretty good. I've gotten skunked."

"What are you talking about?" Ray turned away from the window. "You won the first."

"Well hell, the payoff didn't cover the bet. That's not a win."

"Long-shots, I'm telling you."

"We'll see." Heater pulled Charlie in by the shoulder, spun him around to the track. "Trifectas are where the money is, Charlie. I asked you earlier what you bet. You were one of those poor bastards down there getting drunk and betting to show." He pointed to the people milling around, waiting for the next race. "You had some fun and you lost some money. That's fine. It's the law of gambling: eight dogs run, and three finish in the money. Even if you bet to show, you've got three chances in eight—a losing proposition. So what me and Ray do is bet the trifecta."

"I've bet the trifecta—it's a sucker deal. No *way* you ever win." Charlie said sourly.

"You're right—you can't guess the trifecta. But that's why we *box* 'em."

"I heard you talking about that. Still seems like a sucker deal."

"You know what it means?"

"Sort of," he said, unconvincingly.

"All right. When you box dogs for a race, that means you pick a certain number of them—we play five dog boxes—and you bet all the combinations of those five dogs. So if three of your five are in the trifecta, you win. It puts the odds back on your side."

"Wait, that's not a two-dollar bet, is it?"

"Hell no. Everybody'd bet it then. You bet all the combinations, so you pay two bucks a pop—a hundred and twenty for a five-dog box."

Charlie whistled. "That's a hell of a bet." He considered Heater's situation. "So you're already down 400 bucks?"

"No, you don't think of it like that. You come, place your bets, and watch the dogs. I don't give a shit what the running total is—all I care about is the final total, right? You're not gonna win every one, so running totals aren't worth a damn. Look, Ray here won the second and fourth. What'd you win on the second, Ray?"

"Nine hundred."

"All right, nine hundred. And now," he looked at the thirty-foot wide scoreboard across the track, "he just picked up three and change. It's the fourth race, and he's already made his nut. If he were betting race-by-race, he might hold pat now. Instead, he's placed all his bets, so he's just going to relax, win another race or two, and pad his winnings. Me, I just think of it like I'm going to win the eighth, ninth, tenth. You never know which races you're going to win—that's why you bet 'em all."

"What happens if you don't."

"Doesn't happen."

"Bullshit." He spoke without thinking, then looked at Heater. "Sorry."

Heater chuckled and let go of Charlie's shoulder. "You lose sometimes. Me and Ray been coming to the track for about ten years. Bet two-three times a week. Whatdya think Ray, about three, four losing nights a year?"

"Yeah, about that."

"Out of how many?"

"What's that, like thirty, forty?"

Ray nodded. "Yeah, ten percent, say. You lose one night out of ten."

"Come on." He knew they were bullshitting him, he just couldn't figure out how. Or why.

"Think he's full of shit, don't you?" Ray grinned.

Charlie took a sip of warm beer by way of response.

"Want to bet on it?" Heater was looking out the window. He made the offer nonchalantly. "Here." He turned around and pulled a paper-clipped packet of 2-inch betting receipts from his briefcase. He removed the three losers, and dropped them on the floor. "These are the rest of my bets for the night. You keep 'em. If I don't win back the balance of the bets, you keep anything I do win. There's that first race winner for sixty bucks in there already."

"And if you do win?"

"You give me tonight's fare free."

Charlie considered it. He expected to lose if he went in on the bet. Somehow, though, he couldn't see how Heater had rigged it. On the other hand, losing a night's fare wasn't a very big deal. Heater had already paid him a buck fifty for the day. He took a sip of plastic beer. It wasn't like he was really working anyway. Maybe worth it to see how Heater was running the con.

"I'm willing to bet just to see what the scam is. I think there's gotta be a scam."

"Good man." A clap on the back. "Hell, it'll be more fun this way, right?"

Heater won the seventh, but only modestly—$350. Charlie was secretly delighted and was now actively pulling against Heater's dogs. He needed $800 more in the last three races to break even.

Just before the eighth, Heater leaned over. "See? Fun, right?"

Ray won the eighth and added $800 to his winnings.

"See, Ray won again. I'm telling you, five dog boxes."

"You need an $800 race, though. In the next two." Charlie noted with what he hoped was neutrality. "Maybe this is the one in ten."

Heater grinned. "Nah, I'm feeling pretty good about the tenth. Got a shine on a little brindle name of Bombay Fire people are going to overlook. Big payday."

They both looked out at the track.

The ninth was a wild card. Heater had bet on medium- and long-shots, but apparently the crowd saw the same thing he had, because two of his dogs were coming off as the favorites. When the pre-race favorite finished second, he was coming in at 12-1—but Heater hadn't put him in the box. The trifecta paid $1200.

By this time, the "show" bettors had trailed off, drunk and broke. The betting pool was back down to about second-race levels, so it was going to take Heater's long-shot to put him in serious money. With about five minutes to go, she was coming off at 11-1; not bad.

"See," Heater said, pointing a fat finger at the board.

Ray was manic from his night, and Heater and Charlie listened in silence as he told a story about his brother-in-law's new boat. Two of Heater's other dogs were medium-shots, one was fairly long, and one was a favorite. Charlie guessed he'd need Bombay Fire and at least one of the medium-shots. The announcer closed the gambling and the handlers started to load the dogs into the starting boxes. Bombay Fire danced away from her handler for a moment, and then dove into the box.

"There she is, my little brindle," Heater said. "Coming off thirteen to one."

| 16.

"You think that's really his name, Heater?" Carlos eyed a bank shot on the five ball.

"You don't have the angle." Charlie's eyes were peering from the edge of the pool table.

"I think he's got it." Lapierre, with less interest, leaning against the wall.

"I'm telling you, the physics just aren't with you."

"Watch and learn." Carlos tapped the five gently off the rail, just in front of Charlie's nose, and watched it dribble toward the corner before losing steam a couple inches short of the corner pocket. "Damn. But the physics were there."

"Nope. If you'd hit it hard enough to knock it in, you'd have lost the angle."

"Piss off—it was easily makeable."

They looked at Clay for a ruling. "Inconclusive," he judged.

Carlos picked up his beer and joined Clay on the wall. "What do you think—is he a dangerous guy?"

"I don't know. I tell you though, I wouldn't want to get on his bad side."

"Maybe our next movie should be about a bookie," Clay suggested.

Charlie, lining up a shot. "Actually, you look a lot like him. Younger."

"Gambling is one of the most ancient professions." Carlos, retreating into speculation. "In fact, the argument could be made that it's the oldest profession—not prostitution. Exchanging money for sex is a fairly advanced concept, but gambling. . . ."

"Gambling depends on money." Lapierre noted.

"No, think about one caveman saying to his buddy, 'If I can hit that pterodactyl with this rock, will you give me your share of mastodon?' Rudimentary gambling, like kids."

"What about, 'I bet you your woman that I can hit that pterodactyl with this rock.' Gambling and pimping at the same time."

"Co-emergent professions—nice. But they'd have to have the idea of ownership first, so I think it's unlikely."

"What are you talking about? Men jealously guarding their women? That's as ancient as mankind."

"He's got you there," Charlie said.

Charlie sank a difficult angle shot, but missed the simple follow—twelve in the corner. Carlos smirked on his way back to the table. "Where were the physics there, Charlie boy?"

Charlie joined Lapierre on the wall. "How much work do you do for Heater these days?"

"Driving?"

Without thinking, he answered, "Yeah." He considered Charlie's answer further. "You do other work?"

"He doesn't call me for fares very often, but about twice a month he has me run collections for him."

Carlos, poised over the three ball, straightened up. "Collections? You pinch hit as a bookie?"

Charlie shrugged. "Oh, for God's sake, I'm not Vito Corleone." He nevertheless took the opportunity to take a theatrical, Godfathery sip of beer. "When Heater's car was broken down, I took him on his rounds a few times. Got to know the routine. Now, once in a while when he gets busy, he gives me a call, and I take a spin around his other businesses. It's very small time stuff. A cashier at the towing business wants to put a ten spot on the Ducks, that kind of thing. I just run the meter and he pays me that."

"Sure, that's how it starts out," Lapierre goaded. "But pretty soon you're taking C-notes, maybe a car title. Before you know it, you're out with Heater at 2 am packing a lead pipe."

"He's probably in too deep already." Carlos cracked the three, rattling it into the side pocket. "He's like a rat in one of those humane traps. He's munching on the cheese, but he doesn't realize *there's no way out*."

Charlie put down his beer, scratched his cheek, and did his best Brando. "What have I ever done to make you treat me so disrespectfully?"

Toward the end of the di Paulo-Munro battle, two biker types slid a quarter under the rail. But when Charlie scratched on the 8 ball, they decided to abandon the table outright. Charlie bought a pitcher of stout and they took a table in the dim back corner of the pub.

More small talk, and then Charlie noticed Carlos eyeing a table across the bar, at which two young women drank and smoked. "Munro didn't hear you," he told Clay. "His mind seems to be elsewhere." Lapierre followed his eye line. Nodded sagaciously.

"I don't have to devote enormous amounts of my brain to take in your prattle." Carlos, offering the no-look rebuttal, keeping his gaze on the women. "I have plenty of cerebral cortex left over to peruse the establishment while listening."

"The establishment?" Lapierre winked at Charlie. "I'd say you were perusing something else."

"And I don't think your cerebral cortex has anything to do with it."

Carlos sighed and looked at the juveniles giggling across from him. "Yeah, things could be a little more active on certain fronts. Not like you bastards, with your fine women."

Clay tried to wipe the grin off his face. "I thought you had a girlfriend in DC."

"Nah, we broke up last summer."

"Ah."

Carlos—tall, dark, and interesting-looking, like a half-Panamanian Jeff Goldblum. His luck with women ran in spurts. Strangely, he tended to appeal to short blondes—not that there was anything in particular short blonds had in common. Yet of a handful of past girlfriends, all but one were short blondes. The outlier, a short redhead. His last girlfriend was the youngest daughter of a Utah congressman. In addition to traditional height and hair color, she was Mormon, dooming the relationship. A dry patch since.

"I'll come around. Possibly tonight." He glanced back at the table. "You and Jen seem solid."

"True."

"What's it been, two years?"

"Three."

"Wow." He took a contemplative slurp of stout. "And di Paulo has made good."

"Quite good," Lapierre raised an eyebrow and studied Charlie's face.

"Short and bandy-legged and he always has a babe on one arm."

"It's the cabbie thing—he appeals to their lower instincts."

"Or maybe the artiste thing."

Charlie frowned.

"However he does it, Janie's a score." Lapierre elbowed Carlos.

"He better not rest on his laurels, though. I think *I* see her more often than he does."

"You have more time to take my girlfriend out when you're unemployed," Charlie said, more sharply than he intended. The conversation had turned his mood dark.

"Careful, di Paulo, you don't want to turn into the jealous type." To Carlos, "I didn't know you hung out with Janie."

"I'm teaching her to play pool. She likes to go out in the evenings, but di Paulo's in his cab."

"If she were short and blonde, I wouldn't let you near her." Charlie tried to be more positive. "As it is, I'm keeping a close watch on you."

Carlos stood. His eyes were on the bar, where one of the two young ladies was now standing. "Speaking of, if you'll excuse me. Maybe I can find a substitute pool player so Janie's boyfriend can rest easy." Her tresses were not naturally blonde, but Carlos set off to try his luck anyway.

In the VMC, built in an age before showers, apartments were equipped with a massive clawfoot tubs, big as boats. An immense industrial-age boiler heaved day and night in the basement, promising scalding water for every tenant, every radiator. They could hear the rumble of fire through the pipes. Two in the morning and Janie and Charlie were soaking.

Janie, longer and softer, was in the back. Her legs wrapped around Charlie, toes poking out of the water between his knees, nails painted sparkle green.

"Charlie." When she spoke, he could feel her voice resonate in her chest. He didn't answer.

"Charlie."

"Janie."

"Tell me."

Instead, he raised himself into a crouching position and balanced as he reached out for the window. Janie's eyes followed his slender, straining back down to his butt, curled and resting on his heels. A grunt, a wobble, and then he got it to lift. Cool, wet air streamed in. As he settled back into the water, she reached down to the floor for her wine glass, considering for a moment the idea of dumping it on his head. She decided on a deep, aggressive gulp instead, and sent Charlie's head bobbing.

After she returned her glass with a tink to the floor, she locked her feet and started squeezing him between her legs. "Talk."

"There's nothing."

She squeezed harder, past playfulness. Now digging in, angry.

He grunted. "I'm just cranky."

She let out a quiet little shriek of frustration, squeezed him one last time, and then pounded his chest with her hands, making a satisfying clomp. "It's your fucking movie. I'm so goddamn tired of that fucking thing."

Then she remembered the wine. A swoop of her arm and out it went over his head. There had only been a mouthful left in the glass so it wasn't much of an assault.

They sat for a few minutes, both their bodies tense. Janie watched a red bead run down Charlie's neck and pool in the little hollow formed by his collarbone. He sat forward, away from her, and the drop ran down his chest, out of her view. She looked away from him, out the crack in the window into a densely misty night. The suspended water gave the streetlight a little yellow halo. A wind was blowing down the river from Camas, where the paper mill scented the air with pulp and chemicals.

What *is* that smell? It's gross. Like garbage."

He inhaled, picking up the mill, but also the mist and the wet, lingering spring that stayed through June in Oregon. When he had first moved to Portland, he'd asked his girlfriend Molly the same question about the air, acrid on days like this, still and foggy. He repeated to Janie what she'd told him. "It's the smell of Oregon."

"Good Lord, I don't know what the hell I'm doing here."

A short silence and then Charlie said, "It's just frustrating, that's all I feel. Frustration. There's not anything to say."

"It's your own fault."

"I know."

"You have options. It's your own fault for not taking them."

"Yeah."

It was a slow argument, an all-day argument, revisited and abandoned. In one form or another, it had been going on for weeks, since shooting had ground to a bankrupt stop. Neither of them was even sure anymore what the argument was. They didn't know how they'd gotten into it, or when exactly, or how to get out. Just that, at times like this—when they should have been focused on the sensation of slick skin on slick skin—it was the argument they felt, between themselves, intercepting the joy of the moment.

In the wooden editing cell, getting a primer from October. An initial orientation for Charlie, after which he would attend a hands-on course on the subject. October was talking about the audio track, in what seemed to be some incredible level of detail. But only a small part of Charlie's brain, the region devoted to social appropriateness, was listening.

"Far different from Super 8, because you don't have to worry about sound continuity."

The social lobe told his mouth to speak: "Right."

For Charlie, the editing tutorial had the aspect of hypothesis: this is what you'd do if you had a film to edit. The film he did have, which now dominated the other, non-social part of his brain, appeared to be doomed.

He was effectively out of money, but most of the first segment was in the can. Money was an issue, but it probably always would be. The condition of filmmaking. No, the difficulty wasn't in getting film into the can, it was with the film that was already there.

"But that's why you filmed room noise, to pick up ambient sound . . . ."

Nodding.

The film wasn't an abject failure—it was just below average. (Which might have been worse—there would be so much less conflict in abandoning hopeless crap.) It was a failure of successful sculpting. In the abstract—and even in the Super 8—it wasn't a bad film. But the change to 16mm had simultaneously made the film too real and too artificial. In a movie about the artifice of filmmaking, the grainy, muddy Super 8 film stock, like a vision from the quaint past, was a central asset. In living 16mm color, the viewer lacked the visual cue that he was watching commentary. It had lost its coherence. He had selected the wrong block of wood; now the bowl he carved was cracked and leaky.

"You see how it curves there?"

His brain did not respond quickly enough. Now his full attention was on October, looking back at him. "Yeah?"

"Are you all right, Charlie?"

"Yeah, I'm tired, I guess."

"Well, that's really most of it, anyway. You'll get the full picture in class."

"Right. Good."

"Take your footage, though—Chris may use it as the example, and then you'll be editing and learning at the same time."

He nodded. "That would be great, wouldn't it?"

🎬

His eyes instinctively went to the answering machine, hoping to see encouragement from a blinking light. None; Janie had not called. He went to the fridge and retrieved the final beer—an unappetizing Weinhard's Ale left over from a visit from Clay. He cursed the cobbler's poor taste.

From the bedroom he collected all ten extant reels of film. There was a new one from Pinsky, which he left on the desk. He arrayed them chronologically in front of him on the coffee table and then took a drink from the green bottle, beaded with sweat.

Sour. The beer, the look of the film. He took another drink for confirmation. For a moment, he considered pouring the beer over the arranged film stock. But he knew he liked the image of this more than the actuality of it. Perhaps if he had a camera handy to *film* it. . . .

Instead, he left the canisters where they were and went to the sink, into which he poured the remaining beer. He rinsed the bottle, put it on top of the fridge with a growing forest. Each worth a nickel, but it was premature to redeem them yet. He took a short walk to the Kienow's on 14th and found a more suitable libation.

Back in front of the film, box of beer at his feet, he leaned back to dial Janie.

"Hi. Sorry I missed your call—I must be out. Just leave your name and number and I'll get right back to you."

He waited on the line for a beat, then hung up. She knew he had the night off, and there had been talk—but no plan—of getting together. He checked the time—6:23. Not a particularly auspicious sign. After a restorative stout, he'd call back and leave a message.

Five beers and a thirty-minute doze later, he jerked awake to a still, black apartment. Exactly three hours since he left a message. Earlier, after polishing off a beer, he'd placed the empty bottle on a case of film, one each. In the darkness, their glossy surfaces reflected odd bits of light, like a miniature skyline. He reached down for a fresh beer, now lukewarm, and then stood to turn on the light. His first thought, seeing that five canisters remained unbottled, was that he had some work to do. Then he had a different thought.

A trip down old Oti to the recycling nook by the rear door. There, in a cranny between wall and dumpster, were planes of cardboard—boxes broken down—ready to be carried away. They were mostly worse for the wear, but two computer-paper boxes were in fairly neat shape. He selected the more pristine of the two.

Back in his apartment, he perched on the edge of the couch. Like a fruit picker, hands flying, plucking up bottles and film canisters; glass into the honeycombed beer case, film into the newly reconstructed computer box. The film landed in satisfying thuds, the bottles clattered and shook. He paused for a long pull on the stout.

From the bedroom he returned with an armload of film supplies: cables, filters, notebooks, talcum powder (for Lapierre's shiny pate), a Polaroid camera, a ring of Polaroid images, gaffer's tape, and the new reel of film. All but the tape he dumped into the box.

The box came with its own lid, a kind of quarter box that fit on top like a cap. He taped up the lid, then strapped additional lengths on for aesthetics. Then some more. He paused to consider the box. Another long gulp for fortification and a trip to the stereo for accompaniment. Then, to the requiem of Miles Davis, he set about taping the box and lid until it was fully black.

When he finished it, a quarter hour later, he pulled a final length of tape off the roll and sealed up the tomb. He interred it around the corner of his couch, next to the wall.

The telephone rang.

He had just sunk into the couch with a fresh beer, and for the first three rings, he planned to stand and answer it. But at the start of the fourth he changed his mind and waited.

After the fifth ring: "It's me. Got your messages, but I wasn't feeling social. I just had a hot bath and watched a movie. *Sex, Lies, & Videotape*. Pretty good. Anyway, I didn't want you to wonder. I'm going to bed — call me tomorrow."

He groaned. Bed indeed. Put this delightful evening out of its misery. He swayed toward the bathroom, catching sight of the box out of the corner of his eye. After he had brushed his teeth, he put the remaining beer in the fridge, and then stripped nude. Finally, he went back to look at the box. Like him, naked, but not as attractively so. He went to his bedroom and returned with two items: a partially melted skull candle and a framed 5 x 7 Vic had sent some Christmases ago of himself. Markings to identify the grave: death and failure. A bit heavy-handed — possibly even pretentious — but he was drunk and feeling sorry for himself. He grinned grimly.

When he flicked off the light, the yellow pulse of the answering machine blinked at him from across the room.

Reel Three

| 17.

A brilliant morning, the late June dawn pouring through Janie's window. It was the first clear day in six weeks, and some part of her brain, long before waking, recognized the sunshine as soon as it peeked over the horizon and into her window. She came gently to consciousness. Through the window all she could see was a patch of sky, clear blue.

The feeling of warmth and comfort and safety.

She spent a few minutes in half-sleep before the thought of coffee called her out of bed. As the pot was heating in the kitchen, she made two telephone calls. The first to work, to call in sick. The second to Charlie.

She counted fifteen rings before she checked the time—6:24. He was home, just deeply asleep. Eventually he answered, groggily.

"It's me."

"Janie? Everything all right?"

"I can't do it any more."

He knew what she was talking about. He waited on the phone, listening to the pulse in his ear, to her breath. They waited, neither wanting to speak. Thirty seconds, a minute.

Charlie watched the clock flip to 6:25. He broke the silence. "All right."

He could hear her begin to cry. "It's just too hard. I woke up this morning and I didn't feel shitty. It's the first time I haven't woken up feeling shitty in weeks, Charlie. I can't do it anymore."

"I know."

"You're a lovely man, but we're just not having fun anymore."

"It's my fault, I've . . ." He didn't know what to say.

"It just happened. No one's fault." He had a visual image of her hair, mussed from the morning. He could see her sitting in her armchair, a green mug in her left hand. He closed his eyes.

"Maybe I'll feel better later. I'll call you tonight, just to check in." Then she hung up.

After sitting on his bed for a moment, he went to the window and removed his daylight-blocking blanket. The sun was catching the windows of buildings across the river, sending back square fragments of light. Sunlight had a different effect on him, making his head swim, driving out thought and mood. He watched the buildings downtown for a moment, then decided to put the blanket back up. He went to the couch and flipped on the television.

As the hours passed, his head went from swimming to ache, caffeine-deprived. In the mid-afternoon, during a talk show, he began to cry. An unsatisfying, rattling cry that left him hollowed-out and insubstantial. He continued to watch the colors flash on the screen until he noticed the light shafts were no longer coming around the edges of the blanket. Sometime later he relocated to the bed and fell into a deep sleep.

He woke the next day, unrefreshed but restless. He bathed and had a cup of coffee in front of the flashing lights. It was still early; he went to work anyway.

| 18.

Dusk. Four raucous teenagers piled into the cab. Two girls and a boy into the back seat, posturing, faking maturity. The girls managed a late-teen pantomime with bubblegum lipstick, miniskirts, and bare midriffs. Alone, they would pass for 16. But the boys—shiny gangsta denims and baby fat—tipped him off. Fourteen at the most.

Then, with dramatic slowness, a tiny kid in radiant Michigan blue warm-ups slid into the front seat with a rustle. "Go." Charlie panned slowly toward the boy. He had somehow grown the tufts of a faint mustache; his style was accentuated by a gold chain necklace and gold watch dangling on a delicate wrist. He did not return Charlie's gaze, but told him, "I'll tell you where to turn. Go."

Still looking at the boy, waiting. With malevolence, the kid reached into his pocket and produced a baseball-sized roll of cash, outer bill a hundred. He held it up, raised his eyebrows, but continued to look forward. "Two stops and back. I got the cash."

Charlie put the car into drive and started forward, following the boy's instructions. Control, in a cab, amounted to safety. Once lost, it was difficult to regain. This was a tweener.

Among cabbies, the issue of packing was a pressing, if rarely-discussed, concern. Advocates put forth the usual argument: better him than me. Protection, safety, security. All a load of crap, in Charlie's view. With a gun at your temple, what's the use of a .45 under the seat? Three cabbies had been shot in the 18 months he'd been driving, two fatally. All because they were reaching for their piece. But, gun advocates pointed out, those cabbies were irritating bastards, if truth be told, and provoked even the unarmed. Charlie studied the boy's sweats for weaponry, but they were too loose. Which was the intent—keep people guessing.

Commotion rose in the back seat as the youngsters became more comfortable. From quiet sniggers and whispers, they were moving to audible declarations. "Damn it, girl, move your fat ass over there."

"Shut the fuck up. Your skinny ass don't take no seat."

The boy guided Charlie to a parking place on the edge of Peninsular Park, beyond which milled two indistinct forms. The boy slid from the cab, shooting a silencing look into the back seat. As he approached them, the forms drew their shoulders in, began shuffling away. They disappeared behind a shed-sized rhododendron. In the back seat, conversation began again a low buzz of whispers.

The meter ticked off a dollar twenty before the boy returned. The forms did not re-emerge from behind the rhododendron.

Two more stops, voices in the back seat waxing and waning with the movements of the front-seater. The final stop, back at the location where Charlie had first picked them up. The boy pulled off a ten and two singles from his roll, handed them to Charlie without looking at him. Quiet from the back seat as the teens filed out. They walked over the weed lawn to a dirty yellow house, silent as monks. The meter ticked again and Charlie shut it off: $12.

Four p.m., a regular, Mildred White. She was a bristlecone pine of a woman, bent low and twisted, tenacious, lively. She lived in a tiny stone house with a crisp lawn that she herself still clipped. The front door was open—the standing invitation for Charlie to go on in.

"Keep your eye on this one." She was standing in the living room, back to the door, keen ears listening for his feet. "He's a clever one. Good to have at cocktail parties, but I'm not sure about president." On the television, a politician waved.

She started a slow turn, wing out for him to take. "Hello Charlie. What do you think of him?"

"He's no worse than anyone else."

"He's no Franklin Roosevelt." She pronounced the first syllable "rue."

"I guess no one really is."

"No." She looked up at him. "Do you know that I shook his hand?"

"Roosevelt's?"

"That's right."

"I don't believe you."

"Yes I did, and I'll tell you something: he was drunk." Mrs. White stopped. "But a drunk Franklin Roosevelt is twice the man of any of these fellows sober."

Charlie accompanied Mrs. White to the door, holding her elbow. As short as he was, and her head was still below his shoulder. Her hair smelled of roses.

"The lilacs are long done, but my hydrangeas still haven't come around. Catch the door, will you dear?" She was in the yard when he turned back around, scampering toward the cab.

Every Tuesday at 6 p.m., Mrs. White went by taxicab to the grocery store. At seven sharp she appeared back in front of the grocery store, three paper sacks in a cart at her side. Once he took her home, he put the groceries away for her while she made tea. After they had finished the lacy porcelain pot of chamomile, she paid him ten dollars. A routine of several months from which they both derived great pleasure. For Charlie, Mrs. White's muscle and will, coiled and waiting for him. For her? He couldn't imagine.

That day an errant trip to Vancouver delayed him and he didn't make it back until a quarter after seven. She was sitting on a bench, face cocked to catch the gentle June sun. She looked at him with a sleepy eye when he hopped out to get her groceries.

"Sorry I'm late."

"I didn't notice," she fibbed.

She continued to sit in the sun while he loaded her bags into the trunk and on the way home, sat the same way, positioning her face to catch the sun rays at a direct angle.

"Every year I wonder if this will be the last spring I see," she said at an unusually low volume. "I won't miss much of this world, but I will miss sunny days."

He caught sight of her wrinkled, arthritic hand resting on the seat between them and reached out to pat it, feeling that language was insufficient. To his surprise, she caught a hold of his hand and squeezed.

Charlie took his time with the groceries, ignoring the money he was losing as he loitered under the coved ceiling of Mrs. White's kitchen. She seemed sleepy and meditative, so he offered to make the tea as well. She agreed, and went to sit down in the living room. He heard the television come on and, a moment or two later, her voice as she talked back to Peter Jennings.

Later, when they were sitting with their tea, the candidate appeared on the screen again. Mrs. White wrinkled her nose. "Just look at his fat face," she said.

Nights speeding by, connected together by murky half-lit dozes. Each afternoon beginning with the recognition of her absence in the bed next to him. Each night in the cab, skirting the city like a refugee frightened of what awaits him at home. And each morning, hoping sleep would arrive before dawn, before his brain started getting ideas of its own.

At 11 p.m., he was meandering through the curling lanes of Laurelhurst. Here, in the center of the city, an early 20th-century attempt at suburban remove: expanses of hilly emerald lawn dotted by white-pillared neo-Georgian homes, kitschy statuary, luxury cars. Charlie found the address—a relatively tasteful craftsman from which he felt certain an airport-bound fare would emerge. For what other reason would a resident of this neighborhood be requesting a cab after nine?

But he was wrong. An old alcoholic spilled out his order as the door swung open. "I need you to go down to the Hot Spot on Sandy, they have a bottle of scotch." He named a brand, not cheap, not expensive. "Tell him Mr. Hooper sent you and he'll sell it to you for $25."

A fastidious man in elegant clothes of an earlier decade, neatly combed hair, leather house slippers. Behind him Charlie saw a spotless, well-decorated home. But this wasn't a celebratory or mourning bottle. The man stood and spoke with the concentration of someone used to intoxication. Someone whose default mode was tipsy. He was a breed of drunk familiar to cabbies, the one-bottle-a-day men. Judicious use, from the coffee shot in the morning to the nightcap in front of the eleven o'clock news (which Charlie could see flickering on the television). Enough to keep him numb, but not too much to keep him from activities of life — mowing the lawn, paying the bills, buying groceries.

The bar was a two-minute drive. When he arrived, the bartender pulled out the bottle, already bagged, without saying a word. The Blazers were in the middle of a playoff run, but only two men were watching. Porter hoisted up a deep three and canned it. "There you go," said one of the men.

The return trip brought the fare up to just $7.20, but when Charlie started to return the change from the two twenties the man had given him, he waved Charlie off dismissively.

"You wouldn't care for a drink?" he asked.

Charlie, considered it a moment. The man smiled, stepped back, and beckoned Charlie in. "Come on," he said. "Just one."

Early one evening, Charlie at home but on the Heater payroll, awaiting further instructions. He turned on the television, flipped around, turned it off. Picked up the phone and tried Lapierre. Busy. Then Carlos.

"Hey, you're home," Charlie said with mild surprise.

"Charlie?"

"Yeah."

"Where are *you* calling from?"

"I'm home. Heater's Nash is down; I'm on call."

"Ah."

"Just killing some time before I head back over to the Ace High."

The conversation paused for a moment. Carlos knew what Charlie was going to ask next.

"So, you heard from Janie lately?"

That was the question. After a slow, fragmented break-up, Charlie and Janie had quit seeing each other. They hung on for a couple weeks in a half-way state between friends and lovers before finally quitting. Not an arrangement of choice or design, but the natural conclusion of their strange interpersonal disintegration. An accidental momentum, like an unmoored boat floating away from the dock, inch by inch. As a certain point, they could no longer hop back and forth between the gap. Watching, as if from boat and dock, as they each grew smaller and smaller across a growing breach.

But Janie, in slight protest to this momentum, had reached out to Carlos. They had become friends, independent of Charlie. A couple of weeks after the last time she saw Charlie, Janie called Carlos up. To keep a line of connection to Charlie, for human contact. They got together once or twice a week to shoot pool or, occasionally, for a home-cooked meal at Harold and Inez's.

Carlos was surprised to find that Janie was happy to talk about Charlie—she solicited it. She asked how he was doing, what he was up to, if he was all right. And always, even if it was the only thing she asked about, she asked about the movie.

It took a month or so before Charlie and Janie discovered that Carlos was relating their information to the other and then the lines were open. A situation Charlie tried not to abuse. But on nights like this one, sometimes he couldn't stand the ache.

"Yeah, I saw her this weekend."

"How is she?"

"About the same."

"What's she up to?"

"Well, she went out on another date."

"A serious one?"

"No, another one of the guys from work. To 'throw him off her trail' she said."

"So?"

"Seems to me she enjoyed it a little more than she let on."

"I see."

"But it's probably not anything."

"Does she look good?"

"The same."

"Hair?"

"Shorter."

"Smoking?"

"I don't think so."

"Well, okay, I've interrogated you enough."

"You know it's fine."

"What are you up to tomorrow night? Looks like I'll be home early again."

"Game of pool?"

"Why, you in a losing mood?"

"Ha."

Under a snarl of freeway by the train station, a quarter to ten. It was a transitional part of town, initially an industrial pocket with ready access to rail. For reasons obscure to Charlie, it had fallen into disuse. Now the crumbling, red-brick buildings served a variety of provisional uses. Some had become storage units, others were converted to warehouses, others served temporary fringe businesses—telemarketing, junk mail, seasonal storage. Still others were vacant and boarded up. The address Charlie had was in the Briggs Building, lit by a single window on the third floor, absent any obvious non-freight entrance. He honked.

A backlit figure came to the window and waved, and a minute or two later the fare came loping out from behind the building. A fiftyish man with wiry gray hair, flannel shirt, khakis. He got into the back and gave Charlie a North Portland address. As they drove through the peopleless neighborhood, Charlie watched the Briggs diminish in his rear-view mirror. The light was still on.

"So what is that place?" He turned a corner and it vanished.

"My studio."

"Oh really? You're an artist?"

"Animator."

"No kidding. Anything I'd know?"

"Probably not."

"Well." Charlie glanced at the man in his rear view mirror; he was looking back at Charlie. "Try me."

"'Sepsis,' 'Oriental Dragon,' 'Advancing Through the Stages.'"

"'Sepsis,' is that the one where it shows old age like a disease, like an infection?" Charlie had seen it at the animation show at Cinema 21.

The man's face didn't change; Charlie assumed he had the wrong film.

"Yes, that's it." Again, no change, but his eyes stayed on the mirror. "Sepsis" was a dreamlike film with a live-action background and stop-action objects and pictures. It reminded Charlie of the surreal works he'd seen come from Eastern Europe.

"What are you working on now?"

"Oh, mostly commercial stuff. You know pay the bills."

"Mostly?"

The man continued to look at Charlie's eyes in the rear-view mirror. "And a short about a story I concocted." He stopped. After every piece of information the man divulged, he stopped to watch Charlie, who was obliged to nudge him along.

The plot, as Charlie coaxed it out of him, was set in a park on a sunny afternoon. The viewer sees the knees of two people sitting on a bench and in front of them, pigeons gobbling up seeds. The knees on the left, clad in denim, tell the knees on the right, smaller knees, bare, what they described as a gypsy folktale. As the story unfolds, the pigeons fly away and objects on the ground—sticks, rocks, litter, leaves, etc.—animate and act out the events.

By the time the animator was finished with the set-up, they were descending the north side of the St. Johns Bridge. This time, the silence between them lasted only a few seconds before the man continued. Now that he was getting interested in the story, his face was starting to contort along with his narration.

"As the tale draws toward its conclusion, the knees on the left— they're knees of the father telling his daughter the story—explain that as soon as his story ends, life ends. Life is, in fact, the theater of a great invisible storyteller. So then, at the moment the left knees finish this final sentence, all the objects go still—you see, the story is over. The right knees laugh and ask if that's the end of the story, and the left knees say 'Yes.'" The man paused for a moment and waited until Charlie looked up at the rear-view mirror. "And then the film goes to black."

They had been parked in front of the man's house for a while as he finished his story. When he was done, he fished out his wallet and paid the fare.

"What do you think?"

"I think you better keep talking."

Standing in the black of his apartment, just after midnight, home for a quick bite to eat. It had become a ritual of his, to calm himself in the silence of his familiar space amid the deep, velvety shadows of night. As his eyes adjusted to the faint light, the room took on definition: floors and glassy television screen first, reflecting streetlights, then the soft luster of the couch, his bedspread visible through the bedroom door, and objects appearing on surfaces like texture. To his right, a window from the north shone with streetlight—the only direct light he could see.

Charlie felt around to the side of the couch until his hand came into contact with his cardboard film box. In the weeks the box had been parked there, he rarely acknowledged it but felt its presence like a living thing. He brushed the tokens onto the floor, then scooted the box around the side of the couch. He didn't open it, just let it sit between his legs while his hands caressed the surface. At the prospect of opening the box, a knot had formed in his stomach; he took a deep breath.

Eventually he opened the flaps, expecting the box to feel cool inside; it was slightly warmer than the room. The hard plastic on the spools of film was room temperature to the touch.

First he unspooled a few feet of Eight, until he felt the end of the leader. When he held up a frame, he could see that there was an image there, but the light was too weak for him to see what it was. He tried a roll of Sixteen with similar results.

The breakup with Janie and the collapse of his film had left him listless and hazy. Or, alternately, with the knot in his stomach, should something remind him actively of either loss. The Janie pain was deeper and more remote and out of his control. But the film— the pain of his failure there was distinct. He rubbed the smooth edge of the film and felt, for the first time, anticipation.

After awhile, he stood up and turned on the light. Behind the couch was a Mary Shaver—one he'd brought back from Arizona. A piece in tans and brown; a desert landscape. Not the desert of Arizona, but the high desert of Reno, flat and barren. The painting made him feel uneasy, which was one of the reasons he'd brought it back. He liked that it had the power to move him. It was like a sand-colored moon. He smiled.

He went back to the box and exchanged the reel for a notebook. Found a blank page and then began scribbling. It was 2:03.

Late fare, 4:38 a.m. The Logan Building, in the armpit of Southeast Morrison and MLK. A delicate cream-brick structure, vintage 1920, that had stood watching the streets grow wider and fuller with each passing decade. It was dingy from burnt fuel, front door hanging open—a tired, dying place that was the last stop before homelessness.

Charlie felt his pulse quicken as he coasted warily along Morrison. He slowed the car to a crawl, considering whether to stop and pick up the fare or gas it and go look for another. At that moment, he saw a bit of movement in the entryway. He lifted his foot off the brake and let it hover over the gas pedal. And then: a wispy figure on the landing, a young Japanese woman lurking like Welles in the *Third Man*. He reconsidered and put on the brake.

At the top of the stairs, the woman stopped to light a cigarette before she came to the cab. She was a combination of motifs, plastic neon and Sam Spade, in red shoes and striped socks, bleached-blond hair and a felt porkpie hat, shoulders draped with a black trench coat. She ambled slowly to the car and slid in next to him.

A struggle to close the door and then she turned to Charlie holding a letter. She pointed to the address and smiled politely. "Okay?"

"Sure."

The air was dry and warm as he turned off empty Morrison to empty MLK. Seven combined lanes on the two streets and not a single car. The Japanese woman slouched down in the seat and propped her feet up in the nook of the open window. They glided through the sleeping city, inhaling the air, listening to the V-8 rumble. From time to time, she took a drag and then leaned forward to exhale out the window.

As they crossed Fourth and Burnside downtown, two men were scuffling on the corner. There were pushing and shoving and screaming but no real violence. To Charlie this was the usual homeless stand-off; it would end when both men had exhausted their energies, without serious harm. But the young woman sat forward and studied the scene with wide eyes. She followed them as the cab continued down the street, craning her neck and watching until they were out of sight.

She slouched again, propped her feet up. A few blocks later and she pointed to the radio and looked at Charlie. He nodded and she started tuning it. She found an oldies station and stopped on "Got to Get You Into My Life."

"Oh!" she said happily.

From then on, she didn't move. She settled back into a slouch and let her cigarette smolder in her hand. Charlie modulated his speed, trying to time it so that the streetlights reflecting on the windshield flashed with the beat of the music. For the duration of the trip, he felt a strange bond with the young expatriate. He wished they could keep driving around, listening to music, inhaling the incense of tobacco. For brief moments, he felt like a tourist to his own city, able to see the features of the landscape as if they were foreign to him, as if the music were a serendipitous soundtrack to his life, to the adventure of his exploration. As if he wasn't a cab driver, but a fellow traveler, looking out at the mysterious, dark city, wondering what was going to happen next.

| 19.

Back in the black, the clock this time reading 1:21. The same landscape, objects forming the same bumpy skin on surfaces, but the answering machine's light this time a steady red glow. He reclined on the couch and looked out the window to the lights of downtown. Bright enough to stand out in the darkness but, he noted by following the shadows to wall and floor, not enough to illuminate the room. And on the end table near the couch, his answering machine flickering that he had a new message.

"Charles, good evening." It was Ava, tongue thick from gin. "It is time we talk about your film." There was a pause and then a thump of wood on wood he couldn't identify. "Your dead film. Call me tomorrow—at a reasonable hour, please—and we'll discuss it. It's time for you to continue with your work." There was another pause and another thump. Could she be building a fire? "Or, if you wish, you could stop by this evening. I know sometimes you eat your dinner at home. Do not come by after one. Goodbye Charles."

The answering machine beeped and clicked and rewound, so loud in the still he wondered if the neighbors could hear. He stood for a moment before scuttling in a crouch to his bedside, hands out to avoid furniture. The alarm clock read 12:12. He considered. Then he crouch-walked back out of the apartment.

Street lights and porch lights but no lights in the windows of homes on Rosa Linda Drive until he rounded the bend and saw Ava's. Charlie imagined the residents of the neighborhood tucked safely in bed, dreaming happy suburban dreams, unaware of the racy French émigré's late nights, just down the street.

He turned off the ignition and sat a moment, giving the situation a final once-over in his mind. A scenario was playing inside his brain that looked a lot like one of Zale's old sexual noir movies. A modern version, with the strawberry-and-cream Ava Rose now playing the role of experienced seducer. Charlie was the man, about to descend into a shadowy pleasure den while cuts of the innocent Janie—herself sleeping, dreaming of pods—provided the tension and weight of moral corruption. The movie as reality, Charlie helpless to avoid it. He got out of the cab.

"Charles—what a surprise." She didn't seem surprised at all, but Charlie was, upon seeing her fully and pedestrianly clothed in beige slacks and a mauve blouse. "Please come in." She turned away and walked toward the kitchen, leaving him to trail behind. Whatever alcohol he thought he heard in her voice on the message was gone now. He wondered if he had imagined it.

If the Zale Theater was the ice palace, Ava's home was the snow chalet: white carpet of dense pile, white love seat and couch, crystal étagère and glass-topped coffee table offset by dark-stained wood— cabinets and bookcases and end tables—jutting up like rocks off the tundra. The kitchen was also white, separated from the dining room by an island range, dotted on the dining room side by a line of ice cream shoppe stools.

"I'm making tea—I'll put some more water on for you. Please, sit," she said, waving at the stools. "I'm having herbal, but I trust you would like some caffeine, hmm? Some Earl Grey, possibly?"

"No, herbal's fine."

She turned, raised an eyebrow, and offered him one last opportunity to linger on the disintegrating fantasy of illicit seduction. He took it, imagined murmuring "Oh, I'm not working tonight, didn't you know?" and watched the movie play one last time. Then he said, "Yes, herbal, please," and abandoned it.

They made small talk while the water heated, then returned to the living room with steaming mugs of chamomile.

Ava went immediately to the point. "Charles, the film. You've let it languish."

"It was no good."

"It *is* good."

"I've given it up. Anyway, that's not the main issue—I ran out of money."

"Of course you did—it goes without saying. Still, that's no reason. What have you been doing to raise more?"

"Oh, not too much. I've tapped out everyone I know."

"So then?"

"What?"

"How are you raising the money?"

"Saving, I guess."

"Charles." Ava looked into her teacup. She was sitting upright, legs crossed primly.

Charlie followed her lead and looked into his own cup.

"You know, Arturo made money on only one of his films. Of the early period, I mean. Do you know which one that was?"

"*Last Cow.*"

"No, that was one of his more impressive financial failures. His only success was called *Mr. Gorostiza's New Bride.*" Charlie sat silently. "You haven't heard of it?"

He had, but remembered the fact only because it was inscribed on a plaque Ava had erected in Arturo's honor at the Zale. "Not really."

"A concession to one of his principal financiers who wanted a happy story. It was based on a popular escapist novel written during the war. Arturo did his best to give it a heart, but it was a sentimental story and made a poor film. It was his third, just after *Last Cow*. He made three more, all flops."

"That's interesting," Charlie said, disinterested and sleepy.

"Do you know who the biggest director was during that time?"

"No."

"Rafael Espinoza. He made a series of popular films. Lots of music and smiles. A Spanish Capra — but destined for oblivion."

"Hmm."

Ava put her cup in its saucer and leaned forward. "I'm telling you this for a reason, Charles, although I can see it bores you."

"No—"

She held up a hand. "Arturo always told his financiers the same thing: do you want to make money, or do you want to make a film? He never mislead them. He managed to make six good films in his life and one masterpiece. Espinoza is forgotten and the money his financiers made probably helped open a motorcycle dealership or a café. Which is the better legacy?"

She appeared to be done. After a moment, Charlie smiled at her, waiting. She didn't say anything more; instead, stood and took his cup.

"Remember what you're doing, Charles — that's what I am trying to say."

When she returned from the kitchen, he stood. "That's what you wanted to tell me?"

"Yes. It is clear you are languishing—that your film is languishing. There's no excuse for that, Charles." She remained standing, so he stood up, too. "So, you don't like the film you shot. You have another?"

He waggled his head indecisively.

She took this as a yes. "Of course. And have you started work on it?"

"There's nothing to work on."

"Charles, who is going to make your films if you don't?" He understood it to be a rhetorical question. She did not. "Well?"

"No one, obviously."

"Here, take this." She handed him an envelope. It was for 'Taxicab Triptych,' but use it however you wish. Every day, Charles, work every day. You will need to find a way to continue. It's time to stop feeling sorry for yourself."

When he got to the cab, he looked inside. It was a personal check for a thousand dollars. He looked in the direction of her house and recalled his fantasy—distantly, as if it had been someone else's. Instead, he mouthed the words "thank you" to her and tucked the check inside the front cover of a notebook on the seat next to him.

Just before his shift was due to begin, Charlie made a stop at Lapierre's. The days were lengthening into summer, so the day didn't yet seem spent. The late-afternoon sun, even filtered through clouds, still had daytime warmth. Peering through the window on his way to the door, he saw the cobbler cobbling, chatting to Jen, who was sitting on the floor next to him, sipping from a can of soda. He knocked and entered the house, roughly at the same time.

"Hey guys."

Jen clucked disapproval at Clay and he told her, "We have to start locking that door."

Fanned out on the floor were nine shoe soles, all left feet, arranged from smallest to largest. Lapierre was cutting black leather into the shape of footballs.

"Lefts today." He squinted at the footballs. "Are those for toe caps?"

"Good eye." He was making a batch of *poniedzialeks*. "You sure you don't want to give up the cabbie game? I think you might have what it takes to be a shoemaker."

Jen had the script of *House of Games* on her lap. "Your shoemaker days are going to come to an end soon." She snapped the script.

Charlie smiled. "Yeah, shoes are not in your future, Yojimbo. How goes the rehearsal?"

"He's got it nailed," Jen answered, in his stead.

"Good. Hey, I want you to look at something." He pulled out a spiral notebook.

"What is it?"

"Just read it. I'll give you a call tomorrow to talk about it. I gotta go drive now."

"You're not recovering al*ready*?" He tapped the notebook.

"Piss off."

"It's only been three or four months."

"You're a supportive bastard."

"Because I'm not reading anything that's just hypothetical, you know."

"Yeah."

"Good man." Lapierre held up a sole. "You sure you don't want to make shoes? You can drink beer while you work. It's a fringe benefit."

"Pssh. Like that's anything new."

| 20.

Gliding up in front of the Munro's, Harold waving from the porch. "Hey Charlie! How come you never come see us anymore?" He had a nice set of longshoreman lungs; Charlie wondered if he greeted everyone at 50 feet.

"Hey, Mr. Munro."

"Inez misses having you for supper. You too busy for us, now?"

Carlos was living in an apartment above the garage. Charlie figured he'd hear the bellowing, so he ambled up the driveway.

"Ah, you know, weird schedule with the cab driving."

"Hey, come up here." Charlie was still thirty feet away, watching the garage for signs of movement. "Come here, I have something to show you."

Charlie reluctantly went to the porch, but stayed in the yard, on the other side of a row of azaleas. Harold had opened the front door and was swinging it and shutting it quickly, like a bellow. "Can you smell that?"

"Even from the driveway I could smell it." Inez was roasting peppers.

"Can you resist it?" Charlie knew that the Munros could melt an entire evening with irresistible flavors.

"All right, all right, Mr. Munro; I'll come over soon."

"What about Sunday night?" he asked, as Carlos rounded the corner.

"Sunday?"

"What do you think?"

Charlie looked at Carlos, who shrugged.

"Yeah, I think I'm free."

"Good!" Mr. Munro sat back down on a plastic-covered easy chair.

"Where you two headed?"

"Shoot pool," Carlos said.

They were at the cab. "Have fun," he hollered, waving again.

When they came to the corner of 63rd and Yamhill, Charlie turned right. Carlos hadn't anticipated that. "Hey, what are you doing?"

"Change of plans."

"Oh yeah?"

"I want to take you somewhere."

"I'm a hard-working man, buddy. I gotta have my evening pint and trounce you in pool to unwind. It's the system."

"It's all right, there's beer where we're going."

"First round's on you."

"That seems fair."

As they came to the freeway onramp, Carlos asked, "Well, are you going to tell me where we're headed?"

"Dog track."

"Oh *man*. I don't want to go to the dog track."

"You're going to find this interesting." Charlie jockeyed until he was in the left lane on the freeway, and sped up until a pickup blocked the way. "Seriously. I'm trying something tonight and I need someone along for moral support. Look in the glove box."

Inside were fuses, a Thomas Guide, sunglasses, and a racing form.

"This?"

"Right. Now, I'm going to tell you something, but I want you to hear it all before you start tearing into me."

"That's not an auspicious lead-in."

"Okay?"

"It's a gambling scheme, isn't it? I smell Heater."

"Will you cut it out?"

Carlos grinned at Charlie. "First *two* rounds."

"Deal."

"Okay now, look at that eight dog in the first race." Sitting in the parking lot outside the track. He leaned over and pointed at tiny type underneath the dog's name ("Rosey Lady"). "These numbers here show how she did in her last six races. This is her post, and then this number is how many lengths off the lead she was. She looks like a bad dog, right? Look, in the last six she was only in the money twice—and she finished third both times. You see that?"

"Right, I got it."

"But, if you look, you see that she was racing from the outside both times. She's a late starter, and if she's coming from the outside where the traffic's not bad, she catches up in the end. And in this race she's the eight dog."

"She's kind of a long-shot compared to some of these other dogs."

"That's right, which is good. Because if you're going to win the trifecta, you want the long-shots to come in—there's a lot more money in that."

Carlos rolled up the form and thumped Charlie's chest with it. "But this is all pure speculation, right? You've never actually bet on the dogs?"

"No, it's not speculation. I've been handicapping the dogs for a couple weeks now, as if I was going to bet on them. Learning how to handicap."

"Let me guess—you picked all the winners."

"Don't be an asshole—you never win them all. But once I got the hang of it, I only had one losing day. The odds makers say that you'll have losing days. It's in the averages, though. In the end, you come out ahead."

"By odds makers, you mean Heater."

"Well, Heater. But he's not the only one. Let's go in and I'll show you a bunch of guys in there who are regulars. *They* make money at it. Buncha old guys betting their Social Security checks."

"Right. That's why the track's here—to subsidize the pensioners."

"That's good, man. That's why I brought you here. Your keen critical eye."

"I'm critical, all right."

"Anyway, it's pari-mutuel betting. You just win whatever's been bet. The track takes a percentage on the bets. They don't care who wins. It's all these chumps who come down here to bet on one dog to show who are the suckers. They subsidize the pensioners."

"I need a beer."

Twenty to seven and the track was mostly empty, except for the usual retirees hunched over their racing forms with highlighters and calculators, puffs of Swisher Sweet smoke rising. Charlie nodded wisely.

"We'll get a beer and then place the bets before I lose my nerve."

Walking to the betting booth, Carlos observed, "I guess if you're going to blow $1200 at a dog track, I'm pretty happy to witness it."

"That's all I need."

Once he had exchanged his sixteen bills of green for ten slips of white dot-matrix receipts, Charlie felt strangely calm. He was reminded of the time he'd decided to fast. In that case, the longer he fasted, the calmer and less hungry he became, defying expectation. Here too, he was serene and almost disinterested while watching the races. He also observed that he had come to absolute certainty that he was going to lose every race.

Through three races and no winners. Unsurprising, Charlie noted with detachment. After watching two races at the edge of the track, he convinced Carlos to go inside to the second-floor bleachers. Carlos was manic. He returned before the fourth with a fresh beer (his third) and a lighted cigarette.

"You don't smoke."

"I picked it up in grad school. Nice to get out of the library and into the fresh air when you're stressed."

"No need to be stressed—we're going to be all right." Charlie considered this statement. The first race was the closest of the three, but the prize eight dog got bumped out of the gate and was never a factor. Races two and three he had only one dog in the money. He looked back at Carlos, dragging deeply on the cigarette. "Well, *I'll* be all right, anyway."

"Goddamn, man. Twelve hundred is a lot of money. You could buy a lot of film with that."

"Not really."

"Okay, it would take you a long-ass time to save that kind of money." He wheeled around and poked the cigarette at Charlie. "How long *did* it take?"

"Would you settle down?"

A suspicious eyebrow from Carlos: "Where'd you get the money?"

"The betting boxes are now closed," the track announcer blared over the loudspeakers. "Heeerrreee's Rusty!" As the announcer went into the "here's Rusty" wind-up, a metal arm squeaked around the turn in front of the boxes. When it was about flush to them, the doors sprang open and the dogs piled out. Carlos froze.

"What's your dogs? Who do you have?"

"That four, he needs to move up."

"All right! Come on Mister Four! Let's put a little pepper into it!"

Four faded in the first turn. They watched the dogs race down the back stretch, a group of five breaking away. "Anything?"

"Just two in the front group."

"Damn."

When they came across the finish line, Carlos turned away from the track and Charlie. He looked off into the corner of the bleachers, then produced a fresh cigarette, which he lighted off the one burning between his lips. Without looking at Charlie, he lowered the back half of his butt onto the front edge of the seat, settling into a crouch. Snatched the program from Charlie and turned to the fifth race.

He studied it for a moment. "Who do you have?" Charlie handed him the receipt for the fifth.

"Maybe you weren't the right guy to bring. You're making *me* anxious."

"You don't have the one dog. That's the best dog. *Man,* you should have had the one dog."

"I have a system." He gently took the receipt and program away from Carlos. "Besides which, it doesn't matter—the bets are already made." Carlos remained crouched, so Charlie tapped him with the program collegially. "Why don't you tell me about something to take your mind off the dogs. How's Janie doing?"

Coiled and jumpy Carlos went noticeably stiff, straightening his back. He looked at the cigarette in his hand, seemed to find it repellent, and stubbed it out on the cement floor. "Oh, you know, about the same." He stayed rigidly perched. "Fine."

Charlie watched to see if he'd do anything more. He didn't. "You shouldn't pursue a life of crime."

"What?"

"Who's she seeing?"

"Oh man." Having already pivoted unnaturally on his tailbone to look back at Charlie, Carlos now slid back in the chair. "I don't know his name." Outside, the tuxedoed trumpet player blew a merry tune. They sat silently until he finished, eyes forward. "You know, I knew you were going to ask about her sometime tonight. I think that was actually the main reason I'm so jumpy."

"It must be more serious, not just some guy from work."

"I think so. We haven't talked in a couple weeks. I think she's embarrassed."

"It was bound to happen."

"Yeah."

"I knew you'd give me this news sooner or later."

"Yeah."

His calm mood seemed to detach itself and float like clouds at the top of his head. As he sat, digesting the news, it gathered substance, leadened, and sank down to his belly. They watched the full greyhound procession, down one side of the track and back up to the blocks. When they were loading the dogs in, he said, "Damn."

He sat forward and a moment later the dogs were into the first stretch.

"Wait a minute. Who do you have in this one?"

"That first pack of four dogs — they're all mine."

"I thought so!"

"Holy shit." Carlos jumped up. "Go, you little bastards. Hang on!"

The pack led wire to wire, jockeying all the way for position. It was the kind of close race that brought people to their feet, got them screaming out numbers and names.

As they came down the final stretch, the crowd's volume picked up, reaching a peak as the dogs crossed the finish in a tight pack. "You fucking *did* it. You won!"

Charlie was still sitting. "Let's see what they pay."

"Let me see your ticket — I don't believe it."

There was a photo finish for place. Track officials studied tape. Carlos studied the ticket. The crowd studied the board and debated.

"Look at that. Either way, you're good to go."

"Yep. Let's see what it pays."

Across the track, the big board flashed numbers as the announcer spoke. Cheers and groans rippled through the crowd. The sun was just at the horizon, shining directly back in the squinting eyes of the bettors. They were a week from the longest day of the year. And, next to the word trifecta: $1280.

Charlie stood and clapped Carlos' back. "Life is a funny thing."

"You got that right."

They looked at each other, smiling different smiles. Carlos, the smile of a man who can't quite figure out the magic trick, but appreciates it. Charlie, the smile of someone who realizes how quickly moods change, how events are experienced through such dense filters.

"Come on, I'll buy you a beer," he said.

| 21.

He was picking up the smallest touch of feedback. Imperceptible without the headphones, but it might be audible on the soundtrack. To October, standing across the ballroom, he signed "stop" with the palm of his hand. Elegantly draped shoulders sagged and then eyes fixed on him as he sprinted to the quartet's amplifier.

While he re-checked the sound, October directed. "Okay folks, let's do it like we did in rehearsal." Charlie gave the all-clear. "Everybody ready? Places." Backs stiffened, chins rose, arms embraced. Dozens of pairs of dancers, in tuxedoes and gowns, awaited the cue. Once she was satisfied with the set, she looked back at Charlie. "Sound."

He started the recorder. "Speed," he called back.

She nodded to the center of the floor. "Cameras," she said, waiting a beat for them to begin rolling. Then, "Action!" The quartet began a waltz and after a few bars, the dancers started spinning, an action as inscrutable to Charlie as the movements of schools of fish.

The production was October's, a feature. A well-financed film by indie standards, meaning that she was actually paying her crew. His intent to repay her by working as the sound man therefore somewhat stymied. She had arranged for financing, but then before production decided to shoot on digital video, an emerging technology among indie directors. It flattened the image and cheapened it with gaudy, superficial glint, but he couldn't argue the financials—October was saving fifty grand on film stock alone. The savings she dumped back into the production, inadvertently robbing Charlie of his generosity. Neither minded too much.

The dancers twirled, obscuring a central couple whom Charlie could hear in his headphones. Circling the dancers were two cameras, just beyond a central column of light. The tiny electronic cameras rode on metal arms operated by crab-walking cameramen. They seemed preposterously small to Charlie, tiny, underpowered, the size of his Super 8.

If Charlie had been shooting the scene, he'd have had to do it in just a few takes—dialogue track, music track, close-ups, crowd shots, and establishing shots. No more than two or three takes on each element, and even then, it would be an expensive scene. But October spent all day in the ballroom, shooting several takes at every distance, every angle. She had four cameras on the set, and each probably had an hour or more of footage. They could even watch the footage on-set, on a monitor October had brought for that very purpose. He marveled.

After a nine-hour shoot, cast and crew retired at the Shanghai (Charlie's suggestion).

"So what do you think *now*, Chuck?" October hoisted a tumbler of bourbon. "My DV's looking pretty sweet, huh?"

"Looking sweet is the one thing it's not doing." She continued to smile victoriously. "I'll admit to a few other virtues, though."

"You're just a sour old-school celluloid-head."

"It's the wave of the past."

"Ah, you're just not used to DV. It looks different, but it can do some things film can't do, too."

"I'll see how it turns out before I trade in my Arri."

"That's the Institute's Arri." She clapped him on the back and winked.

In the months since "Taxicab Triptych" had ground to a stop, Charlie had spent more time working on other filmmakers' projects. In that time, he had met even more of Portland's extended film community, most of whom were in the bar with him. Doing sound for October was a rare opportunity to actually get paid—working on film and funding your own, an unbeatable combination. He saw Andrea, Amy, David, and Tony from his own shoots, Russ Washington and Julia Cook, a kid named Tyler. Even Buddy Holly.

Eliza Park, a director notorious for her shocking, sex-charged shorts, settled into October's vacated seat next to him at the bar. She was still in costume—a beaded, off-the-shoulder gown in eggshell.

It looked almost suburban, which was an inside joke for those who knew her customary wardrobe—fatigues and combat boots, black eyeliner, and hair that changed color weekly.

Charlie cocked an eyebrow. "Frilly."

She hopped off the barstool and curtsied. "Don't I look respectable?"

"I believe so."

"You were the only one who could hear Lynn and Joe"—the leads—"how'd they do?"

"They sounded pretty good. Joe doesn't have much range—but he doesn't have much of a role, either. Lynn sounded good, but you really have to be able to see her face to know."

"Cool."

They discussed the shoot for a few minutes, talked about DV (Eliza was all for it), then ordered another round.

"So I'm planning to shoot a project on AIDS."

He nodded. Sounded like a good fit. "You need a sound guy?"

"Actually, I was wondering if you'd do some acting." She paused to gauge his reaction, which was a wince. "It's a small part," she added, hopefully.

"I don't like to act. I'm no good." He attempted a compliment by way of appeasement. "Like you."

"It's an easy role. I need skinny guys to play AIDS victims."

"Easy?"

"Well, there's almost no dialogue."

"I don't know."

"Come on—how often do you get the chance to play a gay man dying of AIDS?"

"It's true, but what if I get typecast?"

She kicked his stool's leg. "Will you at least think about it?"

Over the course of the evening, a good quarter of the filmmakers approached him for various work. He told them the same thing he told Eliza. "Give me a call when you know your schedule."

She smiled, clinked his glass with her gin and tonic. "To successful projects." Then, as she turned to go, she stopped. "Hey, how are things going with your work?"

He shrugged. "Pretty good."

"You have anything going on?"

"Oh, you know—a little of this, a little of that."

"Cool. Well, holler if I can help you out."

"Will do."

A soft creak, pause, and metallic report. Booth making the afternoon mail delivery. This time a single envelope, which Charlie retrieved sleepily, a few minutes later. He recognized the logo, and also the familiar prose.

> Dear Mr. Depaulo,
> Hello Charles, we are sending you this brief reminder that it's time again to submit films for the Portland Film Festival. As an exciting young filmmaker, you . . .

He dropped it on the coffee table and went to the blanket, draped across the window. From outside, a dingy September spilled weakly into the room. He flicked on lights as he went from bathroom to kitchen, yellowing up the dim apartment. Against his strong wish, he'd become an espresso-shop addict. Unable to drink the sour tinned coffee, he was now compelled to buy the good stuff at four times the cost. Clay chided him, asking where his gas-station blend had gone. With a yawn, he dumped out yesterday's grounds and tapped a pile of Mexican Altura into a fresh filter.

He showered, poured out a second cup, and went to the couch. There he reclined for a few minutes before he picked up the phone.

"Hi Vic, it's me. How you doing?"

"Who is this? Is this a prank call?"

"You never get tired of that one, do you?"

"Charlie! How the hell are you doing? I've used that one before? Really?"

"A couple times."

"So what's going on there? What's the weather like?"

"Back to the rain. Not cold yet, though."

"Ha! You oughta come down. It's magnificent: sunny, eighty degrees. Cool mornings, balcony-sitting evenings. Best time of year."

"It's funny you mention that. I actually want you to come up here."

"Now? Why didn't you invite me a couple of months ago when it was the bellows of hell here?"

"That would have been better planning. But I'm inviting you now."

"Well hell, why don't you come down? I'm serious—it's perfect here. If it's money, I'll fly you down; that's no problem."

"No, it's not money. I want you to visit me. It's been years."

"Oh come on, not that long."

"You've been here twice in five years. I'm calling in my marker."

There was a momentary pause, but shorter than Charlie expected. "Five years—really? Well, I guess it's time."

"Good."

"When did you have in mind?"

"I don't know—whenever. I'm scheduled to take off a whole weekend at the end of the month. How about that?"

Vic got his calendar and they coordinated. The weekend Charlie suggested was fine.

"Are you going to stay with me?"

"Don't you still live in that little apartment?"

"Yeah."

"I'll stay at a hotel."

"It's not bad—there's plenty of room."

"Nah, you're a young guy—you want your privacy, anyway."

"Suit yourself."

The conversation wound down and they said goodbye. Charlie got up and poured himself another cup of coffee. He stood in the kitchen and considered the mound of dishes that pushed up out of the sink—at a point very soon, the collection would grow unstable. After two sips of coffee, he poured out the rest and balanced the cup on top of the pile.

Good for one more day.

22.

The first time he drove by, he slowed to a creep as he passed. About eight on a week night, but no one was home.

Two days and two hours later, he made a second pass. This time the cab came to a full stop; he scooted over to the middle of the seat to have a better look. All the lights in her apartment were on. He studied the windows for some visible sign of change, but he could detect not a single difference. The sameness of her building put him in a slightly disembodied mood, as if he might just knock on the door and forget the past four months. He couldn't envision another man sitting in her red living room. The color was her rebellion against the monochrome city; Charlie felt like a partner there. If she had a new boyfriend, was the rebellion over? He watched for a few more minutes. No bodies passed before the windows. He could see no movement at all.

In the days before Vic arrived, Charlie fretted. He found this unusual. Their relationship had a certain quality of unease that he always attributed to his stepfather. Vic played the heavy—it was Vic's life, Vic's city, Vic's personality that drove their interaction. Yet confronted with the prospect of having to entertain, he saw that this cut the other way, too. His life and his city suddenly seemed the object of judgment.

"What's the itinerary?" Clay, working a chicken drumstick.

"It's up in the air. The only thing we've set so far is Monday — everything else is fluid." In front of Charlie, a hamburger, untouched. "I have about fifty things prepared — fifty potentials. I'm just going to have to play it by ear." He took a bite of the burger, sending the patty, tomato, and onion halfway out the back of the bun. Chewing, tamping it back together like a deck of cards. "For example, he gets in at 8:30, which puts us in the car at nine, nine-fifteen. He may be hungry, or he may already have eaten; could go either way. So I have two options ready."

"Um-hmm."

"I was thinking maybe to get you and Carlos out with him one night. Shoot some pool, meet each other."

Lapierre finished the leg and set about cleaning his fingers on an inadequate tissue-y napkin. "He knows how to play pool? I always thought of him as more upscale. Golf, that kind of thing."

"He is, but I think he'll like it. He met my mother at a bar in Reno." Charlie took another bite of the burger, then tamped it together again. "Quite a bit like Heater's place, actually."

"You're not taking him to Heater's?"

"No."

"Good man." The napkin, a greasy foosball, he tucked under the edge of his plate. "Man, that's a shitty napkin." His fingers still glistened. "I'm assuming Heater hasn't made it into conversation?"

"He has, in fact. But nonspecifically."

"Gambling."

"No." Charlie put the burger aside and started in on the fries. "So what do you think? You up for some pool?"

"Absolutely. It would be great to finally meet the guy. Find out if he's really as bad as all that."

"He's a perfectly good guy. I mean, to meet in a bar. You'll like him."

"Yeah?"

"And besides, you don't know how bad you come off in the stories I tell to him."

Charlie did a final clean on the apartment. Two days early. Booth's ancient Hoover he eschewed in favor of a supermarket steam cleaner. Cobwebs out of corners, stove drip-plates scrubbed, even the windows a futile clean (it rained within 12 hours). As a final touch, he hung up two more of Mary's paintings. A 36-inch square in terra cotta and ochre of the Red Spot. In this painting, the tavern had been relocated and placed at the side of a pitted highway in some desolate location. Charlie assumed that she had fused the Red Spot and the Bar X Bar in the painting. The second, just 8" by 16", a landscape in bruised purples and yellows and blacks. A late-afternoon thunderstorm. He liked it because it approximated the aspect ratio of a movie screen.

After he had completed the work, he went back through for a final examination. Not bad. Move Vic quickly into the building and inside his apartment before he sees one of the residents and he might even admire it.

He got a beer and sat down amid his cleanliness.

The scene at the airport was like Charlie's many arrivals in Phoenix, but in reverse. This time Vic came boiling out into the concourse, nearly running down a couple who had stopped to embrace.

"Charlie!" The couple dodged and frowned. Charlie waited while Vic wove his way forward.

"Welcome to beautiful Portland—" Charlie started to sweep his arm up at the glass ceiling, beyond which rain clouds loomed, but as he brought his hand out, Vic grabbed it and started shaking. The left hand thumped his back. "—today's cloud cover is a delicate skin, luminous from the lights of the city."

"Did you practice that?" A step back, not releasing Charlie, slowly starting to drag him down the concourse.

"Yeah. I knew you'd complain."

"Complain? In this weather—hell no! Why, it reminds me of Belfast; how could I complain?"

"I think you'll pull through. It's not Scottsdale, but it's not Moscow, either."

By now they were into the concourse, Vic gripping Charlie's elbow, a two-man racewalk, picking up speed.

Charlie advised Vic to pick up his rental downtown, rather than at the airport. For the complete cabbie experience. He regretted that it was parked in the lot; he'd have loved to pull it forward from the cab queue, but there was no way to engineer such a thing.

At the car, he tried to play it up, anyway. "Headed downtown, sir?"

"You're not going to make me ride in the back seat, are you?"

"No. I don't even make my regular fares ride in the back seat. But if you prefer the Full Monty, you can ride back there." Vic had two garment bags, which Charlie hung in the back seat.

"Trunk's a bit grimier. I'll just put these here." Then he opened the front passenger door. "Well?"

Vic looked briefly around the inside of the cab, his eyebrows a straight line. Then, pulling out of the parking structure into one of several converging asphalt streams, he looked out. The sky was strangely bright from the city lights; an orange-tinted bowl. The air was crisp—not a note of the acrid chemicals from the paper mill up river. The grass was back to emerald after a summer of drying and browning, and the thick bushes and trees had just started to color. At the edge of seasonal death, but the city looked fecund and lush.

"So what about food? Did you get to eat?"

Vic had discovered Charlie's cabbie ID. He was fingering it, right eyebrow finally rising. "No, I'm starved."

"You want to eat first or go to the hotel to drop off your luggage?"

"This is amazing, son. This cab of yours." Charlie looked at his stepfather. He still had the ID in one hand, and he was poking at the radio with the other. Rarely had Charlie ever seen him in a moment of discovery—to him, Vic was always the expert. "What's that? Food or hotel? I don't care." The radio crackled with Mike's voice. He grinned. "Actually, let's eat."

"What are you in the mood for?"

"Whatcha got? Is it all tofu and lentils here? I could do lentils."

"Nah, we're not doing lentils. I thought I'd take you to Jake's. It's a landmark—been there a hundred years. They do steak or seafood."

"Great."

The freeway in from the airport was a chute of concrete, descending downward a deeper and deeper canyon until it split just at the edge of the river. Banking south after Lloyd Center, it rose up on elevated stanchions to reveal the glittering downtown skyline.

"There you go: Portland."

Vic watched the city approach as the freeway dropped them off onto the Morrison Bridge. As they crossed the river, he said, with eyebrows rising, "I don't remember it being this big. It looks like a city."

On the way through downtown, Charlie pointed out the sights. "The freeway used to be on this side of the river." He indicated the green ribbon between the river and buildings of the city. "But they ripped it out in the 70s and put in Waterfront Park."

"Nice."

A few blocks later: "If you look up a couple streets on your left, you can see Pioneer Courthouse Square. It's an open block we call our 'living room.'"

"It's a nice downtown. Clean." He looked out his window and up. "And compact. The blocks are really small, aren't they?"

Jake's was still buzzing when they got there at nine. Vic stopped before they went in and sampled the air. "I remember this smell. What is it?"

Charlie pointed to an industrial orange-brick building two blocks north. The Blitz-Weinhard brewery. "Boiling beer."

"Oh right. They brew beer often?"

"All the time. It's the smell of the city."

Although he was more turf than surf, Vic had the salmon. On the issue of alcohol, he was more recalcitrant.

"You don't want a scotch. You can get that anywhere."

"I don't want a beer."

"It's the best beer in the country."

"If Portland made the best saltines in the country, I'd still want a scotch."

"A pint."

The waitress watched this play out with growing interest.

"Let me consider it while I have a scotch."

"Now you're talking."

While Vic drank his drink (rather leisurely, Charlie observed), they talked about the plane ride and Vic's hotel. After he (finally) polished off his drink, Charlie successfully cajoled him into a pale ale. Decided: "It's not bad. For beer." Then he got the update on the family casino development (remained promising), golf (finally starting to cool down enough to play), and a development in Vic's love life (tentative, slow).

About the time he finished the salmon, Vic took a last swallow of beer and hailed the waitress.

"It wasn't bad, really."

"I didn't say anything."

They both smiled. "Say, when do I get to meet Janie?"

"Ah, yeah. We broke up."

"What? Really?"

"Yes."

"That's too bad, I was looking forward to meeting her." He held up his glass. "Sometimes that happens."

Charlie liked this about Vic: his neutrality extended to subjects Charlie didn't want to discuss as readily as to those he did. "Speaking of meeting folks, I was thinking of taking you out with a couple friends."

"You're the boss."

"Maybe shoot some pool. Didn't you used to shoot pool in Reno?"

"Oh, a little bit. It's been a long time."

"Good. Maybe I'll beat you, then."

"Sure." Here his eyebrows widened in false innocence.

After they ate, Charlie suggested a walk back to Vic's hotel. "It's a few blocks away, but your luggage is pretty light. Nice night."

Along the stroll, he noticed that Vic was uncharacteristically quiet. Conversations were allowed to lapse. As they walked up Yamhill, Vic's shoes tapped on the sidewalk—for long moments they were the only noise either man made. Vic studied the buildings and storefronts, slowing or stopping when he found something interesting. Conversation came when Charlie pointed out something or Vic had a question. Then tap tap tap tap.

At the hotel, a doorman offered to take the garment bags.

"Why don't I let you go here. You can get checked in and have some time."

"All right."

"I'll give you a call in the morning. We can coordinate."

"I'll probably sleep in a little. Vacation, you know."

"Of course. I won't call early." Under the yellow lights, Vic's tanned skin seemed dark against his shirt. A couple went into the hotel, scanning him for a moment as they passed by. It occurred to Charlie that they might take Vic for a European—an Italian or Greek. He was dressed in natty white slacks and a cream linen shirt. Definitely not an Oregonian.

"I'm glad you invited me up, Charlie. Good to see you in your natural environment."

"I'm glad you're here, too."

"All right, then. Have a good night."

"You too, Vic."

Ten-thirty and the VMC was a lively place. A green station wagon was double parked on 13th Avenue, attended by a knot of admirers who flanked both sides of the car. Darlene, of apartment 309, was leaning against the back door watching the street scene and smoking a long brown cigarette. Generally, when he got off work the building was dark and silent, but now most of the windows were lit with the flickering light of television sets.

Charlie was also lively, it being only midafternoon his time. From the fridge he pulled out one of three stouts, pondering whether he should run to the store for more. Possibly. He'd drink one and see how he felt. He wandered out to the balcony to watch the station wagon party in the interim. The voices of the people were perfectly clear in the warm evening air.

"The other station." A man on the far side of the car was leaning through the passenger-side window.

"This is it," said the driver.

"No, this is the oldies station. Go up the dial."

"I'd get a cassette player," offered the man next to him.

A side conversation started between two men on the driver's side.

"Earl Scheib'll do it for $99."

"Doesn't need it."

"No rust?"

"That's what he says."

"Well, the paint's dull."

"He shouldn't waste his money on that. There's no rust. I'd get a cassette player."

Charlie listened for a few minutes, then went back inside. He flipped through the stations on the TV and shut it off. Went for another bottle of beer, paused again, then sat down.

The image of Vic stopping to look at a granite lintel came to his mind. Vic, silent, interested — a new Vic. He took a drink of his beer and considered his stepfather.

Vic stayed for four days. He picked up his rental car and spent the mornings exploring the city. On his first evening, Vic joined Charlie and his friends for a game of pool.

As he had with Charlie the night before, Vic took a back-seat role, letting the younger men drive conversation. He was relaxed and comfortable, and joked with Carlos and Clay.

"All right, Clay has a girlfriend, so what about you, Carlos?"

"Not at the moment."

"Not at the moment."

"No." They were leaning against the wall. Vic rattled a cube in his empty cup; Carlos took a sip of beer. Grinned at him.

"Holding out?"

"That's right."

"Biding your time." He nudged Carlos with an elbow and winked. "Yup, that's how I used to think about it, too."

They played three games of eight ball, and then had to try to defend the table when a couple of regulars tucked a quarter under the rail.

Clay tapped in the final ball, winning game three. "All right, who's playing? I won with Vic and Charlie, so I'm in. Who wants to play with me?"

"Vic and Carlos won the other game," Charlie said. "What do you think old man; you up for defending the table?"

Vic took a cue from Charlie and started chalking it. "I was defending tables when you were still eatin' pretzels off the floor, junior. I'm in." They won the game easily, Vic tapping in the eight after a difficult bank of the 12-ball. He smiled gently at Charlie, letting his eyebrows do the gloating with a wiggle.

The next day Charlie took Vic around town, alternating between sights of the city and of his life. Surprisingly, Vic seemed as interested in the cab stand as the rose test garden; in the wooden editing room as in the labyrinths of Powell's Bookstore. The evening following that, they went to a showing of *House of Cards*.

On his final full day, Vic toured the wine country in Yamhill County. Charlie had arranged to rendezvous with him around five for an early meal before taking him to one last place.

While Vic was sampling Pinot Noir in Gaston, Charlie dropped by Lapierre's. Two by the Caprice's dashboard time.

"Either Vic's on his best behavior, or you've been pulling my leg for five years." He was cobbling in the living room, another fan of shoes in front of him. This time brown oxfords, lefts again. He was drinking a Rainier.

"I don't know this guy. He's a different man."

"Well, he's a pretty cool man, if you want to know the truth."

"No kidding. Maybe it's the climate. This guy wouldn't have been a half-bad father."

"Neither one of you is dead yet."

Charlie sat next to him on the floor and took a drink from Clay's beer.

"Help yourself."

"Do you ever make rights?"

"You probably didn't know this, but the left shoe is actually the 'gateway' shoe. First you get 'em hooked on it, then you sell 'em the right. At a big mark-up."

Charlie reclined on a heap of leather scraps, smiling at the joke. He picked up a piece from the fan Lapierre had started and studied the work.

"So how's it going? You're having a good time?" Lapierre asked.

"I am. It's been nice to have him in town. He's actually been interested in what I do."

"Did you take him to the Film Institute?"

"Yeah. I showed him around, introduced him to October."

"Huh." He took the beer back from Charlie and took a drink. Put it back down on the other side of his body, away from Charlie. "How about tonight?"

"I think it'll be cool. Especially with the mood he's in."

Charlie watched as he cut out a strange piece that looked like half a butterfly. When he'd finished cutting a perfect mirror opposite, he took a long drink from the bottle, depositing it near Charlie. There were only a couple swallows left. "After you finish that beer, what say you go fetch me another?"

"I'm not thrilled about it." Charlie took a drink and put the beer down next to Lapierre. Then he stood and went to the door.

"Hey, what about a fresh beer?"

Charlie pointed at the bottle. "You're not done with that one. I left you a swallow."

The final meal was on Charlie, at his own request. Rainbow Thai, at 32nd and Belmont. Partly because of the location—just down the street from the Zale—but mostly because Vic had never had Thai food.

He was skeptical, but Charlie cajoled him. "I am willing to bet money that you'll love it."

"Love it?"

"That's right. Love, not like—it's that good."

"Sold."

A converted house, the dining area was split between three rooms. They were seated in what was formerly a bedroom.

"You know how I said Portland's not really a city?"

"Yeah."

"I'm reconsidering. I've been in Phoenix so long I've forgotten what neighborhoods feel like. Old homes, a downtown. Portland's got all that, it's just small. It's like a miniature city."

"It's funny, because it also feels like a small town—the people, I guess," Charlie said.

"True, both."

Charlie was working on a mild Pad Thai, but Vic had gone for a spicy green curry, despite the waitress's warning. "Very hot," she had told him.

He brushed her off. "I like hot. Hot's good." Then to Charlie. "She doesn't know I live next to Mexico; thinks I'm like one of you palefaces."

"It's different than Mexican."

"Pah."

A few bites in, and Charlie could see it was hitting him pretty hard. Vic took the cloth napkin from his lap and sopped his sweating forehead.

"I told you."

"What, this? Hell, this is just medium spicy." He took another bite. "I love it."

The Zale, as always, looked dingy and small. Two of the lights were burned out in the marquee, leaving Marilyn Monroe's surname dim. A double showing: *Some Like it Hot* and *The Seven Year Itch*, both, Charlie knew, from her private collection. For a reason he couldn't divine, Ava loved Marilyn.

As they approached, Vic squinted. "So this is the famous Zale Theater. It doesn't look like much."

Charlie, recalling Molly, advised, "Just wait."

A fair queue by Zale standards—11 people. Vic started for the twelfth position, but Charlie caught him by the elbow and guided him toward the door. "I gotcha covered."

To their left, unnoticed, the notebook paper with pink marker. But on the door as they entered, a sign Vic couldn't miss. In typeface, on a wide slit of paper: "Local films screening tonight, 7 p.m.—regular schedule to resume tomorrow. Price: $3."

"Wait a second. What do you have going on?" Vic's right eyebrow climbed his forehead; Charlie nodded to the door.

Vic was surprised enough by his stepson's subterfuge that he didn't immediately notice the theater. As Charlie whisked him through the foyer and into the theater, he was trying to find an indication of what he was about to watch. In the center section were several blocks of reserved seating, each marked with colored ribbon. Charlie guided him to the black section where he saw Carlos and Clay and another twenty people he did not recognize.

Their arrival caused a restrained commotion—a smattering of applause and low cheers that set off a chain of high whispers. Charlie sat Vic next to Carlos, then introduced him to a few people in the section. Some of the names he had heard, most he had not. The woman sitting on the other side of Clay was Janie Prescott. She stood up and offered her hand. A very firm shake.

"So what the hell's going on here?" he whispered to Carlos.

"Surprise."

"You're in on it?"

"I knew he wasn't telling you anything."

"Did he tell you anything?"

Carlos watched Vic's face for a moment, smiling. "I'm in on it."

Vic sat back down and digested things. For the first time, he looked around the theater. To accommodate the chatty event crowd, Ava had the lights on as bright as they would go, diminishing somewhat the frosty effect. Vic was nevertheless impressed. He leaned over to Carlos. "This is quite a place. I'd hate to try to keep it clean."

"No kidding. Somehow she does."

After a few minutes, Charlie returned with a woman dressed in black slacks and a white silk blouse. Vic didn't need an introduction. He stood to greet her.

"You must be Ava."

"Yes. I'm pleased to meet you, Mr. di Paulo."

"You caught me by surprise here. Charlie made it sound like an off-hand decision to stop by."

"Charles is an inventive young man."

"I think it's more than that."

"Yes."

"I'm looking forward to it—whatever 'it' is."

"Yes, and thank you so much for coming. I believe you'll enjoy it." She offered her hand—softer shake, softer skin than Janie's.

"Thank you for introducing yourself. I've heard a lot about you."

Ava paused for a moment, touched Charlie on the shoulder, and started to scoot out into the aisle. "Yes, I've heard quite a lot about you, too."

For the next few minutes, people filed into the theater and found their seats. At just after seven, Ava appeared at the front of the theater. She picked up a microphone from the stage, but stayed down on the floor level. "Good evening. Please, take your seats. Thank you." Charlie slid into the seat next to Vic. "Thank you and good evening. Tonight we have three films to screen for you, two dramas and a documentary. I believe it will be an enjoyable experience." The crowd, apparently used to Ava's locution, offered polite applause.

"The first film is called "Red Fort," by a director well-known to many of you here: Russell Washington. In the film, Mr. Washington examines the state of historic preservation in one of the world's most historic countries, India."

"Our second film is by a newcomer, Julia Cook. It is just three minutes long, but I think you'll agree that the time is well used. Miss Cook calls the film 'Sparks.'"

"Finally, Charles di Paulo has a short film he'd like to share with us called 'The Puddle Variations.' Some of you saw a rough cut of this film a few weeks back, so you are no doubt as anxious as I to learn what Mr. di Paulo has done. Will you please give them a hand? Thank you."

Vic leaned over. "Charles?"

The first film was a slightly tedious documentary, though Vic thought it looked professional. He had seen few documentaries, however, and he wondered if they were all tedious. The crowd appreciated it, and the images of India were fascinating, at least. "Sparks" was a strange concept piece he couldn't understand. It seemed hip and young, like something MTV might show.

After the end of each film, they sat in a murmuring theater while a projectionist cued the next one. Waiting in the dark after "Sparks," Vic found that he was anxious. He hoped that the film would be good, that he would understand it well enough to offer a plausible compliment to Charlie. He hoped that if it was good, Charlie wouldn't resent his failure to invest in it. And also, he noted with surprise, he was anxious about what the crowd would think. He hoped they would love it.

The opening shot was an arabesque of gold and black—a beautiful image, but Vic couldn't identify what he was looking at. The shot held for a few moments, long enough for his consciousness to become aware of sound trickling into the theater. A truck's rumble, distant voices, footsteps on the floor above them. The image began to widen slowly, moving left as the camera drew back. The arabesque became a border and then a frame: a painting. For a moment he was confused—this wasn't a movie about a cab driver. When he could see enough of the winter palette of blacks and blues, he recognized the roiling strokes as Mary Shaver's.

He reflexively glanced at Charlie in the dark and whispered, "What the hell *is* this?"

"Shhh. Watch."

The camera zoomed out to reveal a wall hung with Shavers, all fitted together like cobblestones. As the frame roamed across the wall, the sound of a radio came in from the left, a low, atmospheric tune. Eventually the camera pulled back far enough to reveal a figure seated in front of an easel, painting. Behind him, a score or more of paintings. Vic smiled—it was a great image.

The shot was filmed almost in profile, but with the painting tilted just out of the camera's sight line. The painter was played by Clay, but Vic saw instantly that the posture was Mary Shaver's. She always painted hunched over, with her face very near the canvas. The film cut to a tight close up of the painter's face. His eyes were focused in sharp attention, his brows furrowed just slightly in the space above his nose. But the rest of his face—mouth, cheeks, forehead—were relaxed. Vic used to marvel at this same look on his wife's face—intense but serene.

The camera cut to an extreme close-up of one of the paintings on the wall, a patch probably no wider than a couple inches. At that distance, the canvas lost coherence. It was a jumble of textures and random color. The film then cut back to the painter, now in a slightly wider close-up. Vic was struck by how cleverly Charlie had used sound in this essentially static scene. The music had ended, and again random sounds drifted in and out. A telephone, more traffic noise, the creak of the stool, a slow exhalation, the drone of a plane. Somehow, these sounds kept the narrative intact.

The film cut back and forth between an ever-widening shot of painter and painting, held together by the continuity of sound. After several cuts, the painting began to come into focus; the viewer had a sense of the smaller components that now blended together to form the whole. The artist stood up and studied his work, and this time the camera showed the full painting.

Another Mary Shaver, and Vic realized why the film's title had seemed familiar to him. The lens revealed a barren landscape—a low-profile perspective with a dirt road in the foreground. The gray of the road was a lighter shade than the sage hills, tinged with purple, that rolled out toward the dark horizon of the charcoal sky. 'The Puddle Variations' were a landscape series Mary had done that were connected only by a single element—a puddle. The desert floor after a storm, the flat, black-tarred roof of a vast industrial building, a patio of bricks. Water highlighted each of the paintings in the series, but in this one—he was sure it was Variation #3—there was no puddle. The painter studied his work for a long moment and then walked off.

Hours or days passed, and the artist studied his painting. Passing by on the way to make a cup of coffee, then standing in front of the painting with a steaming mug. Coming from outside, standing in a dripping raincoat. In his robe. Talking on the telephone, distracted as he reached out to touch something on the surface. Periodically, the camera cut to shots of the canvas. These scenes passed by in a semi-montage, though Charlie kept the audio running as before, with a very faint overdub of the music the painter had earlier been listening to on the radio. This technique had an unsettling effect on Vic—he didn't like how it slowed the film down. But it did focus his attention on the painting, he had to admit.

The film faded from a shot of the canvas into a murky wheat-colored frame that eventually resolved into an oak floor. A dollop of sunlight lit the lower right corner of the frame. In the background, Vic again heard the ambient sounds. This time the noise of the painter seemed accentuated—his breathing, the creaking of his chair, the tick of the brush against hard surfaces. The scene cut very briefly to a medium shot of the artist painting again.

The last scene was introduced by four sharp noises, like claps. The image was back on the patch of floor, but now the sunlight had crawled up to the upper left corner of the frame. The film cut to a long shot of the wall of paintings. The artist was reaching down for the painting; he stood up and hung it on the nail he'd just driven into the wall. He stood back to look at it briefly, and then the camera started zooming in. It continued to zoom in and the painter walked off-frame. The audio of ambient sounds drifted away, and the music from the radio rose.

As the camera zoomed in, the puddle was back where it belonged, in the painting's foreground, reflecting the light of dawn. As with Mary's other Variations, it reflected the sky—this time a lighter region, unseen, beyond the edge of the canvas. The light it reflected was an icy blue-gray, which Vic had always marveled at— somehow that puddle unmistakably communicated dawn. The rest of the painting was cast in deep, saturated colors, seeming to absorb light. Vic had always understood that the paintings were accentuated by these puddles, but he had never recognized how the soul of the painting was captured in them. They were like windows that let meaning shine into the painting. This was, of course, the point of Charlie's short.

The screen flicked black, and the credits (the few that there were) rolled to music. After the final title—"A Cab 133 Production"—the music stopped, but the screen stayed black. There was final creak of the painter's stool, and the film ended.

Charlie arrived home relatively early—just before midnight. A moment of both languor and clarity as he stood in his apartment, listening to the night. After the screening, a largish group had retired to the Barley Mill. A Monday, though, so they called it a night around eleven. He floated home on three beers and a post-adrenaline hangover, feeling like there ought to be more. The evening hadn't even ended and already he had grown nostalgic for it.

By way of having something to do, he decided on a shower. Also to remove the stink of cigarettes.

The screening had drawn a good turnout. Far fewer people worked on "The Puddle Variations" than "Taxicab Triptych," and yet the latter's failure hadn't soured them on seeing it. Even Roger, who couldn't see why Charlie was wasting precious funds on Puddle when "Taxicab Triptych" was poised for completion. (Roger remained in denial.)

At the Barley Mill, relief seemed to be the reaction of choice. October, newly-dyed maraschino red, kept an arm on his shoulder like a proud sister, vindicated for supporting a worrisome little brother. Clay was sheepish, and as the beers warmed his mood, eventually proud. For Carlos, the relief was not in the film's success, but its completion, which he regarded as a miracle. He still wasn't sure Charlie hadn't been putting him on with that dog business.

Vic's mood he could not divine. As he had been the whole trip, Vic seemed vaguely surprised. Even more quiet than he'd been the first three days—a melancholy resulting from his wife's paintings? Mary was one of the few points of emotional connection for the two, and he could see the distant grief in Vic. Once he had made a clarification—"you didn't destroy your mother's painting for that, did you?"—he spent the evening listening, mostly, smiling, agreeing, patting Charlie's back. He even drank beer.

Janie departed the theater as soon as the credits ended. Earlier in the evening, he spoke to her once, briefly. After a greeting, he keenly observed—seeing her alone: "You're alone." (To which she had said, inscrutably, "Of *course*.") After the film, her cheeks were wet and her eyes were red. On her way out, she caught his eye and mouthed the words "it was wonderful" to him. Recalling this made his stomach tense.

Through the window, a ray of streetlight caught the lower half of his Truffaut poster. As he looked at the photo of the movie set on the poster, his mind wandered briefly to the cameraman. He was operating a machine that looked like a riding lawnmower on a hydraulic lift. What were those things called? He was then reminded of the time he sat outside Janie's apartment and envisioned a shot through her window. He would have needed something like that machine to rise up smoothly outside the house and swoop down like a crow to look into her red living room. What if you had a fleet of those machines, he wondered, posted at each window of a house? You could ride up and down and follow the people around inside. That might be an interesting way to shoot a film. Had Hitchcock done something like that?

As his thoughts meandered dreamily, the image of visiting Janie's apartment for the first time entered his mind. The vividness of that experience, like he was experiencing it freshly. As he thought about the moment, which now caused another painful clenching of his stomach, he let it meld with his thoughts about filming through windows. His mind began re-imagining that memory as if through a camera's lens. As if he were simultaneously living and filming it. He saw them through the window, though this time in the third person — through the lens of a camera.

But how, he wondered, could a filmmaker communicate that kind of clarity, the slowing of time? Not to show two people in love, but what it was like to be in love. He recalled the sense of his mind being completely unfiltered and open. The images of her room were sharper in his mind than they were in real life. They flashed: adobe walls, blond wood coffee table, the picture of a girl spinning in a raincoat, a crystal doorknob.

At the time, she had asked, "Trying to figure me out?" But that wasn't the right question — at the time he wasn't figuring at all. He was enjoying. It was one of the few times in his life when he wasn't thinking. To show that on film — he wondered, was it possible?

He went to his desk and found a notebook. Then took a blanket from the bed and went to the kitchen table. Hunched and hunkered in yellow cotton, he began jotting notes. Writing as fast as his hand could go, he scribbled thought fragments in three categories — shots, plot, themes. Before an idea for a shot was fully written, he'd think of how this lent to a theme. Then the plot would appear, invitingly, incompletely, and he'd write a few notes down. Then another image would come, then another.

After fifteen minutes, a title randomly burst in amid the jumble. He wrote it down at the top of the front page, but before he'd completed it, he was reminded of both a plot element and a larger theme. He made a quick notation in the margin so he wouldn't forget the theme, then wrote an idea for a scene. Then went back to the plot —

An hour later, sleep started to pull on his body like glue. He put his ballpoint aside, leaned back in the chair, and tucked his icy hands inside the blanket. The groan of the building, a car rattling by. He looked back over the first page, then sent a hand darting out to turn pages as he read through what he'd written.

Well, maybe not. It was all right, but who knew? A bit gimmicky, too thematic and symbolic. He tended to work in theme more than plot, he observed. He pondered "Puddle." It wasn't too symbolic. A nice, straightforward plot, successful and perhaps evocative, but not too art-school-y. Yes, the plot first, then the theme, that was an antidote to his tendency. After the final page, he leafed back again to the beginning. There was the title that minutes ago seemed so brilliant: "Time Stops When You're in Love." Oof— he winced and scratched it out. Better no one should ever see *that*. He leaned back in the chair and tried to think of a better title, lapsing soon into a doze.

He woke, then yawned and stood, his mind residually pondering what he'd just written. Lights off, and in to bed. His eyes followed the streetlight to the poster again, but they never had a chance to focus. The glue claimed him.

Fin.

About the Author

Jeff Alworth is a founder and editor
of the political website Blue Oregon.
He has written about politics, beer,
movies, and Buddhism. In the more
distant past, and in corners remote
and forgotten, he published poetry.
The Puddle Variations is his first novel.

www.ingramcontent.com/pod-product-compliance
Lightning Source LLC
Chambersburg PA
CBHW032028240626
47154CB00003B/832